CW00381322

A Cloud Can Weigh a Million Pounds

A.D. Stephenson

The Paddy McAlpin Chronicles: Book One

Best wishes,

A. D. Stephenson

For all who have enjoyed Friday Football,

and of course, the real Paddy.

* * *

Prologue

It is said that a cloud can weigh a million pounds, yet gazing upon them in the gentle light of late afternoon, most will only ever see their majesty, an oil-painting rendered alive, crepuscular rays creeping down to earth to illuminate joy and beauty for the beholder. The glowing golden imprint lingers in the mind long after the wind has dispersed their physical form to far away climes, leaving nothing but the charm and romanticism of another balmy day. What is ignored is the unparalleled power and hidden depths of strength held deep within, rolling gently by, undisturbed, but waiting to be unleashed in a torrent of force. The cloud in this case is Paddy McAlpin.

On another side of this divided city, the light of the evening has begun to dim; the man in the suit strains his eyes to check the paperwork one last time. As promised, profits were significantly up, the deal struck towards the back end of last year having come to instant fruition. He looks assiduously through the paper trail that has been elaborately created and hopes it will be enough to keep the authorities off his scent. Little does he know the sequence of events he is about to set in motion, nor could he ever expect the source of his inevitable downfall.

Chapter 1: The Semi-final

THE TUNNEL REVERBERATED AROUND PADDY, THE HAIRS ON THE BACK OF HIS NECK ERECT AND TINGLING AGAINST the collar of his deep emerald shirt. Days like this made him proud to be Scottish, proud to be playing for, no, *starring* for, Claston Celts – a club had been a part of him since the moment he came into the world. An almost imperceptible turn of the head to his left revealed his opponents. Paddy meant no disrespect to the players of Dundee United, but he knew that they had little hope of victory in this match. Paddy knew that many bookies had already paid out on a Celts victory and most had stopped taking new bets on it, such was the overwhelming task that faced the men in orange and black – not that he had tried to bet on his own team; he'd dabbled in that once or twice before, but on the previous occasion had come too close to being caught betting on matches he was playing in (only to win, such was his confidence, he would never have thrown a match). A ban now would signal the end of his career: the ticking on that particular clock was already too loud for his liking.

And then the drum started. A deep booming from the bowels of the stadium that intimidated many a player of lesser stature than himself. For Paddy, the slow, steady beating of a war drum was just a part of a big match day's festivities. And he'd had plenty of those. From his early days with Claston Celts, to the time spent playing in Hamburg, Paddy had won every conceivable honour, from the team victories of the Bundesliga (four times in the six seasons he was there) and the Champions League (three times), not to mention the Europa League (Hamburg hadn't qualified for the Champions League before he'd joined the club, but he'd made the best of the situation in his first season there), to the individual honours and triumphs, including receiving the Ballon d'Or five years in a row and vastly diminishing the reputation in Hamburg of their previous British import of the late 70s.

It was seen as insanity by all commentators when Claston Celts made an offer to re-sign their former wonderkid at the end of his contract in Hamburg, and Paddy had had offers from the biggest clubs in Europe: Real Madrid, Barcelona, Juventus, both Milans, Paris St Germain, both Manchester clubs and three London clubs, as well as the enormous financial temptation of a move to China. Paddy, however, knew his heart lay in Claston. There would always be a part of Paddy that yearned for the challenge of playing in the biggest leagues against the best players and he had weighed up how much he would miss that challenge very carefully when he made his choice to return home, deciding in the end that his real ambition was to drag the domestically-dominant but perennial European under-achievers of his home-town club back into the big time.

The hit to his reputation of the move had concerned him. Going back to Scotland realistically meant not being a consideration for any further Ballon d'Ors and would take him out of the international limelight, something he had relished for half a decade. And although money should never have been a consideration (he had more than he could spend on himself in a lifetime already), he could not help but think about how he **deserved** to be amongst the top-earners in the world, something that he always knew Claston Celts could never offer. Upon weighing it up though, he realised that his mother was as comfortable as she would allow him to make her, still living as she did in the small flat that he had grown up in, refusing to leave despite Paddy's pleas. His ex-wife was living handsomely, much to his frustration, after their bitterly acrimonious divorce many years earlier. And other than that, there was no one else to look after but himself. Yes, the money he had already accrued would see him through. Plus, he would still be earning far more than the Scottish average salary on a weekly basis.

All that was history now, and he had proven himself right (as he knew he would do) when he first pulled on the famous emerald and black stripes of Claston Celts during his homecoming season. And now, as the season drew to a close, there was still a few things to wrap up.

Paddy was well prepared for this match, certainly the biggest of the season so far. It had been frustratingly rearranged twice already, once due to the famous Scottish weather and once due to the more unusual reason of the

4

discovery of a huge hornet's nest in one of the stands on the morning of the match. The other semi-final, played two weeks previously, had been a turgid affair. The Celts' city rivals, Claston Wanderers, had eventually ended 1-0 winners over Aberdeen in what could only be optimistically described as agricultural football, although Paddy thought that might be doing a disservice to the essential role that farmers played in the UK economy. He had watched that game with a sense of ennui, his eyes often glazing over as he struggled keep himself awake at the lack of entertainment on offer. He knew that football shouldn't be played like that, that it was as much an entertainment business as a sport. And he was ready to entertain, as he always was.

He took a sip from his water bottle. The club provided team bottles, but Paddy knew not to trust them, supressing a shudder as he thought back to his youth days and the laxative prank that he had been the sole victim of. No, he wouldn't fall for anything like that again, and was now well-known for having his own drinking receptacle at every training session and every match. He would take it out onto the field and place it in the bottle holder in the dug-out himself. His teammates knew not to touch it but he was still unwilling to leave it alone when he didn't have to. The litre and a half bottle (or magnum as Paddy insisted on calling it) was a top of the range Japanese import, fully insulated and resplendent in a glossy black finish on the aluminium outer, the initials PM subtly embossed in dark grey on the side, the company logo in Hirigana in the same shade of grey on the base. Paddy never had learnt how to read or pronounce the company's name: he just knew quality when he saw it.

The referee strode forward, leading the players onto the field like the Pied Piper playing his merry tune, gently retrieving the ball from its plinth on his way past with a delicacy that would usually be reserved for the handling of fine glass ornaments, baby animals or explosives. The two teams, Claston in their dark emerald and black stripes, Dundee United in their striking orange, followed close behind, ready to do battle. Paddy took a deep breath as he crossed the white lines of this hallowed field, absorbing the cacophony of the crowd, feeling the rumble of the drums seep into his soul. He had played and won in such famous stadia as the San Siro, the

Santiago Bernabéu, Old Trafford and Stade de France, all with their own unique atmosphere, but for him, any stadium where Claston Celts fans were singing his name was the real theatre of dreams. He ran toward the centre of his half to prepare for kick-off; he would be playing in his preferred position, as a dominant box-to-box central midfielder today. He had successfully filled in as a marauding full-back or clinical centre forward previously and knew that reprising these roles might be on the cards today. He played both those roles better than anyone else in the squad and only wished he could play three positions at once. Without warning, he shuddered and blinked his eyes twice as an otherworldly feeling swept through him. He didn't believe in being nervous, so shunned the sensation and prepared for the game to start, absorbing the cheers from the crowd, already at fever pitch despite kick-off still being minutes away.

Without warning, the ball was at Paddy's feet. He smiled an easy smile and rolled it back to the centre spot, ready for kick off, only to see an opponent seize his caressed pass with a look of surprised glee and start bearing down on him. What was this joker doing? Paddy wondered, letting him have his moment on the ball before the game began. Paddy was alerted by a piercing cry from his manager, the self titled "Big" Jim Fallanks, an overweight, burgundy-faced man, formerly a Scottish international (as he so he proudly crowed, winning a single cap in a friendly match), remonstrating with him for giving the ball away, urging him to win it back. In his confusion, Paddy could only watch in horror as the brightly-shirted Dundee United players played a series of intricate passes, splitting open the Celts' defence like a machete coming down hard on sugar cane. They would not normally be so exposed, with Paddy their customary shield when defending as well as their outlet to start their attacks. In a matter of seconds that felt like hours, the ball was in the net and the Celts were behind. The stadium fell silent, the air sucked from the lungs of everyone watching on, the tsunami drawback before the deafening crash of water, and then the explosion of sound from the Dundee United fans who could not believe their eyes. The Celts fans simply sat in silent disbelief.

As the ball made its way back to the centre circle for the Celts to kick-off, Paddy was aware of a low droning noise, the hum of conversation from the Celts fans, aghast at what they were witnessing, tentatively allowing the question to rest on their lips but not quite escape just yet: was Paddy McAlpin at fault for the goal, and more worryingly was he past his best? Joel Johnson, the Celts' young, cocksure centre forward, a brash, prickly young man who seemingly spent as much time coiffuring his hair as he did practising his shooting and wanted everyone to call him JJ, was not so subtle in his assessment of the situation.

"What the fuck was that, Paddy?" he howled as he walked by to take the kick-off. "Ah think ye mebbe a bit old for this game now." Paddy shook his head and turned away from the young whippersnapper before he lost his temper and acted in a way in which he might come to regret. He still upheld respect for his elder players and was disgusted by Johnson's vitriol toward him. The boy had always hated when Paddy, playing out of position as a forward, was selected instead of him. At times like these, Paddy knew he had to be the bigger man, and invariably was, much like the elder statesman who listens carefully before weighing in with well-considered wisdom, compared to the brash, newly-elected activist who shouts the loudest to be heard, but then has nothing of substance to say when given the opportunity to speak.

Johnson would mature one day, but for now he seemed intent on embarrassing Paddy, fizzing the ball just beyond his immediate reach directly from the kick-off. Paddy was up to the challenge and coolly controlled the wayward pass, the smile on his face replaced with the look of steely determination that had made him such a fans' favourite in Germany. As he was closed down, Paddy made to shimmy right, his quick step-over selling his opponent faster than discounted haggis at the Claston Saturday morning market, but before he could readjust his balance and accelerate off to his left he found himself on the floor, his right thigh having given way and the whole of his leg tingling with the numbness of pins and needles. He jerked his left leg to the ball, managing to play it to William Wark, one of the two central defenders that had been so easily dismissed for the goal. An intense feeling of fatigue overcame Paddy as he hauled himself onto his feet again. He tried to move forward up the pitch to join the rapidly-developing attack, though he felt a sluggishness in his limbs, as if he were running underwater.

The sounds of the crowd faded; all that remained was the sight of the ball at the end of a long tunnel of haze. Paddy watched on, unfeeling, unmoving, as Johnson received a crisp pass on the penalty spot – surely an instant equaliser – but no: the young striker skied his effort well over. Paddy turned away again, suddenly aware of the saliva flowing freely in his mouth, the sweat beading all over his body. It was all he could do not to throw up his pre-match breakfast of a well-fired roll topped with square sausage and potato scone.

His knees buckled and he went to ground again, this time onto one knee, head down, eyes closed.

"Come on Paddy!" he muttered to himself, "Get it together!" From the technical area, Fallanks watched his star player in bemusement, his loose club tie flapping in the strong breeze that whistled through the stadium. In the distance, the sky darkened and what had promised to be a glorious day of April sunshine for this semi-final now looked to be close to surrendering to the infamous Scottish rain. A quiet word in the ear of his assistant resulted in a vigorous shake of the head, and Fallanks resisted the urge to substitute McAlpin after only 15 minutes of play.

By the time the referee's whistle pealed around the ground for half time, Paddy looked less than a shadow of the Ballon d'Or winner of last season and more like a man who had been towed into Hound Point by his ankles. It seemed to him as though there had been little more than five or six plays in the whole half, as if the match were only ten minutes old, and he could not help but wonder where the time had gone. Another shudder jerked through his body and the sound of the crowd disappeared momentarily. Again, he shrugged the feeling away, ignoring the obvious signs of his body, his mind overcoming the signals that were desperately being sent to every fibre of his being. He somehow managed to drag himself into the changing rooms where he slumped into his seat, gasping for a drink, lethargically searching for his water bottle. Around him, his team mates looked on, dumbfounded by what had happened. They were only a goal down, but had been totally outplayed in all areas, Johnson's ballooned effort their only shot of the match so far. Fallanks pulled no punches with his team talk, laying into almost every player in turn, the hapless McAlpin bearing the worst of the barrage of abuse.

"Ye useless sack o' shite, Paddy! What the bloody 'ell are ye playin' at?" Flecks of spittle sprayed from Fallanks' mouth, raining down on the players who sat in silence, heads bowed, carefully watching the floor for an impossible exit to appear and release them from this half-time hell.

"Ye cannae keep the ball, ye hit the ground more times than ye've made a tackle. Box-to-box?" he yelled in exasperation, the fury on his face rising like the crescendo of his voice. Paddy didn't need to look at his gaffer to know what was coming next, but he was surprised by the sudden calm and quiet the furious man raging around the tense and suffocating changing room somehow deigned to summon. If the situation hadn't been so tragic, Paddy would have been impressed with the rare sophistication shown. The change in tone reminded him of when he saw the Scottish Chamber Orchestra play Barber's Adagio for Strings in St Andrews, although clearly lacking all the beauty and finesse of that haunting piece. Paddy blinked hard, trying desperately hard to bring himself back into the moment, though he needn't have bothered, as the next utterance that befell Fallanks' mouth was one that Paddy had not heard for many a year, one that instantly brought him to his senses. "Ah'm gonnae pull ye off, son. Ye've given us nothing this half. Nothing!"

Chapter 2: Oktoberfest

Paddy could only put the swirling feeling that was enveloping his stomach down to the news that he was being taken off. Yet it was a feeling that tickled the outward limits of his own memory. That sense of disbelief that one's own actions had resulted in something so undesirable. It was years earlier, during his first season as a young up-and-comer at Hamburg, that Paddy last felt anything akin to the disorientation that had struck him during the first half.

In a fit of youthful impulsivity, Paddy had assented when a small group of the hangers-on that had so plagued him in his early months in Germany had suggested a trip to Oktoberfest in Bavaria's capital, over seven hundred and fifty miles to the southeast. "Don't worry, Paddy;" he had been reassured, "we won't let you miss more than a couple of training sessions and we'll have you back in time for the match on Saturday afternoon. Just tell the boss that you've got diarrhoea and are staying at home until Thursday. It's only Monday, we'll travel down tonight, get a hotel near Theresienwiese and keep our profile low. Just a few beers and we'll come back up nice and early on Thursday morning. You can't live in Germany and not take advantage of Oktoberfest!"

And so Paddy was swept up in a road-trip that he knew in his heart was a bad idea. That morning, he wracked himself with guilt over the idea of the deception and almost bailed out on the morning of departure. Yet his integrity succumbed to the pressure of his peers, and, like the battle between the rock and flowing water, over time his friends wore him down and he relented, yielding to allow the water to flow over the path of least resistance. Slowly convincing himself that he was someone special, that the rules didn't really apply to him, that he could do what he wanted, he willingly met up with his friends, ready for departure.

Keeping a low profile was the only part of the "plan" that he liked and he had suggested that rather than taking his car: a club-owned silver Mercedes, his friend Fritz should be in charge of their transport. Sadly, Paddy had overestimated Fritz and Jürgen, his companions for the trip: their idea of a low profile was booking second class tickets on the ICE train from the centre of Hamburg to München city, a journey that would be filled with drunken revellers and football fans. Nonetheless, Paddy ignored the instincts that would serve him so well in his future and boarded the carriage, pulling his baseball cap low over his face.

His identity was kept secret for a total of eight minutes; a group of Hamburg fans were taking the same journey and recognised him as their newest signing, singing his name intermittently for the entirety of the journey, much to Paddy's chagrin.

Fritz and Jürgen had kept their word about finding a hotel, though – they had secured a suite in the most exclusive hotel in München's Theresienwiese: The Sheraton. Again, Paddy questioned whether these lads understood the meaning of travelling incognito or of subtlety, but they seemed to be enjoying the experience of basking in Paddy's relative celebrity.

Fritz had had aspirations of being a professional footballer when he was much younger, but his burgeoning beer belly and his ruddy cheeks enlightened Paddy as to the reasons why he had never made it above the Regionnaliga. Jürgen, on the other hand, seemed to have no aspirations at all. He was, in short, an idler. Both had attached themselves to Paddy very early in his time at Hamburg by turning up at an open training session and speaking in perfect English: something that Paddy had sorely missed in his first few weeks away from Claston. This, coupled with their enjoyment of beer and their ability to drink it in vast quantities reminded Paddy of his homeland and made them rather fun to be around. With no real friends anywhere else, Paddy spent more time with them than with his new teammates, something he would eventually look back on with regret as it seriously hampered the development of his German language skills and his integration into the team.

In those early days abroad, Paddy was young and inexperienced: he didn't see how this behaviour was isolating him and preventing him from integrating. All he saw was himself struggling to break into the starting XI and distracting himself, by any and all means. He had gone from being the largest fish in the small goldfish bowl of Scottish football to a regular minnow in the ocean of the Bundesliga and he didn't like it, preferring to ignore rather than face his problems, telling himself that he wasn't being given a fair chance, that these "foreigners" did not understand his unique skills, that he was excluded for being Scottish. As a solution, he, Fritz and Jürgen spent far more time in Hamburg's Reeperbahn than was sensible for a burgeoning professional. More than once they drank so much that they took an *unofficial* harbour tour, with Jürgen as ship captain. More than once Paddy had been reprimanded by the club captain, Jan Schüster, who had done his best to act as Virgil to Paddy's Danté during his early months, protecting him from the serious repercussions that his misdemeanours might bring. Schüster, acting like a patient older sibling, would do what he could to guide Paddy and shield him from the inevitable parental wrath of his manager.

It was thinking about Schüster that had so nearly prevented Paddy taking this trip, the thought of letting down his captain being almost too much to bear. *Almost*. One last time, Paddy had reasoned, and then it would be hard work and professionalism only, words that had echoed around his mind more than once since his move. Thinking that he could enjoy the delights of Oktoberfest quietly, and then re-join his teammates later in the week, he telephoned the club doctor, carefully reading symptoms he had selected from Wikipedia to make him seem too ill to be at training, but not so ill he would benefit from receiving treatment. All had seemed to be going smoothly, until he boarded the train with his idiot friends. Yet even then, rather than abandoning the plan, Paddy continued on his chosen path, unable to see the ramifications of his naivety.

They awoke early, "Best way to get a table," Fritz had informed them. "Be at the front of the queue, then once the gates are open, run to a tent and secure some seats." It had never occurred to them that Paddy had the means to acquire these seats in a much more subtle way, but they, like him, were young and inexperienced.

And so, Paddy did as they suggested. Dark glasses on, baseball cap pulled low, collar of his leather jacket resolutely up around his chin, and when the gates opened, he blew away any notion of a low profile with his incredible speed.

Minutes later, when his friends arrived at his table, breathing heavily, sweating profusely and ruddy cheeked (more so than usual for Fritz), Paddy sat on one side of a long wooden bench with two beautiful young fräuleins – one on either arm – accompanying him. Paddy failed to recognise the irony of his criticism of his partners' subtlety, but was beguiled by the way that these young ladies' dirndls presented their assets. It is fair to say that Paddy rather let himself down that morning.

It was during the first round that he was introduced to the Bavarian maß – a full litre of beer in a single glass, of which the servers can easily carry a dozen or more. Paddy sucked back maß after maß, all the while singing, standing on the table to down his beer and arm wrestling the strongest looking men he could find. All the while, he was blissfully unaware of the attention that he had garnered and the thousands of photos that he had been a key part of. It would take more than the quiet intervention of Jan Schüster to save him from the boss this time.

After hours of drinking and very little food (a whole chicken and some Kaiserschmarrn were mere morsels compared to Paddy's usual calorific intake), he was very, very inebriated. Eventually, his vision cleared and he noticed Fritz had disappeared with the younger of the girls who had so eagerly introduced themselves to Paddy that morning. Through the haze that obscured his vision he thought he could see that Jürgen was being escorted from the premises after losing the ability to suppress his vomit.

Paddy then, was alone. Drunk and rich, but alone.

As he posed for another photo with a band of dirndl-clad young ladies, Paddy decided that that was the moment to subtly head back to Hamburg and the relative safety that he had found there.

Stumbling from street to street, following signs for the Hauptbahnhof (train station was one of the only German words he had learnt) Paddy covered more miles than he could possibly comprehend. He was refused entry from the Hofbrauhaus – no one who has ever been to München could figure out Paddy's route – went for a short swim in the Eisbachquelle in the Englischer Garten, and was almost arrested for public nudity at a wedding party in the city's

Rathaus. And yet even these acts pale into comparison to his next move, which was to board a train. A simple act, you might think. Paddy found the correct carriage for his booking and even the correct seat, slumping down with a sense of pride in his achievement. He didn't, though, find the correct train.

After a few moments sitting in his seat, Paddy felt a wave of nausea flooding through him. Overwhelmed by the urge to vomit, he ran to the bathroom and prostrated himself to Bacchus, head inserted deeply into the Deutsche Bahn toilet. When he awoke, who knows how long later, Paddy was naked for the second time that day, except for his baseball cap. Covered in water – Paddy reasoned that he must have overheated, stripped and dampened himself – he towelled himself dry using the single ply toilet paper provided in such establishments and dressed himself. His clothes had a painful odour to them: he didn't envy the other passengers.

Stumbling back to his seat, Paddy was enraged to find a tiny, frail old lady in the seat that he had booked and loudly declaimed her as a thief and a liar, all in his best and totally inadequate German. Washed, she hobbled from the seat and left the carriage, leaving Paddy feeling vindicated. He fell into an immediate slumber.

Rudely awoken by a deep, booming voice, Paddy lashed out at the arm that was prodding him. He made heavy contact and the arm was swirly retracted. He was once again left to sleep.

The next time he was awoken it was more confrontational. It was not an arm that prodded Paddy, it was the barrel of a rather large, rather intimidating gun, held by a serious-looking police officer, with a train guard (holding his arm in pain) and that vulgar little woman that he had so publicly denounced earlier.

"Fahrkarte?" Nothing more. Hand held out.

Paddy, smiling, inebriated now, rather than incapacitated, thrust his ticket willingly into the officer's hand. A frown.

"Ausweis?" That stumped him.

"Bitte?" Paddy asked, hoping that they would tell from his accent that he wasn't a native and speak to him in his own language.

"Ausweis." The tone had darkened rather severely in the last few seconds. Paddy assumed that they were requiring some form of identification, and he duly complied, supplying his passport, at which the police officer's expression lightened, just a little. "Sprechen Sie Deutsch?" Paddy understood the words, but the accent was thicker than that to which he was used in Hamburg.

"Ein bisschen – a little" Paddy smiled. He knew that by conversing, in German, even a little, that he would be treated well. "Well, Mr McAlpin – welcome to Austria. It seems that you have boarded the wrong train and have struck this man when he attempted to inform you of this." He gestured to the ticket inspector. Paddy realised that this low-key trip was going to cause him some serious trouble.

An hour in an Austrian police cell, a grovelling phone call to his boss, a long journey and a great deal of shame later, Paddy was back in Hamburg. The combination of his pounding head and churning stomach paled into insignificance compared with the bollocking he received, in German, from his manager. He didn't need to know the language to know the seriousness of his punishment. He knew enough to translate "unter" to under and "achtzehn" to eighteen to know he would not be training with the first team for some time. This moment of realisation dawned on Paddy slowly, as one who watches the sun set and then wonders why they are in the dark. And while his hangover dulled his ability to process anything of substance, he knew that he had no one to blame but himself. In many ways, that ill-advised trip was the making of the future great that he became as he swore that day that his focus would never again slip from his career. That was a promise to himself he had yet to break.

Thinking back on these travails, Paddy narrowed his eyes and stared hard at his manager.

Chapter 3: The Second Half

Paddy drew in a deep breath and exhaled slowly once, then again. He was gasping for a drink and looked over to the water bottles but could not see his own amongst the team bottles. Bemused as to where it had got to, he reluctantly took a bottle from the communal set and slowly sipped from it, hoping to project an aura of composure, hoping to hide the fact that his head was swimming, hoping to look like he was feeling normal. In many ways, those deep breaths did have that effect, as if he had given himself the kiss of life. He gently shook his head, laboriously rose to his feet and simply said: "Nae."

Fallanks started to stutter a riposte, unable to comprehend the simple defiance shown by his star player, but looking around the changing room he realised that, despite his appalling first half showing, Paddy still had the backing of the majority of the team. In an attempt to save face, Fallanks backtracked, mumbling how he meant he'd have to bring McAlpin off if he didn't soon improve. Only Johnson seemed upset by the decision to keep McAlpin on, and Paddy was not going to lose much sleep over that.

As the half time break ticked away, Paddy continued to search for his bottle, finally finding it under the kit bag – certainly not where he had left it. Paddy didn't have the energy or inclination to question how it ended up there, he just needed water – lots of it. The bottle felt surprisingly light as he lifted it, even in his weakened state, and it was soon obvious to him that someone had tampered with it. His suspicions immediately turned to Johnson, but even he knew not to touch Paddy's belongings. His stomach churning, he reluctantly retrieved the team bottle that he had previously gulped from, taking a long draught. The water was cool and refreshing, acerbic, almost glacial in its intensity. It cut through the mist swirling in front of his eyes, and for a moment, he almost felt back to his best. The bell rang around the changing room, indicating the players needed to retake the field. Paddy took another long gulp of the liquid refreshment and made his way out for the battle of the second half.

As the game began, Paddy soon felt the slackness of muscles that had been constraining him in the first half. As soon as the ball was out of play, he made his way to the bench for some more water, a pattern that continued throughout the half, and one that, unknowingly to him, saved his life.

Seeing the slight resurgence in form of their star man, the Celts managed to pull themselves back into the game, and wave after wave of emerald and black attacks rained down on the Dundee United goal, but to little avail. Johnson was guilty of fluffing his lines like a drunken amateur who had been thrust into the part of Hamlet at The Globe, missing two clear cut chances that Paddy only wished he had been on the end of. In spite of their dominance on the ball and their chances, the score remained at 1-0 into the 85th minute. Paddy looked up at the traditional clock on top of the Burley Stand, tick tick ticking away the seconds. His legs were screaming at him, and he was momentarily transported back to his school days at the prestigious Thistledown College, and particularly the cross-country season. He remembered well those energy-sapping laps around the school grounds, the thick mud sucking his feet into the ground, and the daunting prospect of another run up Thistle Hill, known to the boys at Thistledown as 'The Mountain', enough to bring the weaker students to a tearful standstill. Yet when Paddy had reached the base of that craggy slope, he had not faltered. Memories of surging efforts, heart pounding, eyes bulging, came flooding to the forefront of his mind. He had taken on The Mountain many times and he had beaten it every time. It was days like that that had made Paddy into the man he was now; a man of immense mental strength; a man who always backed himself to face down all challenges with a glint in his eye, defiance in his heart and gritty Scottish shale in his soul. He had faced The Mountain alone and he had conquered The Mountain alone. This was, he thought, just another mountain. And mountains were made for conquering. He knew that if his team were not going to bow out of the Scottish Cup in the semi-final, it would be up to him and him alone. They were so close to completing an historic treble of the three major domestic trophies and he would not let this chance pass.

Paddy put his first and third fingers of his left hand between his lips and whistled to Mikael Tintoni, the Celts right-back. Tintoni looked up to see Paddy jerk his head towards the centre of the field and Tintoni obediently moved across, leaving space for Paddy to move into to the receive the ball from his goalkeeper. The crowd sensed something magical was about to happen, even with McAlpin in this defensive position. They had seen him play as a marauding full-back plenty of times, had seen him create goals from nothing in a matter of moments. Surely, surely, this would be one of those times. With Herculean effort, Paddy accelerated away from the lazy chase made by the Dundee United forward Ryan Stephens, cutting inside as he reached the halfway line, his change of direction wrong footing his next opponent. Team mates to left and right called out for the ball; Paddy, still moving forward, assessed the situation with an instant, almost robotic calculation and laid the ball to his right, skipping around another Dundee United player, before receiving a pass back to him.

By now the Celts fans were on their feet, urging their hero to achieve what had seemed like an impossible task for the last 85 minutes. By now, Paddy was panting like a dog on a hot summer's day, his immense chest feeling like a caber strapped to his body, weighing him down and sapping the energy from him. He imagined The Mountain in front of him, looking up to its peak. Over the top of the stand behind the goal lightning flashed down onto the moorland. The thunder cracked almost instantly. A gasp from the crowd sounded out, some fans cowered momentarily, covering their head with their arms, as if to protect themselves from the rage of the Pagan gods that had once been worshiped in these parts. The storm that had been threatening to engulf the famous old stadium was not so much creeping now as barrelling in. From the corner of his eye, Paddy noticed a flash of orange scything towards his legs. He could barely move fast enough to avoid the knee-high tackle that flew in. A stud raked down the lateral side of his patella, yet somehow he rode on, approaching the edge of the box. Another flash blinded Paddy, yet there was no thunder. This flash came from within, wrenching open Paddy's head. He started to sway and waited for his legs to give way. The Mountain, it seemed, had finally defeated him.

Paddy thought back once again to those heady school days. Everyone, everyone, had wanted to beat him up that hill, and some had nearly managed the feat. His great rival in those school days, Archie Macnab, had come closest, had even taken the lead once, but Paddy had managed to draw on some super-human strength to claw him back and reach the summit first. Once again, he reached into the depths of his being and stood up straight and tall, bringing the ball to a standstill. Turning away from goal he feigned to lay the ball off to the onrushing James Arrol, before smartly backheeling it into the empty area, turning in an instant and chasing his own pass. The Dundee United goalkeeper rushed towards him; Paddy wasn't going to make it. With an almighty stretch he pushed the ball around the 'keeper, taking it to the byline. He had no angle for a shot. His chance was lost and it seemed that he might not be the hero he craved being after all. Somewhat reluctantly, he rolled the ball across the empty goal, desperately hoping that one of his teammates would finish off the move that he had single-handedly orchestrated. Three orange shirts came running in unchallenged, and all seemed lost, until from between them emerged an emereald blur. Joel Johnson burst through the three defenders to smash the ball towards goal. Even Johnson couldn't miss from that range, and as he fell, Paddy watched the net ripple with the long sought-after equaliser. The defensive wall finally broken, Paddy breathed a sigh of relief, knowing that there would only be one winner now.

The remaining few minutes of the half passed tentatively – neither side willing to commit men forward to seek the equaliser. For once, Paddy himself was content to be a bystander, such was the pain streaking through his body. The full-time whistle pealed through the ground and the teams once again made their way to their on-pitch huddle.

"Much, much better, lads!" bellowed Fallanks at his team. "McAlpin!" he shouted, before dropping his voice again, "Better. Still nothing like yer best, Ah hope you arnae resting on the laurels of yer bloody balloon door. That holds nae sway round 'ere!"

By now, the full eleven looked almost as exhausted as Paddy did: it had been a tough 90 minutes, far tougher than anyone could have expected. Only Johnson looked delighted with himself, and he was happy to take full credit for the equalising goal.

"Ye ken, lads, if it werenae for my goal, ye'd be going home about now. Good job someone on this team still has some hope and wants tae win this match. Hey, McAlpin – did ye see my finish, or were ye tae tired? Ah thought Ah saw ye having a little sit down as the ball went in." Paddy didn't bite, and before anyone else could say anything, Fallanks announced his plans for extra time.

"Ah'm gonnae make a couple o' changes, just in case of pens." Fallanks explained. Paddy knew he wouldn't be sacrificed now. He'd never missed a penalty when it mattered, and rarely missed when it didn't. Tintoni made way for Spelter, Nolan for Dal-Flaato and Smith (T) made way for Smith (K). That's fifty percent more than a couple, Paddy mused, momentarily wondering what life must be like without the classical education he had enjoyed at Thistledown. Then, focusing back on the match at hand, his thoughts turned to the potential issue of using all the substitutes with thirty minutes still to play. We'd better hope no one gets injured now. He took a long, slow drink from one of the team bottles, his own bottle, mysteriously emptied, was safely contained in his initialled kit bag under his seat, back in the changing room.

By now, the storm had hit the stadium, with the Scottish spring rain lashing down on the pitch and the unfortunate fans who were not under the cover of the stand alike. The iron sky had swept a darkness over the stadium and the floodlights had been turned on, four lighthouses rising from each corner of the pitch, beaming down on the glistening grass, lighting the players' way to greatness

The fans' enthusiasm seemed undiminished in the face of the soaking they were experiencing, and the drums soon started up again to welcome the players back out for 30 more minutes. Paddy had taken it upon himself to move to a centre forward position for extra-time, leaving the Celts exposed in the centre of the park, but with a more reliable outlet if the ball should make it into the Dundee United penalty area. Plus, Paddy could barely walk anymore, let alone play the box-to-box role in which he was usually so accomplished.

Within a couple of minutes of extra time starting it became clear to all involved that this game was going to penalties. The rain had sapped any remaining energy from the players and fans, with everyone present just waiting for the time to tick down until the end of the match. A dull blanket had enveloped the match like a well-worn, shabby tartan picnic rug, slowly suffocating the life from the game. The Dundee United players knew that penalties would give them their best chance of progressing, and opted to play a defensive strategy, holding a deep line with ten men behind the ball and just the one outlet in Ryan Stephens. Chances were, he had been told to defend as well, but anyone who had ever seen him play knew that wasn't how he operated. The man had a left foot that struck a ball like a rocket and lived for the thrill of putting the ball in the net: he wasn't bothered with the nitty gritty defensive duties advocated by some to be a requirement of a team player.

The game marched slowly on towards its inconclusive conclusion; no further goals, or even any real chances of note meant the inevitable prospect of penalties. In the Celts' team huddle, Joel Johnson demanded the first penalty.

"Important tae put the first one away!" he said to anyone who would listen. Paddy was down for the fifth, or, if the shoot-out could be won earlier, whichever one he needed to take. The rest of the line-up consisted of Smith (K), Spelter and left winger Gordon McClair, the two subs having been brought on precisely for this eventuality.

The players huddled on the centre circle, some not daring to watch, others looking on with a grim-faced resolve, determined to experience their fate first hand, all desperately hoping for a success that would see them reach the final. Dundee United won the toss and elected to take the first penalty. A shrewd move, thought Paddy, one that puts the pressure on your opponents for every kick, so long as you score your first one.

Yet no orange shirt made the walk down to the penalty spot and the Celts players looked around in bemusement; had they meant to go second? Then a shocking moment of realisation dawned on all who were present other than the Dundee United players; their first kick would be taken by their goalkeeper. The traditional green shirt stood illuminated by the flood lights, a man alone in a sea of tension. The Dundee United fans were hiding their eyes as Galbrinny began his run up, but they needn't have worried as the ball rocketed into the top right corner, shaking the stanchion and bulging the net. No keeper would have made that save, thought Paddy.

It was now Claston's turn. Players, staff, fans – even the catering staff – watched on as Johnson made the long, lonely walk to the penalty spot and carefully placed the ball down. Paddy wasn't keen on the young lad, but he would take no pleasure in seeing him fail to convert this. A couple of Celts players turned away as Johnson began his run up. A second later, Paddy wished he had done so as well, as the ball thundered onto the topside of the bar and ballooned high into the stand. The cheers from the Dundee United players were almost as loud as the groans from those in emerald. Johnson smirked and shook his head, jogging back to his teammates without the temerity to look abashed.

Things were made worse when the second Dundee United penalty was calmly tucked into the bottom left corner, but Smith kept his cool to score and keep the Celts' dreams alive. Another Dundee United goal, followed by a superb penalty from Spelter, followed by a miss from Dundee United. If McClair scored, it would be level. All eyes watched as the left-footed McClair guided the ball straight down the middle of the goal, just off the floor, easily evading the diving Galbrinny. And then, the script was written for McAlpin to finally make his mark on the game as a poor Dundee United penalty was easily saved low to Mark Richards' right, meaning if Paddy could find the net, the Celts would be into the final.

Paddy began his gruelling walk to the penalty spot. His body ached, a fatigue like none he had felt before, another shudder, the strongest one yet, rocking his body. As was true for his whole career, he was determined to reach the summit that lay in front of him. One foot after the other he walked, head down, visualising the ball moving unimpeded into the goal. He imagined the goal as a huge unmissable target, the goalkeeper a tiny insignificant speck. He had always found these psychological tricks to help his confidence and allow him to succeed. But now, the goalkeeper was growing, the goal shrinking. He shook his head, trying to shake up the image in his mind as if it were a snow globe. His legs were seizing up, his neck struggling to hold his head still. Somehow to ball was on the spot and he was running towards it, but he hadn't decided where he was going to place his kick. He tried to stop himself, compose himself, but it was too late. In vain, he glanced up at the bottom left corner, checking where the goal was. His stiff legs finally buckled, no more than one step from the ball and he went tumbling to the ground. Fallanks turned away, biting his lip. For the second time that afternoon, the crowd gasped. If there was one player who would score his penalty, surely it would be McAlpin. As he fell, he thrust out his right foot and made a weak connection with the ball, which started to roll towards the goal.

Paddy watched in horror from the floor. Galbrinny had dived full stretch to the left corner that Paddy had just managed to glance up at during his run up. The ball was rolling to the other corner, but would it even make it to the goal? Galbrinny scrambled across the floor, the sodden, slippery surface proving difficult to get any purchase on, his inertia too much to bring him to a quick standstill. The ball rolled on as Galbrinny finally found his feet and changed direction, diving to his left. It was too late though, the ball crossed the line, barely making it to the net. The Celts fans heaved a sigh of relief. Paddy rested his forehead on the soaking surface and closed his eyes. Beyond the concrete that filled his head, he could just about make out the Celts fans blasting out their unofficial anthem, something a younger Paddy had inspired but had now grown to hate, filled as it were with an arrogance that Paddy did not enjoy hearing.

"It means nothing to me!
This means NOTHING to me!
Oooooooh!
Vienna!"

Chapter 4: The Aftermath

Long after his teammates had removed themselves from the tangle of bodies that celebrated the tense semi-final victory, Paddy hauled himself to his feet, mud from the saturated ground coating his face like the coal dust that had covered his father's face at the end of a hard day's work.

The Dundee United fans had flooded out of the stadium in their droves following Paddy's mis-kicked yet ultimately winning penalty, the Celts fans staying long after to celebrate with their heroes. Yet Paddy did not feel like a hero today: he knew he had played poorly; it was perhaps the poorest performance of his life. There had been whispers that he was not quite up to it anymore. The brutal Scottish press loved to dissect his every mistake in minute detail, picking apart his performances and delighting in tearing down the man that they had spent so long heralding during his time playing abroad. Then, of course, there were the away fans of every club who loved to hate him, targeting him for abuse from the outset of each and every match, some of it light-hearted, some personal and scathing. But during this game, this bizarre two-hour match (and concluding penalties), was the first time he had sensed the rumblings of discontent from his own fans.

Behind the goal his teammates now stood, joining in with the on-going chorus of Vienna from the fans, both players and supporters revelling in their victory. Even the management team had made their way over and were helping to orchestrate this largest, most unruly of choirs. Paddy reluctantly began to head over as well, dragging himself in the opposite direction of the tunnel and sanctuary of the changing room where he really wanted to be now. As he drew closer, he noticed his manager heading his way and determined to point out that his refusal to be substituted had been vindicated, but before he had a chance, Fallanks was accosted by Vicky Kilbride's TV crew looking for an on-pitch interview.

Paddy had always had a soft spot for Vicky since the day she had conducted his first post-match interview many years before, guiding an adrenaline-filled eighteen-year old through the unfamiliar surroundings of live broadcast with utmost professionalism. Their relationship had grown (professionally only) prior to his move abroad, with the pair exchanging cards before he departed, hers to him expressing good luck for his future, his to her a card of thanks, accompanied, of course, by a bouquet of the finest orchids. Paddy had often wondered if there may have been something more between them, and had he not been married to his first wife when they first met (a mistake Paddy now put down to inexperience and naivety), there may well have been, but now, that ship had long since sailed. Paddy had already been married for a second time since his divorce from Tallulah, that partnership ending in a tragedy that he had never spoken of to anyone, and Vicky was now happily engaged to the esteemed writer Dave Gorton. Paddy liked Dave and had enjoyed sharing a pitch with him on a number of occasions in charity matches, both on the same team and as an opponent. Dave was not afraid to get stuck in and was undaunted coming up against professional footballers, relishing the challenge and remonstrating to all about their defensive responsibilities. Paddy suppressed a chuckle as he thought back to the time Dave had even managed to get Ryan Stephens to track back into his own half during Darren Meredith's testimonial match. Deciding to greet his old friend, Paddy made his way towards the pair who were just starting their interview in front of the goal where the decisive penalty was scored.

"Jim, well done, you've made it into the final, although clearly not with the comfort that many were expecting. What did you make of that performance?"

"Well Vicky, Ah think the team did pretty well out there. Those were difficult conditions by the end, but we kept plugging away and, in the end, like Ah always say, the cream rises to the top. Victory was never really in doubt." Fallanks always spoke well for the cameras and at that moment, Paddy wished they could see what he was like when he wasn't being recorded.

"And what about McAlpin? On days like these you must be pleased to have a player of his calibre playing for Claston again." Vicky smiled.

"Well ye'd think so, Vicky, but Ah have tae say that today wasnae Paddy's finest game. We were obviously delighted when he agreed tae come back here to ply his trade, but more performances like that will result in his dropping tae the bench. Nae one is bigger than the team, not even McAlpin. Now Ah realise some fans might think this is madness, but they dinnae see him train every day like Ah do, and Ah think there is an element of him that came back tae Claston for an easy ride, thinking he was tae good for this league. Well, Ah regret to say, he isnae tae good for this league and he certainly isnae tae good for this team." Fallanks smiled his smug smile upon finishing his criticism, as if he had just announced that he had personally orchestrated world peace.

Taken aback, Vicky continued, pressing Fallanks on the positive contribution Paddy had made, "So you didn't rate his input to the equalizing goal today then?"

"Well, Vicky, he did play a part in that goal, but putting the ball in the net is the most important job, and he didn't manage that today, even after I moved him into a more advanced position to try tae get the best out of him. We've really got tae thank JJ for making up for Paddy's early mistake. He was lucky tae stay on at half-time, and he even asked tae come off, because he knew he wasnae up tae it. Ah told him that defeatist attitude would get him naewhere, although in hindsight, maybe Ah should have... what's the word?"

"Acquiesced?" Vicky put in politely.

"Yes, if Ah had a-quest to his request, we might well have run out comfortable winners in normal time. He even tried tae miss a penalty and got lucky that Galbrinny, who Ah think had a very good game, went the wrong way."

Paddy had heard enough. Furious, he turned on his heel and made his way back to the tunnel and the changing room. Paddy had always considered that Fallanks had never known how to manage a team, yet this public criticism was unheralded, even for him. Arguing live on TV might get him some extra attention, but it wouldn't help anyone, and more importantly, he needed to get the weight off his aching muscles and increasingly numb feet.

Whilst the players around him celebrated in front of their fans, Mikael Tintoni could not help but notice that the usual star man was not amongst the joyous victors. Whilst he, Tintoni, had been off his game that day, had been for a number of weeks in truth, he knew Paddy had been worse and would be the one to draw the critics, hiding his own failings for another day. He wriggled free from the tight grip that held him in the team huddle and turned just in time to see Paddy making his way back towards the changing room, alone. Tintoni had always looked up to Paddy and felt it to be a personal insult at seeing the great man disappearing without a friend at the end of a match.

Although he was considered Italian, and had grown up in Italy, his mother was from Hamburg, and it was Paddy's poster he had had on his wall as a child. When Hamburg had signed McAlpin he wasn't yet the global superstar he later became, just a kid with (reportedly massive) potential. The Oktoberfest debacle looked as though it might have brought a swift end to his time there, but instead it seemed to be the making of him. Within a season, the fans knew that they had something special, a young, imposing player who had started his time in Germany primarily as a right back before moving into his now customary central midfield role. From the end of that first season, Paddy had improved all those around him, raising the standards of the whole team and bringing so much to the game that he loved playing. Even something so simple as his long, flat throws had been like nothing Tintoni had seen before, and his desire to get forward and score whilst never forgetting his defensive responsibilities had mesmerised the young teen.

After his many years of admiration, becoming teammates had been like a fantasy. Tintoni had come to Scotland from Italy, where he had been struggling to break into the first team at Fiorentina. His mother had held a season ticket at Volksparkstadion for many years, even keeping it for a year after she left the city and the country to move to the beautiful city of Florence with her new husband. Tintoni, still very young at the time of the move, had no choice but to grow-up following two teams; the crisp white of Hamburg and the rich purple of Fiorentina.

And then, at the age of 21, Tintoni had received an offer to join Claston Celts. After a lengthy and tough discussion with his manager, where he was told the harsh reality of his (lack of a) future in Serie A, he decided to take the plunge and head to the sunny climes of Claston. The culture shock was more than the young man had expected, and after just a year he was ready to move back to Italy, or perhaps try his luck in Germany, when the shock announcement that McAlpin would be returning home was made. Tintoni could not quite believe it. He had always assumed that McAlpin would go on to Real Madrid, Barcelona, maybe even Juventus, so seeing him return home was a dream come true for Tintoni.

On the first day of pre-season following Paddy's return, Mikael was a nervous wreck: desperate to meet his hero, to impress him, and terrified of showing himself up as his peer. Tintoni had always been a quieter member of the squad, preferring to stay back after training and work on long passing, or maybe see the fitness team for an extra strength session. Claston life was so different to what he was used to in Florence.

It was with great relief and almost embarrassment when Paddy strolled up to Tintoni on the training field later that morning to introduce himself (as if anyone in football didn't know that rugged face and steely eyes) and compliment him on his prowess as a full-back.

"Looks like Ah might not have tae play at right-back nae more," he'd said, laughing kindly, "Ah just hope ye dunnae try yer hand in midfield, or Ah mebbe out of a job."

Tintoni had made a fool of himself, laughing childishly in his state of awe, but Paddy had instantly made him feel comfortable, encouraging him to join in the team socials, to which he had duly obliged. Their Hamburg connection was a big part of their professional relationship, and the two would talk together, in English or German, about the merits of the tactical system utilised by the top German sides in contrast to the other top sides across Europe. Paddy was clearly a man who knew football and loved to discuss it, but also a man who knew how to bring the best out in people.

Tintoni would never forget how much the man had helped him when he was new to the club and felt a sense of regret at how he had let his hero down that day. He decided to jog over to join him in the changing room but hesitated. Paddy was friendly, but he was not a good loser, and today would go down as a loss in the ledger of Paddy McAlpin. He continued to watch as Paddy disappeared down the tunnel, his fate awaiting him, and turned to re-join the rest of his team in what was, to him, now a false celebration.

Getting back first meant Paddy was able to enjoy the showers alone, turning the water up to scalding levels. His thick dark chest hair, previously matted with mud that had seeped through his shirt was now flattened onto his strong, muscular torso, the water turning his olive skin red with its spiking heat, a million hot needles of catharsis. The scalding water eased the tension in his muscles, but not in his mind. He was still reeling after being thrown under the bus by Fallanks when his manager and the rest of the team eventually came in.

Paddy pretended not to hear them and continued to stand, head down and facing the wall, the water now cascading onto the back of his neck and running down his body. Paddy was renowned for his upper body strength, but right now he felt as though he could hardly lift the bulk of his own limbs. He had no idea how long he had stood under that water, but he did know that something wasn't right and now simply wanted to get back to the comfort and excessive luxury of his home: the sprawling Cowie Estates.

One by one, players started filing into the shower, clearly in jovial spirits. Beers were passed around and Joel Johnson even offered one to Paddy. Paddy was not averse to a post-match beer, in fact he'd read that the carbohydrate content of humankind's (debatably, depending upon whom you asked) oldest alcoholic beverage was the perfect recovery drink, barring the slight dehydration side-effect, and he'd lived by that advice ever since. Playing in Hamburg had certainly helped ingratiate this as the norm and he had enjoyed many victories (and defeats) with a few litre glasses of Konig Pilsner. But not today.

Paddy stepped out of the shower without another word, ignoring Fallanks, and went to start dressing himself when a soft, clipped female voice called out to him.

"McAlpin, please report to the physio room for your random and compulsory drug test."

Chapter 5: The Drug Test

The cheers and jeers from the rest of the team rang around the dressing room. Though it was a part of every big game, and many smaller ones, players dreaded being called in for a test after a match. It meant waiting in a cold, sterile room while some quack ran who knew what tests on your urine. It was bad enough on a normal day, and to Paddy, this was no normal day. He wanted to get home, sharpish, try to forget about the game, forget about the interview from Fallanks, forget about the whole sorry affair of his performance. He wanted to hit the weights in his home gym, to sweat away his sorrow, to remember who he really was, and most importantly to forget the shell he had become in the past three hours. His muscles were still, perhaps not screaming, but certainly yelling from a distance, like an angry man across the bay as you row away in his dinghy. Still, Paddy knew the pain of a workout was the catharsis he needed. Self-discipline, and when necessary, self-punishment, were some of the cornerstones to his success.

"Never get ahead o' yerself, lad!" his father used to say to him. "Because lemme tell ye, the moment ye do, someone'll be right there tae bring ye back down tae earth!" Paddy had remembered this advice well over the years, in particular the day after his father lost his battle with pneumoconiosis: The very same day Paddy had won his first Ballon d'Or.

He'd been all smiles at the ceremony, the news of Matthew McAlpin's death not yet public knowledge. But Paddy had held no interviews afterwards and had seemingly disappeared from the ceremony before any of the celebrations had begun. Vicky Kilbride was the only person who knew the truth of where he had been that night, Paddy having finally contacted her following the 17 missed calls and 12 answerphone messages she had left him. Their conversation was matter of fact, unemotional, and strictly not for public record at Paddy's insistence. Within minutes of his name being announced and collecting his award, Paddy, clutching his trophy close to his heart, the glimmer of a tear forming in the corner of one eye, headed to his hotel gym. Barricading himself in, he lifted as much as he could. Again. And again. And again. Carelessly placed by the door, the golden orb watched on, and somewhere, breathing freely, Matthew McAlpin smiled.

Back in the changing room, Paddy pulled up his pants, lightly towelled his hair and slid on his trainers. Tintoni gave him a sad smile, a sympathetic look that he could not help but feel a deep appreciation for. Joel Johnson grinned with glee and slapped his team's talisman on the back, laughing him out of the changing room to suffer his fate. Paddy left without a word and wandered along the corridor to the Physio Room: densely populated as it was with a massage bed, a shelf with various gels and rubs and a few anatomical books, a small desk with a magazine on it sandwiched between a couple of chairs and finally a hastily erected screen for privacy. As he walked in he caught sight of Galbrinny on his way out, having obviously completed the same procedure that Paddy was now here for. The doctor who had called his name sat patiently behind the desk, her dark hair falling easily around her shoulders, sharp eyes behind the thick-framed square glasses that accentuated, rather than hid, her attractive face. As Paddy entered she stood, revealing her small stature. She was dressed informally and was unfazed by Paddy's minimal attire.

"Mr McAlpin, I am Dr Piero" she began, "as you are undoubtedly aware, we require a drug test following today's match and you have been randomly selected." Her tone was formal, professional, her voice soft and welcoming, but to the point. She held out a cup for him. "If you could kindly..."

"Piss in yer cup... Ah ken. Ah've done this a thousand times before." Paddy said dissmively. He was not normally so terse during these screenings, especially with such a delightful doctor as the one who stood before him today, but then, this was not a normal day for him. He was thankful when Dr Piero continued as professionally as she had begun.

"Well, yes, that's right. You can use the toilet behind the screen there. I'm afraid I will have to ask you to keep the door open. You understand that I cannot let you leave the room without receiving your urine sample," she paused before adding, "even though it seems obvious you don't have a secret supply of clean urine on you." Paddy managed a weak smile before Dr Piero continued. "The whole testing procedure should not take long. You can wait here whilst I do the analysis."

Paddy tried to apologise for his tone, but the words failed him, and instead he took the cup in silence and moved behind the screen. It seemed like an age before he managed to produce the required 45ml of urine. From the other side of the screen, he could hear Piero writing something on a pad, the scratching of her pen an unwelcome reminder that he was not alone.

Paddy emerged from behind the screen, sample in hand. He always hated the moment when he handed over a cup of his warm urine to another human, but this was an inevitable part of his chosen career. The doctors involved knew the drill just as well as he did, and the moment usually passed with dignity for both parties. This occasion was no exception, with no words uttered by either until after the sample had been placed inside a large open-topped plastic box and the testing equipment had been laid out on the massage bed.

"Right, Mr McAlpin. This shouldn't take too long, then you can finally get yourself home. I'm sorry that you had to be kept here today."

Paddy nodded in reply, slumping down on the as-yet unused chair to wait. Occasionally a pen scratched on paper and through it all the clock on the wall ticked away unceasingly whilst the doctor worked. No other noise could be heard as the pair sat together in proximity but alone in every other way. Through the small window Paddy could see that the rain had stopped and the clouds were beginning to clear. Perhaps he could yet find a moment of joy in the darkness of this day.

The minutes ticked on and Paddy waited. Piero continued to work almost silently, with the irregular rustling of samples being bagged and notes being made the only puncture to the rhythmic sound echoing from the clock. Then she spoke, not quite to herself, but not quite to Paddy either.

"That... can't be right."

Paddy sat up and looked towards the mumbling doctor, but she did not return his gaze, absorbed as she was in the work she was doing. Her brow was furrowed and she scribbled some unintelligible notes before crossing them out and writing some more. Paddy leant over to make for the magazine.

"Mind if Ah read this while Ah wait?" he asked. The young doctor didn't look up or even reply, but waved her free hand non-committally. Paddy took this for a yes, grabbing the glossy mag and laying his eyes on his prize: a month-old copy of Highland Life. Ah well, Paddy thought, it's better than a two-month-old copy… He settled down to read a magazine for which he was clearly not the target audience. Adverts adorned every double-paged spread, mostly for make-up, perfume, beauty products and the like. There were stories about interior design, the latest Highland restaurants to eat in and fashion advice. Paddy flicked through hoping for an article of "Sex tips to drive your man wild" or similar, but was duly disappointed. Only one article piqued his interest, a biographical article about Doris MacLeod, nee Doris Cochran, successful Scottish self-made millionaire and an inspiration to young Scots lasses across the country with aspirations to own their own businesses. None of that really interested Paddy particularly. The only reason he read on was because Doris was the wife of Donald MacLeod, chairman of Claston Celts' city rivals: Claston Wanderers. Paddy kept reading, hoping for a reference to the Wanderers' poor performances, perhaps a mention of how he, Paddy McAlpin, had dominated every recent match between the two sides, but once again, he was disappointed. He threw the magazine back onto the table carelessly. Piero was still hunched over her work, immersed in it completely. Paddy puffed out his cheeks with a deep, frustrated exhalation and continued to wait.

Finally, the silence in the room was broken. "It can't be…" she said again, this time more quietly, to herself. She seemed unaware that Paddy was still in the room.

"Dr Piero?" Paddy asked, but again she waved her hand dismissively in his direction, not taking her eyes from the testing equipment in front of her. Paddy sat back and waited. His eyes felt heavy and the sound of the pen gently etching the pad of paper on the desk was soporific like the sound of rain or a crackling fire. Dr Piero stood up and removed her jacket before returning to her seat, looking Paddy up and down as she sat. Paddy smiled and raised his eyebrows in interest. At this, she stood again, and sauntered towards the nearly naked McAlpin, her hair bouncing gently, her eyes unflinching. She removed her glasses and had a good long look at him for a second time. Paddy tried to stand but couldn't. He seemed stuck to his seat. The alluring form of the slim young doctor manoeuvred closer, gently pulling her white fitted tee-shirt tantalisingly up from her waist, revealing a narrow, tanned navel. The shirt moved higher and higher and Paddy waited with trepidation for the delights it would reveal. Perhaps there might be some good to come from the match yet. Dr Piero's voice called out his name, gently at first.

"Mr McAlpin…" Paddy bit his lip.

"Mr McAlpin!" Paddy woke up with a start. Dr Piero was still sat behind her desk, fully dressed, looking directly at him. He crossed his legs in an attempt at some semblance of modesty.

"Dr Piero, are ye done?" he asked, resolutely maintaining eye contact.

"Well, yes and no," came the unhelpful reply.

"What do ye mean?"

"Well, yes, I've finished the testing and can confirm that you do not have any traces of performance enhancing or illegal drugs in your system."

"Tha's a'right then." Paddy said. He glanced up at the clock and shook his head. It looked like it said 18:37. How long had he been in here?

"Well, not quite." Piero replied, curtly, looking back down at her notes. "I'm sorry the testing took so long, but a couple of anomalies came up. Firstly, the test initially showed up traces of Ketamine." Paddy tried not to look guilty of anything, although he was pretty sure that he had not taken any ketamine, at least not for a very long time. He needn't have bothered with his poker face though, as Piero didn't take her eyes from the notes she had written, crossed out and then rewritten. She continued.

"However, there was something not quite right about that result, so I ran another test, this time isolating the hydrochloride section. I had to nip outside to my car to get some extra testing equipment. I hope you don't mind that I didn't wake you, I assumed you were exhausted from your match, but now I know the truth." Paddy shuffled his weight in his chair. He was certain he hadn't taken anything he shouldn't have done, but worried about what news the results might bring.

"Anyway," Piero continued, "it turns out that what I found **isn't** ketamine." Paddy breathed a sigh of relief. "In fact, it isn't anything I've seen before, although I **can** tell you that it is some kind of anaesthetic. What is worse, there are tiny traces of the heavy metal compound thallium ethoxide. It's rare to see such a compound in anything, let alone a drug that is administered to living creatures. It's not something I have ever been aware of in my line of work, but perhaps it has made some headway in veterinary circles. I'm surprised you managed to walk in here, Mr McAlpin. In fact, I'm flabbergasted that you finished the match at all, let alone scored a somewhat unorthodox winning penalty." She smiled at her reference to the game. So she was watching, Paddy thought gratefully, before remembering that it probably would have been better if she hadn't seen his performance that afternoon. Dr Piero waited just a moment for a reply from Paddy, but with none forthcoming, she continued.

"Now, I think I know the answer to this already, but have you been feeling particularly tired today? Any aches and pains in your muscles, or perhaps episodic black-out periods?" Paddy processed the symptoms slowly. He didn't feel the need to explain all the details and simply nodded in assent. "I think you've been drugged, Mr McAlpin. I obviously can't tell you why, or what the intended outcome was, but the drug was probably administered orally, most likely in liquid form. Have you eaten or drunk anything that no one else has been exposed to?"

Paddy thought about his Japanese water bottle and cursed himself for his unfounded suspicions that someone might play a prank on him with communal water. Instead, someone had used the fact that he never drank from the team bottles to get to him. He had questions and wanted answers, but mostly he felt anger. He needed to think, to get away from the stadium, away from everyone associated with professional football.

Thanking Dr Piero, Paddy left the physio room and went back into the now-empty changing room. His stuff had been scattered, no doubt a prank pulled by Joel Johnson, he thought with anger. He dressed, stuffing his belongings into his kit bag, and headed out. He knew exactly where he would go.

Chapter 6: Ascension House

Ascension House Council Estate – this small suburb to the east of the city of Claston was Paddy's birthplace. When asked, Paddy always named his home as simply "Claston". Not out of any feeling of shame or embarrassment, you understand: most people had never heard of Ascension House, even more would have difficulty placing it on a map and Paddy disliked having to repeat or explain himself.

The suburb grew out of the ashes of The War (the second one) when country folk began to flock to the cities and those poor souls that couldn't afford the luxury of the city centre or the green pastures of the popular Hillpoint to the south had to find alternative options. The expansion of Claston city had begun – those people with the means to do so packed the townhouses and bought up valuable tracts of farmland; those that lacked those very same means headed to places like Ascension, many of them pawns for the company directors who sat in shining offices and sent the low-lives down to the local mines to haul countless quantities of coal.

Ascension: the word itself was a dirty joke aimed at the impoverished. It was an infection on the city, a blight on the population that the government allowed to happen, and those in power profited merrily from its creation. From looking the other way when building contracts were agreed with unscrupulous firms to the taking of bribes, the fat cats in the council building were just as guilty as anyone for the creation of Claston's slums. Corruption was rife, with those trying to make a change hampered at every step until their resolve, like that of the people they aimed to help, was broken. And like an infection that remains untreated, these suburbs grew and grew, spreading east and north, pushing outwards and upwards and clogging the skyline with cement and steel. There was money to be made here, sure, but not for those that needed it.

Ascension House was named for the day that it was officially opened by the Mayor: Ascension Day, the twenty-second of May, 1952. Members of Parliament, the city's gentry and those people who had invested in the building of the areas, as well as the associated press, gathered in the lawned square in the middle of the dull grey rows that comprise Ascension's centre. Cigars were smoked, champagne was quaffed and a ribbon was cut. Applause. They then piled into their Fords and Vauxhalls and headed west and south, to their townhouses and apartments that overlooked the tributary where the Brew river joins the mighty Clast or the green fields of Five Trees Park, leaving behind the sad emptiness of this land that would fill slowly, but would eventually be overrun by families of ten (or sometimes even twelve) in two-room flats. Squalor and dilapidation were inevitable from the very first sound of the popping corks and the clinking glass.

From the first, the writing was on the wall, initially figuratively, later literally. The government had been demolishing slums and making promises of prosperity just four years earlier and if The Bryce Plan to build cottages on a green belt and rehouse the city's poor sounded utopic, it was. The plan soon changed and Ascension began to do literally that: the tenement buildings of the first wave of construction soon became tower blocks and, as the buildings reached for the sky, the population forgot how.

It was in one of those tower blocks that Paddy was born on the 4th of June, an unseasonably hot day even for early summer in Claston. His mother didn't make it to the hospital – his father was not present to drive her (his whereabouts on that day have ever remained unclear). Aoife McAlpin felt her waters break whilst she was scrubbing the toilet. Never one to abandon a job half way through, she began to work tirelessly on the bathroom mirrors, sink and tub, before the pains of labour became too overwhelming and she lurched towards the front door, hoping that the wait for a bus wouldn't be too long.

Paddy's mother was known for her strength, her bravery, her tenacity, but not for her luck. Overcoming the increasingly regular contractions in the blistering heat, clutching her monumental stomach with one arm, she waddled along the corridors and into the lift, and that is where she remained.

The building, already creaking and straining when it was built, had lapsed into a state of disrepair that only those who have experienced real destitution will truly understand. Using the lift had always been a particularly grim experience, but the

McAlpin family were resigned to living on the 13th floor of their building and a heavily pregnant woman, deep in the throes of labour could hardly be expected to take the stairs, so to the lift she had begrudgingly shuffled. Many of the buttons were broken and had to be operated using a coat-hanger that was always left on the floor of the lift. Occasionally, some of the neighbourhood boys would use the hanger to send the lift to the top floor, then exit swiftly taking that most useful item with them. People on the top floor were then forced to take the stairs or to provide their own hangers – not an easy choice. On this occasion, though, Aoife found the coat-hanger undisturbed and, after 30 seconds or so of reaching between her legs with all the grace of a stranded turtle, was able to retrieve it and press the option for the ground floor. From there it was only a near two-mile walk to the nearest bus stop that would take her to the city hospital. The lift, though, only made it to floor 1 and ¾, where it groaned, growled and gave up, leaving Aoife stranded between two floors and in agony.

Part of Paddy's many successes owed to his gargantuan frame: it was the reason he had been able to play so easily at full-back, dictate midfield from box to box, create and finish chances as a striker, and even play in goal once or twice. This would just not have been possible without having a towering physical presence. As a man, he is a mountain, as a baby he was a colossus. Aoife spent six hours in that lift, screaming and pushing and shrieking and gnashing her teeth. Paddy clung on, as if resisting the entrance that the world offered to him in Ascension House. Aoife's screams could be heard echoing in every direction, reverberating through the tower block she was imprisoned in, and while it wasn't unusual to hear a woman scream in Ascension, to hear scream after scream without respite was unheard of. Usually, their husband relented in his cruelty, or their will is broken much faster than that and she reaches a state of learned helplessness and the screams stop. This earth-rending sound though, caught the attention of at least one resident as unusual and eventually the local police force dispatched a group of heavily armed police officers.

The police were an unwelcome intrusion in Ascension: they were required to take the highest levels of care whenever they were brave, or foolish, enough to step onto that

38

unhallowed ground. They were spotted immediately, and the daytime criminals heard the signal from the trained watchmen and scurried back into their burrows, hiding their mug-shot faces from the police, lest they end up on the receiving end of a fist or a boot. The police were lucky themselves though; the local gang were in the south of the city, carrying out some carnage and the only violence in Ascension that day was the kind that happened in their absence.

When the police followed the sounds of the (by now) sobs to Ascension House's lift they saw scenes that shocked even the hardiest of them. Aoife lay on the floor of the lift, the doors having been prised open by one officer's ingenious use of a discarded bumper moments before, surrounded by the remnants of her birthing, holding an unusually-large infant child in her arms. No one at the scene has since had the desire to describe the squalor that they saw, and no upstanding member of society would ever wish to hear about it. The child was wrapped in the only piece of cloth that Aoife could find after she had forced his frame from her body: a soiled Claston Celts shirt from 1977, on the back, the barely-discernible number six: the number famously worn by Claston Celts hero Bobby Duncan.

Sergeant Alfie Galloway was the first brave man to step forward, but he didn't speak politely or calmly enough for Aoife and she tested his riot gear with a few well-placed handfuls of gravel and glass from the floor of the lift, which ricocheted off him and showered his colleagues. He wasn't fool enough to repeat his mistakes, so he adopted a more conciliatory tone and approached her gently, offering her a swig from the flask that he kept in his jacket pocket. As she took that, he relieved her of the considerable burden of her new-born. Moments later, they were on their way to the police van (all available ambulances were being used in the aforementioned operation in the south of the city) and were speeding towards the city hospital. As Aoife drifted into a daze, she asked the officers what kind of vehicle they were in and Sergeant Galloway whispered to her, whilst holding her hand "Ye're in a Paddy Wagon, Aoife, and we'll be at the hospital soon."

Chapter 7: The Poisoned Stud

It was to Ascension House that Paddy returned in his moment of dismay. Fans' discontent was still ringing in his ears when he heard Fallanks denouncing him in the press. Life can be hard in the public eye, but when the man who should be willing to stand in a firing line to protect you can't be trusted to have your back, then how are you supposed to strive, to seek, to find, and not to yield? The drug test was the final straw; Paddy had never taken performance enhancing drugs, and though he had, as a younger man been willing to partake is some recreational (and illicit) activities involving powder or pills at parties, those days were mostly all behind him. At his worst, he did not always know what he had taken, but he did know not to mess around mid-season and get caught. To find out that someone had tampered with his hydration supply in what was a clear (and mostly successful) attempt to negatively affect his game brought about a fury in him that he had not been susceptible to for many years. Now, disconsolate and requiring solace, Paddy returned to his first home.

He daren't take The Jag into the estate: even though he was revered here, there were always some chancers and some wee urchins that grew up without the proper guidance and became Wanderers fans. Wanderers fans that might take the opportunity to mess with such a wonderful vehicle. On top of that, the desperation of those living here would sometimes break the unwritten rule: do not steal from your own.

He needed to clear his mind, so, having driven The Jag across the city and parked it three miles from the edge of the slums, he began to trudge toward his old stomping ground. Slung across his back was his kit bag: he never went anywhere without it. Inside, the usual: a football, his boots, team tracksuit, his now not-so-trusty Japanese water bottle, a signed copy of Total Recall: My Unbelievably True Life Story, by Arnold Schwarzenegger, and an old DVD of the classic 1986 film Highlander.

Although he hadn't seen it for many years, Paddy could still recite most of the lines from his favourite movie. He carried the DVD everywhere in the vain hope that someday soon he would be able to relive the finest fantasy-action-adventure film set in Scotland that had ever been made. As for his reading material, that was just down to the fact that Paddy liked Arnie: on many occasions he had opined that the Austrian was the finest actor of his generation, and he had once performed a one-man performance of Total Recall for his teammates at a Christmas do.

Regardless of his current saturnine disposition Paddy exuded cool, even on this dark day. His black leather jacket covered a tight, midnight-blue tee shirt that accentuated his muscular chest and huge arms, their bulk laid bare by the thin cotton material. His black and white houndstooth trousers hugged his renowned calf muscles, ending somewhere between mid-shin and ankle, leaving a little flesh to be observed. He had turned up the collar of his jacket and wore dark aviators in an attempt to walk unrecognised through the estate, but all was in vain: those Ballon d'Ors and league winners' medals brought the double-edged sword that is fame along with them. Before he had even reached the optimistically named green, more of a dusty desolate wasteland, he heard his name called: "Paddy!" He kept walking, increasing his pace – normally he had time for his fans, but even though this voice was a higher timbre that the usual twenty years plus men that hollered for his attention, he had no desire to talk.

He walked on, white leather trainers crunching as he strode through a pile of discarded own brand vodka bottles. Not uncharacteristically, this area of deprivation was stricken with the plague of drugs and alcohol. "Paddy!" There it was again. This woman didn't know when she was being ignored; mind you, Paddy was used to being pursued. He picked up the pace, his march practically the speed of a layman's jog. "Paddy Duncan McAlpin. If ye keep walking away from me Ah'll tell everyone about that time ye used my maw's hair curlers to give yerself a perm!" Stopping, shocked, Paddy finally clicked who his pursuer was: Claire Duggan, a former girlfriend of his – if you could call her that – from primary school. And wow, she had changed.

The first thing that struck him was her eyes: they were always beautiful but Claire had finally realised how to use them to her advantage; her lashes were longer and thicker and her brows heavy and dark, drawing all focus onto those opalescent orbs that sometimes shone sapphire, sometimes streaked gold, giving her gaze an unforgettable quality. Often, when they were young, Paddy would initiate a staring contest: he told her that it was a game, but he simply wanted to gaze into her eyes. He had adapted his moves somewhat since those days, but when he looked at her, the memories of those moments came flooding back.

She had an athletic build, which, Paddy surmised, indicated that she was an athlete of some kind. She walked with confidence and stood with one hand on her hip, the other pushing her glossy sable hair back out of her eyes. Paddy was impressed: but then, he remembered her fondly. She, it seemed, was less infatuated with him than other women. She didn't have the giggling coquettishness that afflicted most of the women he came into contact with, and when he reached out to hug her after all these years, she broke the embrace before he did.

"Paddy, it's been a long time." She said it without emotion; just a simple declaration of fact. "Ah saw the game today; ye were shite. What the hell happened?"

He had forgotten this about Claire: she wasted no time on pleasantries. What she said was true though, it was a game to forget. It was a *day* to forget. "Thank ye for all yer sympathy, Claire: Ah've missed yer wit." She laughed at that and in that moment, her resilience was broken.

"Ah've missed ye, Paddy. It's been so long." Now she held his gaze and he saw a lump rise in her throat. He'd missed her too. They'd parted on good terms, which was more that could be said for many of the women in Paddy's past. When they met, they were attending the same primary school that welcomed all and sundry from the district, but Paddy had been noticed by a roving scout from Claston Celts one morning while he practised his skills on the green. In lieu of a ball, Paddy was doing keepie uppies with a discarded beer bottle, taking care to ensure that the unbroken end was the only one with which he made contact. The scars on his friends' feet and heads indicated their relative lack of success with this, but nary a child in Ascension shirked the challenge. Paddy's skill was undoubted and it was one Bobby Duncan – former Celts stalwart, now chief scout – that called him over and set him on the path to success.

From the rickety, tumbledown shacks of the local primary, Paddy was taken to the prestigious Thistledown College: not only did his access to education improve, but it also meant that the commute after school would be easier and he could train pre- and post-school day. Paddy and Claire had tried to stay in contact, but this was before such technologies of the internet and mobile phones became so ubiquitous, so, in the end, like many fledgling friendships, they simply drifted apart.

Claire's eyes ran over Paddy's shoulder, taking in his curves. He could feel her purr. Her eyes rested on his kit bag and she smiled: "Ye got a baw in there?" He narrowed his eyes, confused. Then it dawned upon him: she wanted a kickabout. Paddy was surprised, having no recall of Claire playing football in their past. He shrugged his shoulders involuntarily, always pleased to champion football as the people's game, and not confined to tired gender stereotypes. And though a part of him would always see the women's game as inferior, he was well travelled enough to be accepting of the inevitable changes that constantly transpired in an ever-changing world. Maybe this old flame, this first flame was the one he'd been looking for?

Paddy knew now why he was instinctively walking to this place; the pitch where he'd honed his skills was just 40 feet away. This was the only patch of grass, other than the square for miles around. The local kids had stolen a couple of goalposts from a rec centre years before Paddy was born and he had benefitted from the pilfered fruits of their labour. Day after day, night until morning, Paddy stood on that pitch and pinged shot after shot into the top corner of the rusting goalposts. The brick wall, not three feet behind it, imperilled anyone who was fool enough to sprint towards the edge of the pitch, and many concussions and split heads from the sharp competition that invited those to that arena had happened that way, but Paddy used the wall to his advantage. The lack of a net meant that he could use to wall to help him retrieve the ball more easily and it was this kind of planning that developed Paddy's accuracy. Now, Paddy and Claire walked, shoulders close, hands almost touching, towards the field.

For all his muscular, hulking frame Paddy had delicate feet, which allowed him the grace and balance of a ballet dancer on the football pitch. More classless players tried to foul him out of a game but he simply rode their challenges without effort, swaying past their clumsiness: a rapier to their machetes, far quicker and more deadly in his precision. This detail benefitted Claire, albeit briefly.

In her desire to speak with Paddy she had dashed out of her house (she still lived in Ascension House, though its misery had not withered her beauty) in her slippers and followed him for quite some time. This was not appropriate footwear for her to kick a ball about with and wasting their precious time together by going back to her place before they were both ready to do so seemed foolish. Anyway, her feet were just one size smaller than Paddy's own, so he fished out the white boots that he used for training. His teammates at Hamburg had bought them for him; he didn't go in for fancy boots, preferring the traditional black (white boots were for show offs), but the fact that they had had them custom made, with the word "Paddy" on the left boot and "Box2Box" on the right was a nice touch. His teammates, in their enthusiasm – so much for German efficiency – had accidentally ordered two pairs of the same boots. Paddy took both gratefully, and donated the other pair to a charity for rehoming stray dogs. This pair, kept out of sentiment more than anything, were the pair that Paddy handed to Claire so she should showcase her skills. Paddy would be alright in his trainers: he was one of the greatest footballers of all time, so he could handle this.

Claire broke into a sprint with the ball at her feet, dancing around broken bottles, used condoms and needles – you didn't want to fall over on this pitch – she impressed with a rapid step over and a drag back and was in the process of pinging a pass in Paddy's direction when her left foot slipped from beneath her. Paddy rushed over, closing the distance in no time at all; her face was ashen, the vivacious beauty from a moment before a distant memory. Sweat covered her face and he could see patches of moisture pouring through her shirt. Paddy checked for a pulse; her heartbeat was faint. His call for an ambulance felt fruitless, her eyes no longer registered any life, but he felt compelled to do so: what else could he do – he wasn't a doctor and he didn't want to lose her again after being so captivated by her beauty and charm. He held her tightly for an age, the life vanishing from her body, him trying to hold it in as he squeezed her, and then, in the distance, he heard the sounds so familiar to Ascension: the sirens approached, belatedly.

Chapter 8: The Station

"Ye dinnae have tae say anything, but it may harm yer defence if ye dinnae mention, when questioned, something which ye later may rely on in court. Anything ye do say may be given in evidence. Start from the beginning, Mr McAlpin." The young detective spoke slowly, his gentle Scottish lilt a welcome sound to Paddy's ears, instantly making him feel more comfortable in this harsh, sterile environment. He was still unsure how long he had sat at Ascension with Claire, had no idea how the police and ambulance had known to arrive at the spot that would form a place in his nightmares throughout the rest of his life, yet arrive they had, and now he was here, in the police station, being forced to recall something he could not remember or scarcely believe had happened.

Police interrogation rooms had come a long way from his youth: gone was the slop bucket in the corner and the blind spot from the cameras that the police utilised a little too freely, he thought. Nowadays it was all fresh grey paint (why did they keep the paint so fresh, he thought, and shuddered. He knew the answer) low-ceilings, windowless doors, steel-reinforced locks and solid core masonry blocks. Ostensibly, these measures were to protect the integrity of the investigation: the fresh paint meant that there were no distracting marks, the low ceilings made suicide more challenging and ensured that space was allocated for important rooms, such as extra holding rooms; the windowless doors, according to the bobby who brought him in were for his own protection: if anyone were to see him speaking to the police, they may think the worst. Paddy *did* think the worst – if no one can see in, then of course there are opportunities for the cops to exploit all that secrecy. All avenues for escape were closed off: even the air vents were sealed with a thick wire mesh. Escape wasn't on Paddy's mind though, which had reached a state of eerie calm; his eyes, though red, were vacant. He knew what had happened, he had recognised the symptoms that Claire experienced – they had happened to him just a short while ago.

"Ah can tell ye exactly what happened! If ye check mah blood, ye'll see that Claire and Ah have suffered from an identical problem." Paddy explained the circumstances that led to him being collected by the ambulance and transported to a cell once Claire had been pronounced dead. Throughout his tale, the young detective listened carefully, nodded respectfully, noting down the key points. Upon the conclusion of Paddy's statement, he put his pen into his top pocket, nodded and thanked Paddy. He looked at the camera in the corner of the room and pursed his lips. Paddy knew from his body language that this discussion wasn't over.

Before a minute had passed, the door reopened and a much older man, clearly of some importance, walked in. From the lines on his face and the collection of small scars around his temples, it was clear that this man had seen plenty of action throughout his time on the force. Paddy, as student of injuries, could clearly see that the marks were made by small projectiles flung at him from close range. The remainder of his face was obscured beneath a thatch of thick, black stubble – greying at the edges. He towered well over six feet – a lesser man than Paddy would have been easily intimidated in this man's presence. He had given his life to the police: that much was clear. This conversation would be very different from the one he had just had with the young bobby.

"Mr McAlpin: Let me introduce mahself, Ah'm Detective Inspector Galloway and Ah will be leading the investigation intae what has become clear is the homicide o' Claire Duggan." The thick Scottish brogue reminded Paddy of his father's deep, authoritative voice. "We had the belief that ye may have been the perpetrator o' this crime, but from yer statement it appears that ye were, in fact, the intended victim. Ye may recall that we took a sample o' yer blood at the hospital, Mr McAlpin, though ye were, understandably, rather distressed at the time. Mr McAlpin, Ah can confirm that that sample corroborates yer version o' events and that Claire Duggan was nae more than a tragic and accidental victim.

"We now need tae compile a list of suspects. Is there anybody that ye can think of that might want tae do ye harm?"

Paddy laughed at this: he could think of millions of people that wanted him to be harmed. Wanderers fans had never forgiven him for the countless goals he had scored against them in the league, cups and – most painfully of all – in Europe, when those two Scottish giants were pitted against each other in the quarter finals. And not only them: St. Pauli fans hated him for his time at Hamburg, just as the Werder Bremen fans did – millions and millions more, all hating Paddy for his brilliance. Football was a passionate business, but surely that passion would not lead to an attempted murder... Outside of that though, Paddy had more localised problems. Due to his chequered history with women, in his flings and liaisons, Paddy had acquired quite the list of men and women who would love to see him get his comeuppance. In addition to that, Paddy's teammates had often revered him, but his individual success meant that they were more often wildly envious of him. His manager had just embarrassed him in the press, and Joel Feckin' Johnson was clearly desperate to see him fail. Could Paddy accuse any of those people though, without any proof? No, not to the police – Paddy had the same code as all the men and women that grew up on Ascension.

"Nae. Nae. Ah'm beloved, or mebbe ye dinnae ken who Ah am, bobby." He spat the last word, more out of habit than hatred. Old habits surely do die hard, and a boy from Ascension is taught certain things from a young age.

"Ah ken ye well, Paddy Duncan McAlpin. But it seems that *ye've* spent so long away from home and *ye've* neglected to take *yer* head out of *yer* arse when ye got back so *ye* dinnae ken *me*. Take a good look at my scars and – if ye ever call her anymore – ask yer mother about Detective Inspector Galloway."

Paddy bristled at this: any mention of his mother riled him to his core, and, even in his mellowing age, Paddy was quick to anger on his best day, but he could see from the Galloway's demeanour that it wasn't his mother that he was insulting. Galloway left the room without another word and re-entered a few moments later, holding a manila envelope. The flashing light on the cameras had noticeably stopped: this was an important man, after all. Paddy thought he may be in for a beating – the police did this when the mood took them – but Galloway was calm, eerily so.

"Ah shouldnae do this, Paddy. This is a murder investigation, but Ah need yer help. Our investigation has already hit a bit of a wall, red tape and such. In this envelope are the results of the blood tests for ye and Ms. Duggan. Ye'll see that there is a foreign body in there, one that ye willnae find in any lab in Scotland."

At this, Galloway reached into his pocket and dropped an object onto the table in front of Paddy, who recognised it immediately: 15mm in diameter, aluminium, with gold plating and a screw to attach it to the boot – this was a stud from his 'Box2Box boots'. Intriguingly though, a long, thin protuberance extended from the screw. It was long enough to pierce the sole of the boot and enter the foot when a bit of pressure was applied, but not so long that the discomfort would be noticeable: not to someone well-versed in pain like him... or, apparently, poor Claire. This was the way that she was killed, with a poisoned stud. Paddy hadn't worn these boots on the pitch though: someone must have tried to cover their bases by administering the drugs to him by injection, as well as in his water bottle. But who could hate him so much?

"'Tis a drug, Paddy," Galloway continued "or, more accurately, a toxin. 'Tis manufactured, not naturally occurring, ye ken? We have identified a few places that make this drug – all o' them down south. The company that intrigues me the most, the biggest manufacturer, in fact, is OptimoPharm. The thing is, Ah ken that the courts will refuse tae issue a warrant, at least not anytime soon; something about them having too much political capital fer us tae just stride in there and kick down the door. A civilian though, having a look around. Tha's a different matter entirely. Ah think ye might be able tae find some information for us. Fer you. Paddy, if we work together, we can find out who tried tae murder ye – but ye have tae be smart: dinnae take any risks ye don't need tae.

"Head tae Berkshire... and Paddy...say hello tae Aiofe for me."

Chapter 9: The Long Drive

Upon returning home late that night, Paddy was resolute. The seriousness of the situation had gone beyond the realms of football and he determined to get in touch with OptimoPharm that next morning. Looking through the documents Galloway had handed him revealed a phone number for the company, but Paddy was no fool: he knew that a phone call wouldn't allow him to use his wit, charm and considerable physique to wow the receptionist at OptimoPharm, the company that Galloway seemed so certain had made the fateful tranquilizer. No matter though, it was the perfect excuse for him to flex his other muscles: his driving muscles.

He awoke just before dawn, as was customary in the McAlpin household. It was a trait that he'd inherited from his father, along with his sparkling smile and rarely used, but highly infectious laughter. "Paddy," his dad repeatedly lectured, "ye can spend yer life sleeping, or ye can spend yer life winning – Ah ken which one Ah chose." At this, his father would look proudly at the gleaming paraphernalia that covered the walls: trophies for a huge range of sports (not to mention his pub quiz trophy collection) glistened proudly in the light of the cramped surroundings. With that, and a look that brooked no arguments and cemented his point more securely than the correctly chosen 20mm crushed stone used for aggregate. Paddy knew a thing or two about aggregate, and often thought that those jokers that used 30mm stones were asking to die in their beds, and that was not him. And so, a life of early rising, and success had begun.

He knew how to dress for an important occasion too, and to Paddy, every occasion was important. His finely pressed corduroy trousers (boot cut) hugged his perfect calves and squeezed his manliness in a way that only his first wife had ever managed to recreate. A leather jacket was draped across the back seat: it was always sensible to take some protection against the rain and from his adoring fans. His shirt was classic: the finest white cotton, with French cuffs and a wide collar teased the ladies (and some of the gentlemen) with just a

50

whisper of chest hair, not a lot, but enough to get them purring like The Jag on the motorway. The pièce de résistance though, were the Italian leather shoes, made by Giancarlo: the iconic buckle is a symbol of elegance, masterful craftsmanship, modern design mixed with traditional style. His teammates didn't get it, but Paddy had been born this way – an icon among men. He often thought that once his career was over, he would relocate to Milano and work the catwalks. Who wouldn't want to see him in the latest fashions?

It was in this outfit that Paddy strode into his garage and marvelled at how the light reflected back at him from that most holy chariot. Paddy recalled the first time he had ever beheld it: a party at the home of legendary strip club owner Eldon Crawford: the heir of a once-great family that fell from grace after it was alleged that they had publicly supported a certain Balkan chap in the purchase of some armaments. Eldon, though, was rather a smart man: despite his lack of capital, he made the all-too uncommon deduction that men seem to love naked women gyrating on stage and thence had made his fortune. Despite his sound economic mind, Eldon was not able to save the family home and the Crawford name would never quite recover its shine. Unlike the Jaguar XJ, of course – that shone like the moon at its zenith. The dark metallic look and midnight blue finish drew looks from all, and when Paddy saw it at Eldon's party, he had to have it. Right then and there he offered Eldon anything that he wanted for it and Eldon's desires ran deep. He wanted no cash for the car; no. He merely wanted a favour, one that he could redeem at any moment. In his youthful ignorance and highly-paid career, Paddy had assumed that he could buy his way out of any favour he was asked. Over the years, the realisation of what he had agreed to slowly dawned on him, and to this day he is still waiting for that dreaded call, the demand for the payback of his one true love.

As he slid into the seat and ignited the engine, Paddy chuckled at the notion that every growl made his heart skip a beat. This is what the girls must feel like when they're around me, he mused, stroking his granite-like jaw. He pulled out of his garage and proceeded through the gates, tearing away from his countryside retreat of Cowie Estates.

He didn't believe in "Satellite Navigation" – he had been heard to refer to it as "covencraft", a phrase he borrowed from his mother – so he pointed his car south and let his memory do the rest. He followed the cobbled streets and porticoed houses of his village, following the twisting lanes until he saw the signs for the M74. Though he was in a rush, Paddy never drove down south without taking the route through Warrington. The undulating curves of the M6 after crossing the border were familiar to him and he slid down through the lakes like a skilled rafter navigating their favourite section of white water. Even so, on a cool spring morning he'd get an even bigger kick seeing the boxy cobalt IKEA rising out of the mist. Built on the bones of his ancestors, you had to admire what the Swedes had done to the affordable home furnishing scene. Despite the joys this section of the journey brought him, every journey there past the towering warehouse was tinged with sadness and anger.

Paddy's ancestors had been railway pioneers, at least in the words of his maw. He had learnt the truth from his uncle Frank: pioneers they were not; they had worked their fingers to the bone laying tracks for the bloody English and had died in destitution. Paddy's family's blood was in this town and though they had literally laid the foundations for Warrington's success, they had received none of its Midas-like riches. Their bones lay in the unmarked graves of Warrington's pockmarked hills, as is the case of all the Scottish poor that had the temerity to die outside their homeland. Paddy would never make that mistake, for though his talent and skill had graced the Bundesliga for a few years, he always knew that Scotland was his land, and tried to never leave it for too long: certainly not long enough for him to do something stupid like die.

For every metropolis like Warrington, there were a thousand minnow-towns. As Paddy crossed the border he groaned: he'd have to see them again. Lancaster, Morecambe, Preston, Bamber Bridge, Wigan (bloody Wigan 1-0 merchants, Paddy called them) and, after the stop for a pint and a pie in Warrington, maybe a trip into IKEA for some brutalist artwork or some flat-pack piece of genius, he would have to go through Knutsford. Paddy hated Knutsford. His ex-sister-in-law from his first marriage had lived there and whenever he and Tallulah would visit she would always regale him with tales of the high street and of Tatton Park: the Tudor hall that housed its own maze. Stupid English funhouse, Paddy called it. What's the point of a maze, he wondered to himself. If I wanted to get lost, I'd go to Barcelona or Madrid – one of those cities where no one speaks English and I can't read the language. There was one upside to Knutsford, though: while his ex-wife was buggering about in the town centre, he used to guide The Jag to Gauntlet Birds of Prey Eagle and Vulture Park. There's something majestic about those birds and watching them tear carcasses apart stirred something in him, something dark. He could never stay for long for fear that the animal instincts stirring in his being would bubble over and release themselves into the wild.

He resisted the urge to take the turnoff at Junction 19; instead, Paddy roared the engine into sixth gear and glided past a stuttering Ford Ka that was wasting space in the middle lane. He peered across as he passed and immediately forgave the driver: she was quite the beauty. His recollection of her, though, lasted as long as the Ka in his rear window and she soon disappeared into the foggy ether of his memory, along with the string of close encounters that he'd had throughout his adult life.

Town after town flew by, like so many of Paddy's gorgeous first-time volleys. Holmes Chapel, Sandbach, the fake Newcastle and Stoke-on-Trent (whose team, in recent years, had seemingly used Paddy's technical ability to formulate a special throw-in training regime). All those and more disappeared in the blink of an eye as The Jag roared out a warning to the inferior machines around it.

Paddy knew this road well: he had often ventured into the lands of disgrace; the home of the auld enemy – usually to purchase supplies for his more *adventurous* parties – and he often found himself on this stretch. He had stopped at every service station along the way, keeping extensive, detailed notes of what he found in each. Over the years one clear winner emerged: Norton Canes. Now, Norton Canes service station may not look like a five-star restaurant, but Paddy didn't want crepes and canapés at 9am – he wanted meat, starch, fat. Those were the principal ingredients that Paddy needed for a long drive, and he knew the drive ahead was just that; the people of the Norton Canes branch of Fresh Food Café and Costa Express knew him well and they recognised the roar of The Jag as it pulled into his reserved parking space (right near the entrance, adjacent to the disabled parking bays).

Approaching the counter, he was greeted by Marlene: a young, comely woman, maybe 23 years old. No future, clearly, but a fun diversion to kill the time after ordering – and before consuming – a hearty breakfast. No time for that today though. She flashed her usual smile and Paddy noticed that she had fewer teeth than the last time they had danced the disabled toilets tango, and he was momentarily whisked back to that moment. He still bore the scars on his hands from the passion of their... let's call it lovemaking, though that is a generous term for the animalistic rutting of those few minutes. Both of them were sated; both of them were bloody. Both of them were forever changed.

Marlene arched an eyebrow, questioning him in the way that they both understood. Paddy's smile and brief shake of his head broke her heart, just a little, every time he did it, but today the shake was firmer than on most occasions and she understood: she had seen the last game and knew something was wrong. Her passion could wait for the man at home; however damaged he might be, he would have a responsibility tonight – no one could fill Paddy's shoes in bed, but anything is better than the palpable absence that is left once you have had, and been left by, him.

"The usual?" A nod.

She sashayed towards the back, ignoring the short order cook that prepares the meals for the masses and summoned someone altogether more comfortable with a spatula. A square sausage, with a side order of haggis, neeps and tatties was placed in front of him, accompanied by Marlene's disappointed sigh. He smiled at her, ruefully. It wasn't through any lack of desire that he couldn't spare her the time this morning; he had never lacked for energy in that department.

The man from The Costa Express trod the path to Paddy's booth and deposited a coupe glass onto his table. The familiar scent of mint leaves, rum, lime, champagne and bitters floated to him. It was never too early for his Old Cuban friend to join the party, and *this* man could make a fine cocktail. Paddy often wondered why this man wasted his life and his talent here, rather than running a speakeasy in New York, but once he had found this place during his extensive research tour, Paddy never deigned to ask the gifted mixologist; he simply enjoyed the opportunities afforded by the failure of others' imaginations.

Once he had gorged himself on meat, carbs and a rather delightful champagne cocktail, Paddy left his usual small stack of notes on the table and nodded at Marlene as he passed her, whistling, and climbed back into the only girl that could ever *really* satisfy him. In one swift motion, Paddy whirled his car 180° and pulled back onto the toll road, heading south.

He still had over a hundred miles to go, but after a breakfast like that, he figured it would take him less than an hour. The scene in front of him blurred; not from any excess of alcohol – Paddy consumed more than one cocktail before his *flying* lessons, so that wasn't going to shake his concentration – but from the speed of his beloved motor. Just like Marlene, and so, so many others, whatever Paddy asked of her, she provided. If he wanted to do 100mph, The Jag did it, even on the outskirts of Birmingham where the bobby infestation was infamous. Those police cars though, could they really catch him? Certainly not if he didn't want them to, and no one won a race against Paddy when he was in the mood; not even those young guns coming through the academy who were boasting about taking his place in the Claston Celts team next season. "Nae chance, ye wee shite," Paddy spat, to no one in particular. He didn't mind the youngsters per se, but only the ones who showed him the appropriate respect, Mikael Tintoni, for example, or recent academy graduate Antoinne Barclugio. The other little kids who earned extortionate sums before they'd done anything to deserve it and had egos that dwarfed their abilities aggrieved Paddy, who still valued the system that was in place as he was coming through into senior professional football where the young players squired for their seniors.

"Come on, Paddy," he barked. He wasn't concentrating on the road, and at this speed that could mean death. He slapped his face – hard – and rubbed his eyes. Flashing along the side of the road were the signs that pointed the way, like big, blue, silent Sacagawea. Signs for the "great city" of London, the much less great "city" of Coventry and that centre of book-learning that came so naturally to Paddy: Oxford, flashed before his field of vision. In another life, Paddy felt he would have been a thinker – he knew he had the capacity, his nine Standard Grades told him that. He only failed Mathematics, and no one had ever needed Pythagoras after the age of 14, so he didn't regret losing focus on his studies for a moment. In another life, though...

As the exquisite beauty of the North Wessex Downs began to fade and the sign for Reading appeared, he steadied himself for his arrival (he was momentarily distracted by a sign for the UK Wolf Conservation Trust just outside the city but he made a mental note to visit that another time – perhaps he would take Marlene...) and, pulling his hat (swiftly retrieved from his glove compartment) down low over his face, quizzed the locals about the whereabout of OptimoPharm's manufacturing plant. He needn't have bothered: the two huge stacks that cast a shadow over the city should have been clue enough and the local pointed towards them as if they were an albatross that hung its wings around the city's neck. Paddy ventured forth undeterred.

Chapter 10: Paddy's Discovery

OptimoPharm's manufacturing plant was a combination of two of Paddy's favourite kinds of architecture: the glass fronted, Deconstructivist entranceway exhibited a lack of harmony between humanity and nature, seemingly created to enhance the discord and fragmentation of the land in which it was built, yet the origins of the building were crafted in the Beaux-Arts style, with intricately-carved white marble archways and soaring pillars. Clearly, this building was not originally a manufacturing plant, but possibly a seat of power or a countryside retreat for a powerful family who had since fallen from grace. If Paddy had peered a little more closely at the plaque that adorned the grounds, he would have seen an ornate letter C beneath the foot of a fearsome-looking lion: the Crawford family crest that should have been familiar following his past dealings with Eldon.

Paddy, though, was absorbed in his task: he had to find a way to gain information about the production, sales and distribution of a deadly toxin, with no legitimate way to do so. He had no badge, or court-ordered mandate; all he had was his charm and his quick wit. His celebrity wouldn't help him here, in fact, it could severely hinder him. The last thing he wanted was for anyone to know that he was snooping around – if someone were trying to kill him, he wanted to keep his head strictly below the parapet.

Walking through the door, Paddy pulled his aviator glasses out of his pocket and put them over his eyes: this was the only form of disguise – other than his trusty hat, though that seemed inappropriate in a building such as this – that he had thought of bringing. In his own way, Paddy was a clever man – a learned man – but he was not a spy and this kind of subterfuge didn't come easily to him. What he did know, what he had learnt early on in his career, was that people see what they expect to see. It was Bobby Duncan who had told him those immortal words: "If you look like you should be there, people will think you should be there." That lesson about performing on the pitch with more experienced players also held so much sway in every walk of like. Projecting confidence, he walked to the service desk, coughing politely.

From an almost imperceptible door in the space behind the desk a young woman appeared. Paddy took a moment to look at the signs that indicated the names of the offices, in the hope that he could bluff his way through. He affected the English accent that he had had to assume during his time playing in Germany. It had taken him a while to become fluent in German and Hamburg's residents couldn't understand his thick Scottish accent, so he had taken to speaking with as close to a Queen's English accent as possible. Paddy justified this to his friends back home as the path of least resistance, but it killed him to abandon his culture like that. His gift for deception would serve him well here though, he felt. "Hi there, my name is Simon Winterbottom. I represent Reflivax Pharmaceuticals. You may not have heard of us: we're a small company, still making headway in the industry you understand, but one with considerable backing looking to expand rapidly." Paddy hoped his spiel sounded legitimate and continued confidently. "Anyway, I'm looking to speak with the CFO about an important business deal and he asked me to come in this afternoon for a chat. Could I head up to his office?" As he stopped talking, he took a calculated risk and removed his aviators. He held her gaze for a moment, placing his hand on top of hers. If the words didn't work, Paddy reasoned, it would be unlikely if this slight show of physical affection would fail. Women usually loved this kind of act from Paddy and he had learned that physical interaction could be far more powerful than the most carefully constructed words; he just had to hope it would work without her realising exactly who he was.

He watched her carefully, breaking eye contact only to glance at her name badge: "Sally Carruthers – what a beautiful name." Paddy instantly winced at the clichéd line he had just trotted out, but to his relief, like a poorly-made dam in a torrential storm, her resistance was broken. Her cheeks became flushed, she smiled and leaned towards him, whispering in a faint voice: "Mr Winterbottom, I'm afraid our CFO, Ms. Schwarz is not in the building today, but her assistant, Brian Anderson is available. Perhaps you'd like me to call him?"

Paddy paused for a moment and returned his sunglasses to their rightful place, resuming his disguise in case of CCTV or unexpected personnel arriving. The order of the things she said seemed wrong to him: a woman as Chief Financial Officer and a male assistant? Once again Paddy reflected on how the world had changed so much around him and, occasionally, his morals imbued into him by his father left him feeling a little out of touch in modern day Britain. He realised that he needed to update his thinking, to change his circle of friends: spending all that time with the lads on the training pitch didn't allow him the space for personal growth, but Paddy knew that that wasn't an excuse and vowed to tackle this misogyny that was embedded deep within him.

Ignoring this momentary conflict, Paddy assented willingly. Even he had not expected to gain admittance this easily. For hours in his car he had neglected to plan, simply relying on his charm and on pure dumb luck to aid him in his extraction of information. In this case, he had been successful, but how long could he live on a wing and a prayer? When the very trusting Ms. Carruthers gestured for him to take a seat and disappeared to make him a coffee, Paddy pulled out his phone and did some research. It wasn't immediately obvious exactly what OptimoPharm produced, but in order to get beyond the first few minutes of the meeting, Paddy surmised that he would have to show them that he was not simply a minor businessman; he would have to be a serious financial prospect for them to listen to him, let alone leave him unaccompanied for long enough to find any information. All he knew was that he was looking for a toxin: well, couldn't most pharmaceutical products be regarded as toxins in their base form? Paddy felt unprepared, and that wasn't a feeling he was used to. For the first time in many years, a seed of doubt had been sown in his mind as to his ability to achieve something.

He heard, more than saw, the doors to the lift opening. Inside was an incongruous setting, something that more than eclipsed the peculiarity of the exterior of the building: the interior of the lift was lined with brass, with golden Venetian-style mirrors adorning each wall. The opulence was off-putting and threw Paddy off guard for a moment, only recovering his composure the third time that Brian enquired "Mr Winterbottom?" This time, more firmly than the last.

Chastising himself, Paddy nodded and smiled. "Thank you for seeing me – I trust that Ms. Carruthers has explained why I am here?"

"She has, but that did not make it any clearer to me. You are speaking to Ms. Shwarz's assistant, so how is it possible that you could ever have had any professional contact with her without me being aware of it?"

Paddy seethed at the condescending tone: he was used to more deference than that, but he had to play a role; he had to be subservient to this little weasel: a mere boy in an adult's world and approximately a foot shorter in stature than Paddy. In a fight, Paddy would bludgeon him unconscious in a matter of seconds, but that was no good out in the open. He had to charm this man, and a plan was forming in his mind.

"What a delectable design for a lift: if I'm not mistaken, it is an imitation of the one found at Kehlsteinhaus, though even more palatial. May I have a closer look?" Paddy strode past the man before him and there were no security guards to intervene; video cameras, yes, but none of them could stop him, and he hoped, none could identify him clearly: he had made sure he kept his face covered with his hands and glasses whenever he had been exposed.

Inside the lift, Brian began his protest anew: "What business do you have here, Winterbottom? I've never heard of Reflivax and have no idea how you came to meet Ms. Schwarz. I insist that you leave immediately." At that, he planted both his feet shoulder-width apart and made a reasonable impression of a man taking a stand. Paddy did his best to suppress a laugh: on Ascension, this man would be a toy for the children to play with; he'd be well-served to cool down.

Paddy forced a veneer of calm and once again relied on charm, not brawn: "I spoke with Ms. Schwarz about a private business transaction – my Reflivax are backed by an Iranian company that is chiefly interested in establishing a partnership with your company to expand our business network. You know, of course, that only 4% of pharmaceuticals in Iran are imported," (Paddy was well aware of the adage that 46% of statistics were made up on the spot, or was is 27% – he guessed it didn't matter) "which is great for our business, but I feel that we can do better: there is a huge disparity between supply and demand – we cannot create enough Amoxicillin"

(Paddy was sure he had been prescribed this once and hoped the pronunciation was correct) "to keep up with our customer base and Ms. Schwarz indicated that you had the capacity to help us. However, if you are unwilling to deal with a company that you've never heard of, then please excuse me..." at this, Paddy turned and made to exit the lift, with Brian spluttering nervously behind him.

"No, please, Mr Winterbottom: of course, please come with me and I will give you a tour of the facilities." Of course, Paddy thought – if I can't tempt someone with my fame or my beauty, money is always an excellent backup.

On the inside of the lift there was surprisingly little detail, other than a delicate etching of the key locations of each floor above the button panel. On the ground floor was the reception and meeting rooms; the floor below led to the analytical labs and the process development suites. Floor –2 housed the "purification level" – a name that perplexed Paddy. Floor –3, the lowest floor, led to the developmental laboratory. As much as those options intrigued Paddy, Brian gently tapped number six: heading above ground to the top floor and upon their exit from the lift, Paddy was again shocked by the wealth that lay in the hands of a previously unknown pharmaceutical company. It dawned on him then that there must be thousands of places like this all around the UK, large, faceless corporations that spent little on wages and product and exploited those people that truly needed help. A champagne socialist was the painful label that he had received from his old friends on Ascension – the ones that had either abandoned him when he became rich, or the ones that became hangers on and were soon dismissed.

Other than his family, no one from the estate stayed around for him too long and they loved to talk about how he'd forgotten where he came from. Perhaps they were right, he mused, reality dawning upon him that he had no idea about how people were oppressed: he had been told that they were and he believed it, but life was too good to obsess about such things when Old Cubans could be brought to you by your butler at any time of the day or night. Paddy wondered if his focus had slipped; the young Paddy wanted to care, but football had been his life and battling societal ills had had to wait. It was in that moment that he first considered whether, just maybe, his successes had changed him, that maybe his vast wealth had turned him into a different man to the one that might have developed had Bobby Duncan not spied him all those years before. Immediately he dismissed the notion as preposterous, but it did not vanish, lingering in the back of his mind, ready to return, bigger and stronger, when he was ready for a true reflection on himself.

As Brian continued the tour, Paddy realised why the owners of OptimoPharm had decided to add on another wing to their production facility: the land itself was beautiful, but the building lacked the imposing grandeur that the glass towers had afforded it. Roughly 100 feet above the ground, Paddy now had a 360° view of the building and the lands that surrounded it. Behind the factory, beyond the edge of the white stone walls and the marble facades lay a labyrinth. Paddy estimated that it must be at least 8 hectares in size – a huge, complex web of hedges and rows. This was not like the maze at Tatton Park, and Paddy was mesmerised by its beauty.

"Ah, I see you noticed it: before the Crawfords fell from grace they made an exact replica of the Labirinto Della Masone by Franco Maria Ricci. I'm sure you've heard of it."

"The Crawfords?" Paddy spoke too soon, unable to keep the surprise out of his voice. Hardly a fatal misstep, but a reminder that must keep his guard up at all times.

"Yes, detestable rabble: you must be acquainted with their history. Ms. Shwarz says – and I've always appreciated her little bon mots – that the only thing worse than the Crawford's history is their present!" At that, Brian tilted back his head and tittered. Paddy was not the least bit amused and thought back to his beloved Jag, but he feigned mirth for the sake of easing his access to information.

"So, Ms. Schwarz said that your company was able to produce over one billion Amoxicillin tablets a year to help us to meet our demands. However, we have even greater need than even that: what else do you produce at this plant?" He realised that he was taking a risk with this question, but was confident that if he were exposed his physical prowess would allow him to escape the building. Those pesky cameras were everywhere though, so that would remain a very final resort.

"Well, we manufacture Ibubrofen and Oxycodone for the most part, as well as fusing thallium with interfelamide to help in the production of computer parts. Perhaps you'd like to see our granulation processors?" Bells started ringing in Paddy's head following the latest manufacturing summary, but he could not think why. Brian gestured back towards the lift, but Paddy noticed the file cabinets in the corner of the room and he wanted to have a closer look. "Maybe later, but first, please do tell me more about the labyrinth."

"I didn't realise that you were a fellow labyrinthophile, Mr Winterbottom. Well, in which case do let me explain the intricacies of this particular piece..."

Paddy saw this as his opportunity to slip away as Brian intoned his sermon – one that was clearly well-rehearsed, and included walking slowly along the circular glass window, regularly gesturing to the complex system of hedges below. *"Inspired by Argentinean writer Jorge Luis Borges..."* Paddy, feigning interest in the labyrinth below, walked slowly in the opposite direction, occasionally uttering fillers to Brian's monologue. In a world of his own, Brian continued around the corner and out of sight, his dry voice floating back towards Paddy, becoming all the while fainter and fainter. This was his chance; Paddy crept across the room to the file cabinets, opening the one marked 'sales records' and took the thickest file that he could: there was no time to be more specific, Brian would surely notice that he was missing. And then the monotonous voice began increasing in volume:

"when Minos decided upon the creation of a Labyrinth, his intentions were sadistic, bestial even..." Paddy stuffed the file up his shirt and buttoned up his jacket; the tightness of his outfit would have betrayed his deception immediately. "inspiration struck our dear architect...." As Paddy returned to Brian, he made his excuses; he would simply love a tour but would prefer that it happened with Ms. Shwarz at his arm.

"I'll make sure that she knows what a gracious host you were though, Brian. Thank you for such a warm welcome." With that, Paddy laid a hand on Brian's arm and gave it a gentle squeeze. Paddy regularly entranced the ladies, but he felt that Brian was not immune to his magnetism either, and Brian's light gasp of surprise at being manhandled only affirmed his beliefs. "Thank you, Brian. I can show myself out."

Chapter 11: The Trail

Waving as he hurriedly passed Sally by, Paddy strode towards his car. He didn't want to spend a moment longer than necessary in that place, particularly as he was now in possession of a second bundle of documents that he had no legal right to access. He gunned the engine of his majestic Jaguar and drove east towards the M4. He knew that this was too much for him alone; chemistry was his second weakest subject at school after mathematics and with the passing of time since those heady days of lab explosion pranks and setting ties alight over a Bunsen Burner to get out of lessons, he knew that this went beyond whatever he could have gleaned from his Standard Grades.

He had another plan though: he had kept his eye on the progress of his peers, even if they were never truly his friends. There was more than one reason why his parents, and the Celts, insisted that he attend Thistledown College: it was the finest school in all of Scotland, and offered him a fine Plan B in case of a career-threatening injury. In his years there, it became apparent that he was surrounded by the elite, and, Paddy being the resourceful (and eventually popular) young man that he was, had made sure not to alienate anyone. A few boyish pranks here and there, some well-deserved beatings once in a while, but only minor scuffles, the odd bit of teasing, all good fun as Paddy recalled, such is life in a prestigious school. Naturally he had always had to maintain a cool distance from most of the other boys: his talents led to a horde of hangers on and he couldn't overexpose himself, but Paddy knew that these boys would be useful at some point, and *this* was that point.

The man he would call upon to help him today was Dr Fergus Wyatt: lead researcher and lecturer at Imperial College London's Institute of Chemical Biology. He would surely help Paddy puzzle out these clues, would almost certainly delight in it.

Fergus (Fergie to Paddy) had aged poorly. His elliptical body reflected one of the two passions of his life (the other being his studies, of course): he was always open to the offer of a cake or chocolate as a boy, and when Paddy saw him waddling across the quad, he recognised him immediately. He was Paddy's antithesis: whilst Paddy was tall, muscular and powerful, with a strong focus on the athletic, Fergus was short, pudgy and weak. His mind was his temple, and it had borne ripe fruits for Fergus, who had become the youngest senior lecturer in Imperial's history. Paddy knew all of that, of course, and was hoping that Fergie only remembered the favourable interactions he had had with Paddy rather than the one less than friendly run-in they had had (or was it two? More? Fergus was the podgy, unpopular one, after all).

It was best not to dwell on those though, Paddy reasoned. No one harbours any resentments from their teenage years, certainly not learned professors like Fergie, who turned to face him at the sound of his footfalls. Paddy took a moment to observe this man: whilst Paddy was still wearing the perfectly-selected outfit that he adorned himself with this morning, Fergie looked like he'd been shopping in the bargain bins of a charity shop. Maybe this was the retro-chic look that Paddy had heard all about but if it was, he wanted nothing to do with it. Fergie had squeezed himself into a pair of too-tight denim jeans, the waist of which strained desperately, like a ship's sail trying to contain a hurricane. The legs of the jeans hung limply, as if they had never met flesh, simply flopping about with no form or function to consider. The shirt could be forgiven, if indeed it were worn on a Caribbean island in the height of summer, but this was late April in London, and a linen shirt in beige should not be adorned on these shores. The *chef-d'oeuvre* of Fergie's outfit though, was the polyester jacket that tugged roughly at his flaccid, drooping shoulders. Originally grey, the colour had faded so sickeningly that it resembled the ancient victims of the succubus Lilith that Paddy had read about in his research of Sumerian mythology; the lining of the jacket was threadbare and gently collapsing in on itself. Again, Paddy was forced to muse about the justness of their society when he compared their clothing, but once more the urgency of the moment dismissed those concerns for him.

Recognition dawned on the face of Dr. Fergus Wyatt. His fingers stiffened and his face began to contort: brows shifting together, face flushing red, eyes narrowing and, all in one

65

movement his arm came up and Paddy felt a stinging blow across his cheek. Everyone on the quad turned to look upon the scene of the assault and the atmosphere was sucked out of the space like an exposed vacuum. Silence followed, with all nearby seemingly incapable of movement or sound.

"Did ye just fuckin' slap me, Fergie?" Paddy growled deeply, quietly, trying not to draw attention to himself and his old schoolmate. "Who fucking slaps another man, laddie? Have the courage of yer convictions and make a fucking fist. Dinnae stand there fucking shaking, ye fucker: if ye want tae hit me, hit me. Ye've got reason tae, Ah'll give ye that, so Ah'll let ye have one swing: make it fuckin' worth it."

Paddy spoke these words firmly, but he wasn't really angry. As he said, Fergus had a fair reason to land a blow on him, but he'd done it publicly and Paddy couldn't allow a slap to stand. A punch, yes, but a slap was the ultimate sign of emasculation, and Paddy wouldn't lose his manhood to this feeble figure. He waited for a moment, but Fergus didn't move. After a pause, Fergus lost all conviction and the adrenaline that had coursed through his veins a moment earlier left him, leaving behind only shame and weakness. He slumped to the ground, sitting cross-legged on the grass, his back leaning against a nearby tree. Paddy motioned to the bystanders with a jerk of his head and, focusing on the suddenly-far-more-interesting ground, all departed swiftly, leaving the two old acquaintances to speak alone.

Dr. Fergus Wyatt, who thirty seconds before was a ball of human rage and was now a broken man, was being held upright on the ground only by the presence of an ash tree that had stood there well before either of these men were born. His face now sported a sullen, guilty look, like that of a teenager caught in a tryst with his cousin, and resolutely refused to meet Paddy's gaze.

"Look at me, ye twat." Fergus did as he was told, though he petulantly informed Paddy that his thick accent wouldn't do him any favours here.

"This is a place for gentlemen, not for savages, and the people here won't respect you with that cacophony you call an accent. I know you can speak well – I saw it when you were playing in Germany – and I thought you had changed. I suppose the saying is true: you can take the boy out of Claston..."

Paddy bridled at this and clenched his fist in frustration. "Sorry, McAlpin! I'm sorry. Please don't strike me! I mean it though: they will judge you. Take care, lest you be branded something less than you are." Paddy relaxed his arm and extended it to Fergus, mending his speech.

"Up you get, good doctor, the same is true for you."

Dr. Fergus Wyatt, lead researcher and lecturer at Imperial College London's Institute of Chemical Biology, took Paddy's outstretched hand and, pulling himself to his feet, let out a groan that will be familiar to all unfit men over the age of 35. He embraced Paddy as he would an old friend. "I'm sorry, McAlpin. You know why I did that, but a gentleman should keep his hands to himself. Come with me, I can see you need to talk." The two walked off together, leaving just the faint outline of Wyatt's considerable behind on the grass as any clue that they had ever been there.

Fergus' office was less grand than Paddy had been expecting and its drabness was made all the more pronounced by its comparison with Paddy's most recent experience of the plushness of OptimoPharm's surroundings. However, that was the scene of a crime, and one that tickled Paddy's moral compass in a way that he didn't like. Paddy was all for the end justifying the means, but sometimes the means required left a bitter taste in his mouth, and the twin manila envelopes that Paddy now carried in his kit bag weighed upon his mind and his body in equal measure.

"Fergie,"

"No, McAlpin. We're not friends: we never were and it's been 20 years. You may call me Dr. Wyatt: I worked hard to earn that title and I deserve the gravitas that it brings.

"That's fair enough, Doc." Fergus inhaled sharply, as if to say something, but then thought better of it. This compromise seemed to work for both men.

"Did you see the news about me this week?" Fergus looked at Paddy quizzically. Of course he had seen the news, but which bit?

"I've seen a lot of news, Paddy. It's happening all the time, after all…"

"The news about me, Ah mean. About the girl that died in mah arms." An almost imperceptible nod followed. "Well, I spoke with the police," Paddy continued. He always seemed to struggle to say that word without contempt, but did not pause in his delivery, "and they told me that I'd ingested the same toxin that killed young Claire. Yae wouldnae know the lass…" At this, Paddy paused, eyes cast downwards. "Do you have any coffee, Doc? I haven't had the chance to hydrate for a few hours: I've been on the road all day." Chastising himself for this uncharacteristic lapse in his hospitality – everything about Paddy's presence had thrown Fergus off kilter – he sputtered,

"Naturally, McAlpin: please accept my apologies, it's been a… surprising day."

He left the office, heading for the staff room where his most prized possession had been relocated: the copper-coated Bella Neapolitana espresso machine. He had set it up in his office, but the dean of the university decreed that it was a safety hazard, what with all the steam that shot from it and spewed into his compact working environment. Fergus saw through that, of course, but there was relatively little that he could do to prevent this – his options were to share the machine or drink *instant* coffee from the kitchen: he couldn't abide either option, but the lesser of the two evils at hand was the option whereby his colleagues had access to his beloved machine. Sometimes, just for fun, Fergus would remove a part from the machine and sit in the staffroom, sipping his coffee and waiting for his colleagues to have a little accident. The hardest part of this process was to feign concern for the poor unwitting fools as they screamed in pain as the steam poured onto their hand or arm. Fergus had never told anyone about this little hobby, and for good reason too. It seems that Paddy's impact on his childhood had consequences more far-reaching than a simple fear of the man himself.

Returning, Fergus held an espresso in each hand, the cups delicately balanced on plates of matching gold leaf. The tiny drink, high in caffeine, was not quite the hydration Paddy needed, but he would not refuse Fergus' hospitality, nor would he turn down the warm rich comfort of the finest of Italian coffee. Fergus hadn't managed to regain his self-control fully, so Paddy heard him coming from two rooms away: the shaking of the cups was the disturbing sound of a disturbed man. The rattling of Fergus returning, reminiscent of Marley's chains, once again reminded Paddy of his own guilt, both of the bad deeds perpetrated on Fergus' body and mind as a boy and of the documents that he held in his possession. Paddy was no expert on the law, but he knew he could be facing some serious jail time for this, and, if Detective Inspector Galloway were asked, he would say that the document outlining the potential producers of the toxin had been stolen from the police station, rather than implicate himself and ruin a lifetime's worth of work. He would deny all knowledge of the documents from OptimoPharm, and why shouldn't he? That was solely Paddy's doing. Paddy was on his own now and would have to live and die by his own decisions. There would be no press team or adoring fans to support him this time.

Waiting for Fergus to sit down, Paddy deftly reached across the meagre office space to lock the door, hanging his jacket across the door's glass window to ensure total privacy. He didn't think to check for bugs: he wasn't that paranoid yet. At the lock's click, Fergus stiffened: "McAlpin, what the hell's going on here?" And so, Paddy told him. He omitted no details, and by the time he had described his actions in OptimoPharm's manufacturing plant, the building was almost completely deserted. The only other people around were the cleaning staff, silently and methodically shuffling their way through the department. Outside, the sky had darkened to welcome the sombre evening. It was then that Paddy laid the freshly purloined documents onto Fergus' office desk.

"I got these two from the police; the D.I. said that these were the results of the blood samples taken from Claire and myself. He reckons that we have traces of the same toxin in there, though she had a much higher dose than they found in mine. He couldn't tell me what it was though, only that I should have a look at OptimoPharm. I can't see what's so important in there, Doc, I don't know what I'm looking for. Please, help me."

"Ah, McAlpin, this sounds like something I really don't want to get involved in. If I look at these papers, I'll be committing a crime; in fact, I'm pretty sure even knowing that they exist is a crime." He pushed the papers gently back towards Paddy, stopping when he saw the man's huge hand come down to rest on the top of the two envelopes. He looked up, straight into Paddy's eyes and knew there was no refusing him. He voiced his thoughts, unnecessarily, "I can tell you'll never leave me until I help you, will you?"

Paddy's expression showed his meaning clearly enough: hands on his splayed knees, a dark look in his eyes and lips pursed. He shook his head, just perceptibly enough for Fergus to see it and waited, staring deep into Fergus's soul.

"Shite man, give them here then," and Paddy pushed the envelope towards him. After perusing them for a few moments, Fergus' eyes narrowed and he inhaled deeply, slowly. "Jesus, Paddy – have you ever heard of thalelamide?" Paddy frowned. "It's a compound of thallium and interfelamide. Thallium on its own is incredibly deadly if ingested, but when mixed with interfelamide it's mostly used in the manufacturing of computer parts! This sort of thing should be nowhere near a human being's blood stream." Fergus was sweating and shaking anew, far worse than the scare that Paddy gave him had produced. His face matched his jacket's pallor and moisture was showing through the polyester and beading on his forehead. He wiped his sleeve across his moist brow, the sweat leaving another darkened mark on the grey jacket, and took a breath: "McAlpin, you don't seem to understand – look at the numbers here: the amount in your body was about the right amount to incapacitate you, maybe a little bit on the short side for a man of your size, but certainly enough to cause you some problems; it would have looked like you'd had too much to drink and you should have collapsed on the pitch. There's no way you should have managed to finish that match! But look -" and here Fergus animatedly thrust the sheet into Paddy's hands. "Claire's dose was 14 times higher than the one you received. McAlpin. Someone tried to kill you."

Paddy had suspected as much, though he secretly harboured confidence that even the dosage that killed Claire would have left him fine after a cup of tea and a kip, but this revelation shattered even his exterior of cool. Moments passed without either man speaking, without a cleaner passing the door, without the slamming of a car door or the honk of a horn. Fergus took the initiative, feeling that he was becoming more and more involved in a plot that he wanted less and less to do with: "McAlpin, you said you had two lots of paperwork?" That brought Paddy back to earth; he'd forgotten about his stolen cache for the moment, the shock rendering him completely inert. He pushed the other envelope into Fergus' reluctant hands. This pack was thicker, containing over a hundred pages, double-sided, single spaced. These were the accounts of OptimoPharm. In the wrong hands, these documents could make someone very wealthy indeed. Neither Paddy nor Fergus were interested in that at this time, though: they wanted a similar goal. Paddy to learn what he needed to depart and catch the man who was stalking his shadow and Fergus to be rid of Paddy. The problem was huge, though: the sun had set and the day was well gone. Fergus professed to Paddy that he could not work through all those papers that night and promised to contact him in the morning. "There are plenty of hotels in London, McAlpin: find one that suits you and leave me your mobile number. I'll call you if I find anything interesting. I need a strong drink and a few hours in which I don't have to look at you."

After Paddy had left, Fergus blew out his cheeks, still slumped in his chair. He reached for his phone and made a call.

Chapter 12: The Hotel Bar

Paddy made his way to The Savoy in central London: a place that he'd stayed many times before on trips to the capital. He loved the suite that he often used, with its solid marble floor and the Jacobean-inspired furniture, all dark wood and ornate carvings. Particularly pleasing to him was the heaviness of the drapes, all the better to extinguish the light of the outside world and sleep all the more deeply. However, it was not sleep that drew Paddy tonight – he needed rejuvenation after a long day, but not from the succour of sleep – he had seen the hotel bar before and knew the opportunities that awaited him: this was the haunt of the married woman, seeking respite from the tired marital bed. After his first few dalliances in the early part of his career, Paddy had stopped asking any personal questions: he understood the truth about women (and indeed men) of this kind – they wanted to take the initiative; they wanted to live out their fantasies of the flesh and act in a way that was frowned upon at home, and Paddy was more than willing to oblige. Seeing Claire, before her miserable death, and leaving Marlene unsatisfied had stirred something within Paddy and he needed to feed the beast that howled.

He headed down to the bar, taking a seat near the door. He didn't want to act like a peacock, displaying his prowess for all to see: he would be more subtle than that – more like a rattlesnake, striking when the time was right. He signalled to the waiter, attired smartly in black trousers, white shirt and a taupe waistcoat, whose close-cropped hair and demeanour conveyed the impression of self-control. Paddy could discern no split ends or flyaways; people respected themselves at The Savoy, and as a result, Paddy could respect them. After the day that he had been through, Paddy was feeling like a change from his usual routine. The waiter recommended that Paddy try Ernest Hemingway's Death in the Afternoon, as he was a fierce proponent of both strong drinks and champagne cocktails; Paddy assented, not wanting to seem ignorant by enquiring about the details of the drink. While he waited, listening to the clinking of ice in the glasses of the other members of this little community, Paddy surveyed the crowd.

To his left, most of the tables were empty, though places were laid as if the head waiter were expecting a sudden rash of couples coming to experience the delights of the Savoy's legendary hospitality. One table, though, was taken and to Paddy's delight it was clearly a couple in the early stages of their relationship, perhaps even on a first date. Paddy loved to observe this kind of situation and there was no negative outcome for him – either the date would go well, in which case he felt himself blessed to be present to witness the successful burgeoning of a freshly-blossomed relationship, or the date would be an abomination, which, if anything, Paddy enjoyed even more. He couldn't say exactly why he enjoyed it so much, but he relished the word schadenfreude, once his teammates had introduced him to it on a night out in Hamburg. The exquisite beauty of seeing someone else suffer, particularly the overconfident or hubristic males: nothing made Paddy laugh so hard as witnessing their misfortune. There was one time, though, that Paddy was ashamed of witnessing, even though the memory of it still brough a smile to his face. He had once observed a date going so wrong, so painfully, excruciatingly wrong, that the downfall of it hurt him even to this day to think about.

The offending couple had been having drinks in a low-class bar in Claston, Paddy sat at a table nearby, sipping from his pint of IPA. He was alone on this occasion – it was one of his days where he required solitude above all things. He didn't need to be alone so much as to not be with people he knew and observing the behaviour of others was rather a therapeutic experience for him. He noticed the stilted conversation, the long pauses and the man constantly swiping the screen of his phone. This dalliance was clearly in its death throes. Paddy sat and listened as the small talk became smaller and smaller until the date reached its natural conclusion: Paddy had lost all sense of time by this point.

Maybe it was the copious amounts of IPA, maybe it was the heady feeling of witnessing something so awkward, but Paddy was entranced. The couple got up and left the table, Paddy followed them – not too closely, for he was experienced in this type of manoeuvre – out of the bar and towards the main street. As they approached the train crossing that, absurdly, goes through the pedestrianised area of Claston, the siren rang out that indicated a train was to arrive in the next few moments. This meant that the barriers would come down and the couple would have to wait for at least five minutes until the danger cleared and they were able to go their separate ways. In desperation, Paddy assumed, the male companion shouted "Come on, we can make it," grabbing his female partner's hand and attempting to drag her through the crossing before they became trapped. Unfortunately for him, she resisted, slowing his escape.

Again and again he pulled at her arm, encouraging her to rush under the barriers and escape the interminable delay. Again, she resisted. Finally, abandoning any hope that the date might take a turn for the better, he released her arm and jogged playfully through the barrier site. Before he went past the final barrier, he turned to wave his partner for the evening goodbye, rubbing his eyes in a mock-tearful gesture to indicate his sadness at the lack of success of their date. Unfortunately for him he hadn't been paying attention to the train barriers, the second of which descended upon his head with a great thunk; he collapsed to the floor, rendered unconscious by the blow, but falling to safety on the far side of the barrier.

Only Paddy and the female witnessed the outcome of this event and neither were ashamed of the peals of laughter that emanated from them both for the next few moments. Both were doubled over with laughter at the poor man's misfortune, both were filled with joy at the sound created by the blow and both were somewhat ignorant of whether he was actually okay: they were both too preoccupied with their own mirth to check on his safety. They did, though, lock eyes and, seeing that there was a mutual spark, proceeded to Paddy's car, where events took a turn for the better for them both.

Despite the passionate lovemaking that followed, Paddy still felt a severe pang of guilt whenever he remembered the man's prone body as the rather fetching woman reached for Paddy's hand and they strode with great purpose to the car park where Paddy had parked his Jeep. He swore in the years that followed that like a documentary film maker, he would never intervene in a situation like this again.

On this night, though – his thirst for schadenfreude was unquenched: the couple seemed to be engaging in playfulness, she with her hand on his, he with his foot caressing hers. The words were stilted, but the underlying passion was not.

He scanned the bar: couple, single man, single man, small group. Nothing so far. Yet next to the piano sat an exquisitely beautiful older woman, late forties perhaps, whose class and beauty had not faded, and her undoubted sexual prowess struck Paddy like a hammer blow (look at her demeanour: look at the way she carries herself, such confidence, such grace). Her golden hair was cropped short, just below the ear, but curled playfully from the temples. Lines worked around her eyes, but rather than emphasising her age they accentuated it, making it seem more alluring. Her eyes shone emerald, a unique look, which was perfectly complemented by her make up artistry – the reddish hue of her eye shadow attested to her understanding of the aesthetic beauty that she held.

Tearing his gaze away from her eyes for a moment, Paddy breathed in the beauty of her form: age and gravity seemed to work with, not against, her in her quest for perfection. Her slim, sublime form was clear for all to see in her Chartreuse dress, which ended just above her knee, inflaming Paddy's lust. Their conversation was brief. Charlotte, for this was her name – or at least, how she referred to herself; Paddy knew better than to ever question anyone's identity in this situation: most people gave a false name for a one-night stand – took charge of the situation immediately, dropping her hotel room card into Paddy's lap as she walked past, gesturing for him to follow. He did so dutifully.

Their brief time in the lift was one of the steamiest encounters that he had ever experienced. She could manipulate her body in a way that he'd never seen in another woman and she correctly judged his physical prowess: he would have no problem throwing her around like a rag doll, if that was her desire.

Charlotte's room was not as impressive as his own, but she was insistent to carry out their liaison on her home turf. Pushing Paddy onto the sofa, she removed herself to the bedroom, returning with some lighted lavender candles and wearing a purple satin robe, the belt of which she used to secure one of Paddy's arms to the sofa leg. She wanted him to fight for her, or against her. She wanted a struggle.

Charlotte stepped out of her flimsy garment, staring deep into Paddy's eyes. Her body was luminous in its beauty; Paddy smiled:

"It is not only light that falls over the world spreading inside your body
    Yet suffocate itself
  So much is clarity
  Taking its leave of you
  As if you were on fire within
  The moon lives in the lining of your skin"

Charlotte chuckled, enjoying the theatre of her companion. "Pablo Neruda. You're not just a pretty face." At this, she mounted him, using her surprisingly powerful, supple form to excite and entice Paddy, who reached for the lavender candle and poured the wax lavishly onto her body, where it singed her skin. She gasped in delight, deriving pleasure from the pain, her back arching, her toes curled. She returned the favour in kind, leaving nail marks on her conquest's shoulders and teeth marks on his chest until he shrieked in pain. Dominating him, she struck his face with her palm and laid her arm across his mouth. This was her night, though he enjoyed their passion immensely. Paddy was unsure how long he let Charlotte have her way with him, but he was glad for his fitness and stamina as she came back again and again before finally collapsing, naked onto the bed, leaving Paddy to sit alone on the couch, breathlessly.

Hours later, Charlotte lay unconscious still. Paddy stood, naked, surveying the scene. He thought about how he had ended up here, conscious that he was yet to contact Fallanks and explain his whereabouts and his absence from training. He wouldn't worry about that now, not in the early hours of the morning. For now, he was satisfied, the confusion of the previous few days was melting away like the wax that had been so instrumental to his evening's exuberance.

And then a soft buzzing broke Paddy's reverie, and like the setting of the wax, the details of why he was in London set hard in his mind. Retrieving his phone and belongings, he crept out of Charlotte's room, wishing he had time for one more outing. Outside the door, wearing only his hastily-flung-on underwear, Paddy answered the call.

"McAlpin: I've got news for you." It was Fergus. Paddy hadn't expected to hear from him so early. "I went through those documents and OptimoPharm has thousands of customers; their biggest one though, by a very long way, is Ordenadex, who are ordering huge quantities of this compound, more than three times any other customer. They are a computer hardware company based in Bilbao, McAlpin, but even some of the biggest of those wouldn't need thalelamide in these quantities.

"I spoke to an acquaintance of mine, McAlpin, one that I trust. He works in the world economy section of the London Register, you see, and he says that Ordenadex have been investigated by the Spanish government multiple times in the past due to suspected shady business practices, but they haven't been able to make anything of their suspicions. My source says that there's something there, but the company is tight lipped and well-funded. I don't know how you'll do it, McAlpin, but you've got to find out why Ordenadex are buying so much thalelamide and what they're using it for. I'd hurry, McAlpin... I saw something this morning that I didn't like..." At that, the phone line went dead. Paddy repeated Fergus' name time and again into the receiver, but no reply followed. The call had ended.

And so, Paddy's next step was one that led him somewhere he could never have expected when he set out in his Jag less than 24 hours previously: Ordenadex's head offices, in Bilbao.

Chapter 13: AWOL

"It is being reported that the Celts and Scotland superstar Paddy McAlpin has gone AWOL. McAlpin, has not reported for training for at least the past three days. Normally the model professional, McAlpin has not been seen since his arrest following the mysterious death of his old school friend, Claire Duggan, outside the Ascension House estate in the immediate aftermath of the Celts' semi-final victory over Dundee United. Since his release, McAlpin, who was declared not a person of interest in the case, has not been seen. Detective Inspector Galloway of Claston Police has made a statement to reiterate that McAlpin is not a suspect in Duggan's death, nor is he required in any further inquiries. When pressed further, Galloway remained tight-lipped, refusing to elaborate on whether he was aware of Mr McAlpin's whereabouts. The Celts' fans will undoubtedly be hoping for a speedy return of their star player with the cup final not far over the horizon. We'll bring you more on this story as it develops. This is Vicky Kilbride…"

Mikael Tintoni groped for the TV remote and switched off the news, letting out a sigh. He had been feeling troubled for weeks now, more than anyone could know, but the semi-final match had brought things to a head.

Tintoni and McAlpin were not close, but he had always had huge respect for his teammate as a professional and as an individual. He felt privileged to play in the same position (even if it was not Paddy's preferred one) and to learn from the master. Although Paddy primarily played as a central midfielder, he had also revolutionised the full-back role in Scotland, taking the attacking instincts of some of the great Brazilians and adding to it the defensive solidity of a traditional British centre-half. This, combined with Paddy's flair, dynamism, rasping long passes and predatory prowess (of the goal-scoring variety), had seen him score myriad spectacular goals to complement his almost one in three assist record.

After almost one season playing and training alongside his hero, Tintoni had improved massively, something he was quick to credit to the great man. Paddy would often give him advice about positioning, awareness and options. His long-range passing had improved and he was being talked about as a young player to watch. Rumours abounded that he might make the move to England in the close-season, something he was not at all averse to. A conglomeration of Italian looks, thick dark hair, permanent day-old stubble and olive skin, combined with the physical presence of his Germanic ancestry, meant that Tintoni had become quite the pin-up in Claston, particularly with the younger, more impressionable fans. This was something else that Paddy had been able to help him with, and had, more than once, given him solid advice about what Paddy referred to as "the fairer sex".

Tintoni had heard the phrase 'never meet your heroes' many times, but since meeting Paddy he felt his admiration had only increased. There were times where Paddy barked orders and became frustrated with the players around him, bemoaning their lack of effort or lack of ability, but he also knew how to motivate, when to be harsh, and when to be sympathetic. When Tintoni had needed help moving house in mid-season, let down at the last minute by the company Paddy had recommended, Paddy had stepped in, and the two spent the day conversing in German about the unreliability of removal companies whilst lugging Tintoni's few belongings from one flat to another across Claston.

Tintoni was, of course, aware that Paddy was missing, long before the news outlets had broken the story. Paddy had not been seen at the club since he went for his drugs test, with his absence at training keenly felt by all. It was, indeed, Paddy's absence that Tintoni used to explain his drop off in performance. While the other players had managed to adapt better than he had without their talisman, Tintoni's performances had continued to worsen and now teammates were calling him up on his poor control, his wayward passing, and his sloppy defending.

His own poor performance in the previous match had been overshadowed by the uncharacteristic dip in the performance of McAlpin, but it was now clear to the whole squad that something had changed in Mikael Tintoni. He thought back to that day and shuddered, trying to suppress the pain of that memory. He should have helped Paddy more that day. Instead, he had just been thinking of himself, of his needs. Deep down he knew that Paddy was the only reason he was staying in Claston. With Paddy gone, a move to England would suit just fine, despite the trouble it may cause. In some ways, he hoped that Paddy didn't return, allowing him to start afresh somewhere and leave the dreary land he now called home, instantly cursing himself for daring to consider such a stream of consciousness. With so little of the season left, surely he would still be looked at as a good signing by those south of the border...

But he couldn't think like that. His mentor needed help. But what could he do? He admitted to himself that he knew nothing about espionage, nor had any clue where Paddy might be. Thinking around these problems was not something he had ever had to consider before, his life had been one explicit instruction to the next, his every whim seen to by a plethora of hangers-on and money-grabbers, hoping to get a slice of the pie he was about to be served by his next big contract. Had he been more capable of self-awareness and independent thought, Tintoni would probably have wondered why these people could not put the same effort into creating a path for themselves and their own futures as they did to ensure they were right behind him on his, ready to pounce on the scraps that he discarded along the way to his future.

A lifetime of living in the moment, always just a click or a tap away to show what he liked and instantly dismissing what he didn't like had given him one particular skill that could help though, a skill that was shared by many of his generation – how to Raise Awareness. A plan started to form in his mind, a social media campaign, and, wait! He could even take it into the physical world, utilising the media sharks that were eagerly circling the training ground like a school of gathering hammerheads around the rotting carcass of a whale, all desperate to take a bite of that sweet flesh but all wary of being the first to make that most daring of moves.

To Tintoni, that seemed to be the only way to help. Get the media, or at least the public, to side with Paddy, and not with Fallanks. His plan, if you could call it that, as it had the nous of a five-year-old navigating a maze whilst drunk and blindfolded, was simply to wear a Celts shirt with the slogan #IStandWithPaddy emblazoned on the front whenever he went out in public and repeat the very same hashtag at the end of all social media posts he put out there. As a revered and handsome young footballer, his reach was considerable. He even determined that he would seek out interviews with the old-fashioned "traditional" media as a way to defend McAlpin and try to atone for the damage he had already caused, even if doing so resulted in a fall out with Fallanks.

Tintoni opened up his laptop and made to search for a company that could create such a shirt. Noticing his unread email and determinedly ignoring it (as he so often tried to do), Tintoni found himself typing in the familiar web address of his most frequently-visited site, just to have a quick look at the latest odds, before making a start on his task.

Chapter 14: San Mamés

Having got the very next flight from Heathrow to Bilbao, Paddy had made his way to a hotel near the city centre and ventured out to enjoy the warm evening. As he ventured out, it was immediately apparent that there was something happening tonight, the swelling population surely unusual for a normal evening. He was used to crowds, but he normally knew their purpose, normally knew what their collective goal was. Often it was to see him perform his own art, his ballet with a ball. This crowd, however, largely ignored him. Today, he was not the star attraction. The buzz in the air was reminiscent of that around a stadium prior to a match, such was the tense laughter, the apprehension of wondering whether your team would triumph or suffer at the hands (or feet) of another. He watched as the Spaniards, enjoying this balmy evening, headed west, chatting passionately about something Paddy could not understand. The throng were making their way from the Plaza Moyúa towards the lifeblood of this ancient city – The Estuary of Bilbao. Like many major European cities, the presence of a river had been the catalyst for trade and, as a result, the formulation of business and residences alike. This short river of just 72 kilometres was long known in the local Basque tongue as Ibaizabal, meaning wide river. Although the Spanish name Nervíon is happily used by most residents and visitors these days, there are still arguments between proud Basque separatists and loyal Spanish unionists regarding the naming of such long-standing natural features.

Bilbao built its success on the banks of the river, becoming northern Spain's most important port throughout the late 19th and early 20th centuries. But, like many booming cities, its growth had to falter at some point, and as the world became a smaller and better-connected place, the use of Bilbao as an important harbour diminished. The heavy industry took its toll long into the future though, with pollution suffocating the river, destroying all life along this once prosperous stretch. By the time of Paddy's birth, the Ibaizabal had become one of the most polluted rivers in the world. Paddy was pleased to learn that this most human of issues had been tackled in a way that he would have been proud of, and a huge conservation effort by the city had seen the Estuary of Bilbao once again teeming with aquatic life.

Throughout his career, Paddy had never played at the San Mamés Stadium, and allowed himself to become swept up in the bubbling flow of this human rivulet, hoping it would give him a chance to see the ground before he diverted north-east to scout out the offices of Ordenadex. The offices should be easy to find, housed as they were next to the city's tallest building, the imposing, all-glass Torre Iberdrola. As they drew closer to San Mamés, the crowd grew larger, but this was definitely no football crowd. Paddy had heard the legends of how the Bilbao supporters arrived as one in a sea of red and white shirts, each and every fan dressed in unison. But here, the spectrum of colours rivalled even that of the paintings of Spain's most famous artist. And still the air tingled with that sporting electricity. Intrigued, Paddy wandered on, keeping his head down. Although he had never played in Bilbao, he was well-known in Spain, and he could do without the attention of fans. He was aware that his club had no idea where he was – he would have to deal with that later – and the thought of Fallanks discovering his whereabouts through the Spanish media did not bear thinking about.

As Paddy drew closer to the stadium, he could finally see its structure rise above the warm tarmac, the mass of fans milling around the wide-open expanse of concrete, not yet ready to enter the stadium, enjoying soaking up the pre-match-of-whatever-sport-this-was atmosphere. He dodged his way carefully through the crowds, sidestepping large groups swilling beer from plastic cups. This seemed as good a chance as any to enjoy the local cuisine, and Paddy made his way to a pop-up kiosk with the words La Salve proudly emblazoned above the bar. Paddy listened carefully as he waited, picking up just enough of the local lingo to order a beer.

"Garagardo bat, mesedez" he spoke confidently, hoping that this would make sense to the young man who smiled at him. Clearly it did, as the man quickly opened a bottle of La Salve and poured it carefully into a plastic cup, handing it to Paddy. Paddy handed over a note in return, smiling and pointing at the young man, as if to say "for you". The man smiled again, speaking for the first time.

"Eskerrik asko."

And with that brief exchange, their dealings were done, and Paddy continued into the night and towards the stadium. As he drew closer, he was soon impressed with the delicate design, a million white metal icicles that so contrasted these sunny climes, tessellating to create an effect that almost took Paddy's breath away. As he contemplatively sipped his beer he also drank in his surroundings and decided that maybe his mission to Ordenadex could wait until later this evening...

Paddy had not learnt any Spanish in school or since, let alone the Basque that he was unaware was being predominantly spoken around him. His language was limited to English (or at least Scottish), German, a smattering of Italian and the Classics – Ancient Greek and Latin, neither of which had proven particularly helpful to him since he left Thistledown for the final time. But then, something pricked his ears. Above the hum-drum droning of the crowd came the clear dialogue of English. Paddy turned up his collar and pulled down the peak of his hastily-purchased "I ❤ Bilbao" baseball cap and moved a little closer to two women who were conversing in a language he understood perfectly well. Immediately, Paddy realised the reason for the use of English; the women were of different nationalities and needed to speak in a shared language. At a guess, Paddy would have put the taller of the two women as Dutch. She was tall, fair skinned, and had the unmistakable slur on her pronunciation of each leading s. The other woman was harder to place, but Paddy with a gun to his head would have gone for French or Belgian. Her ebony skin suggested a heritage from central Africa, but her speech was more north European, delicate and nasal, and almost certainly of Latin origins. Finally, thought Paddy, those Latin lessons have proven useful.

Paddy drew closer, listening carefully as the two women spoke animatedly about what could only be the sporting event that was imminent.

"He hash sheero chansh!" the fair skinned woman said, waving her right hand across her body dismissively.

"Of course 'e does. Juss look at ees record." The darker woman said dismissively. "'Ee has not lost a competiteev arm wrestle in almost twoo yee-ars!"

"Becaush he hash shpent more time on the treatment table…"

That was enough for Paddy to glean that he was at some sort of Arm-Wrestling Championships. He had to confess that he was shocked at the turnout – he had not known that arm-wrestling was so well-followed and was incredulous to see international fans outside a stadium with a capacity for more than 50,000 people. The crowd around him soon started filing into the stadium, emptying the area around him. He watched as the two women he had seen just moments earlier embraced and made their ways to separate entrances. He glanced down at his watch. It was still only early, particularly for an evening in Spain, just coming up to 7pm. Now the crowd had diminished he could see the posters advertising the first round of matches. He didn't need to speak Spanish or Basque to understand that 20:00 meant 8pm, meaning the event was still over an hour away. There must be an incredible warm up act, Paddy thought with a smile. He was still smiling as he headed towards one of the gates, hoping he could still get a ticket; however, his smile was soon wiped from his face as he saw something that drained his colour, leaving a hollowness within him.

Chapter 15: The Double

Paddy rubbed his eyes like a cartoon character seeing their nemesis survive being crushed by an ACME 10 ton weight. He was utterly incredulous to what he was seeing: His face stared down at him from poster after poster. *He* was supposed to be part of this championship! How could that be? He moved closer to the posters, mesmerised by the giant version of himself that held his gaze with unmoving steel, and started to notice a few irregularities that didn't seem to make sense. The nose was slightly smaller, betraying the time Paddy had had his own nose broken in an academy match scuffle. The eyes were also a different colour, brown, rather than Paddy's deep jade, though both of those minor differences could be explained by clever photo manipulation. Paddy had never entertained the wizardry of what he heard referred to as some sort of a photo shop, preferring to remain untouched in his promotional photos, unaware of, or at least unwilling to consider, the industry standard of post-production editing. Was that what had happened here? It didn't make any sense though. Why would his face be on a poster in a foreign city? What could it possibly mean? Intrigued, he joined the back of the small queue that remained at the only turnstile available to him. They certainly did like to pack you in early at the Arm-Wrestling World Championships.

Eventually, Paddy reached the front of the queue and gestured to ask how much a ticket was slurring out "Una ticketo per fervor?" in embarrassment. The turnstile operator gasped as she saw him, alarming Paddy, albeit briefly.

"Sergio!" she cried, "Oh Sergio!" Tears began to well in her eyes as she rushed around to him, letting him through the barrier without charge, jabbering quickly in what Paddy assumed (correctly) to be Spanish. The little lady ushered him past the fans who were gathering in the concourse, ignoring their disbelief as she rushed by, dragging Paddy along with her. They made their way through a set of double doors, and then another. The lady continued to talk at an incredible speed, and Paddy wondered if she had drawn breath since she saw him.

And then, without warning, she stopped. In front of them stood a towering man, clearly a member of security. The queen of the turnstiles pushed Paddy towards him, muttered something, turned, and left, wordlessly.

Paddy looked around confused, but the lady had vanished (not that she had been much help to him anyway) and he was now accompanied by this new stranger. Again, Paddy was confronted with a language he did not know (again, Spanish), but this time in a deeper, sterner timbre: a voice of authority. The security guard, who exceeded even Paddy in height, although perhaps not quite in bulk, spoke into his wrist, and a moment later two further security guards were rapidly gesturing him into the bowels of the stadium corridors.

Above him he could hear a low murmur of a crowd, not quite the fever pitch he was used to, but certainly one of excitement. The championship warm up must be almost ready to play, Paddy thought, until glancing at a clock he realised his own stupidity. He had forgotten to wind his watch forward an hour; the championship was about to start.

The noise of the crowd grew louder and as Paddy turned a corner he recognised where he was from every match he had played throughout his illustrious career. This was the tunnel and he was about to step out to perform...

Paddy arrived at the tunnel entrance, joining seven other men: large, hulking specimens, not unlike himself. None looked around as he joined the final space in the two neat lines of four, each clearly focussed on their own game. Paddy had barely had time to stand in the queue before the men were marched out to, what was for Paddy, an underwhelming applause, yet looking around him, he saw at least two of his fellow competitors shudder in sight of the big occasion. One crossed himself as he stepped out, kissing his closed fingers and raising his hand to the sky.

The men were led out onto the pitch, where a stage had been erected. There were pitch-side seats and the lower tier of one of the goal end stands was full of fans. Paddy did some quick calculations based on his experience in stadia such as this and estimated there were around ten thousand people in attendance. Small fry to Paddy, who for years had regularly played in front of crowds at least five times the size of this, but impressive for such a minor sport. Immediately, his competitive side took over and a crazy thought crossed his mind; perhaps he could use that mental strength under pressure to his advantage in this absurd situation that he now found himself in.

On the pitch, in front of the north end goal stand, five rings had been set up in the configuration you would see on a die, much like boxing rings, but each with a table and two chairs perfectly aligned to the ropes. Surprisingly, the centre ring was slightly lower than the surrounding four and was empty, whereas the outer four each housed an official, sharply dressed in navy polo shirts and crisp white linen trousers. The clean lines of their outfits emphasised their status as the authority on the important situation at hand. Paddy approved.

Without warning, the lights that were illuminating the pitch went out and eight spot lights flashed on in their place, each illuminating one of the competitors. The crowd fell silent as one by one, a deep voice introduced each man. At that moment, Paddy was, perhaps for the first time, thankful for the exploits of the British Empire. The compere was speaking in English, his Spanish accent faint but noticeable.

"Aaaand our first competitor, hailing from The Netherlands, the Golden Rooster. AART DE HAAAAAAAAN!" Paddy rolled his eyes at the theatre of it all, but a few pockets of the crowd cheered in adulation for their champion. Aart de Haan raised his arms above his head weakly and swallowed, before making his way to the furthest ring from where he was, the spotlight following him like a faithful dog looking for a treat.

The charade continued, with each man being announced amidst a smattering of applause and making his way to his seat, waiting solemnly across from his opponent. Soon enough, Dinis Guilherme Da Silva (Brazil) had left the line and taken his seat. Paddy stood alone and looked towards the crowd, but blinded by the spotlight he saw only the dazzling photons that allowed everyone present to see him so clearly. He waited for his introduction, rolling his shoulders, cricking his head from side to side and shadow boxing. Paddy was an entertainer, and if he was going to be thrust into the spotlight in this arena, he would entertain.

"And now, ladies and gentlemen, the man you all came here to see, the local legend, the Beast from Bilbao,

SERRRRGGIIIIOOOO! BRAAAAZZOOOO-FUUERRRTE!" Paddy took a moment before realising that was his cue, foolishly expecting to hear his own name being read out. The crowd went wild, at least in comparison to the previous names, and Paddy played up to their cheers, conducting them through adagio, allegro, energico and fermata, and finally, as he entered the ring, crescendo. This was his concerto now, he was the maestro, surrounded by his supporting orchestra.

Paddy sat down and faced Da Silva, a smile on his face. Da Silva did not smile back but held Paddy's gaze in a show of defiance at the mistaken home favourite. Paddy wondered whether the other competitors realised that he wasn't who everyone else seemed to think he was. He had no idea how often these men came into contact with one another and could not tell if they would know Brazofuerte if they saw him. Unblinking, he looked back, allowing his smile to relax and then harden into a scowl. His eyes narrowed and he looked on, knowing that this was the real battle. Da Silva blinked and turned his head ever so slightly to the left, still looking at Paddy. But Paddy had sensed the weakness in his opponent and leant forward just enough. Da Silva blinked again and looked down at the table, rolling his shoulders and slapping his face gently. He wasn't fooling anyone, and by the time the referee told the pair to place their elbows by their respective marks to start their bout, Paddy knew he had already won.

All four matches started simultaneously, with the crowd cheering their men with a fervour that even Paddy was impressed with. As he expected, his bout was soon over, his regular workouts and upper body strength proving too much for Da Silva to overcome. Always gracious in victory, Paddy held out his hand to shake that of his opponent. Da Silva, head slumped on the table, looked up at his victorious adversary and hesitated, before breaking into a smile and leaning across the table to embrace his foe. The crowd screamed their appreciation at this, and Paddy played along, lifting Da Silva's arm high into the air to show the fans what a gentleman he had just faced. One by one, the matches around him ended and the losers of each bout made their way back into the tunnel and to obscurity once more. They had had their chance of glory but could only watch on, literally powerless, as fate ripped that chance from their strong, sweaty hands.

The four remaining competitors sat patiently, waiting for the next announcement. After what Paddy considered a quite unprofessional delay, the compere was back and announced the semi-final matches. For these bouts, the two rings nearest the fans were to be used, meaning Paddy had to take his place in a different ring. His next opponent was to be the Ivorian Yannick Pokou. As Paddy walked towards his new seat he looked once again towards the crowd. The spotlights were no longer on and he could clearly see the fans for the first time. He waved and received another cheer, revelling in his newfound fame as someone he wasn't, marvelling at the ludicrousness of his being here. He wondered what had caused Sergio Brazofuerte to miss out on this occasion, inwardly thankful that he had. A tinge of empathetic disappointment shot through his body from his head to his toes, but soon passed without recourse. He had a job to do in Bilbao, but the draw of adulation was too much to resist for a man who had spent over half his life very much in the public eye. Paddy continued on until he was at his new seat. Pokou sat waiting, elbow firmly placed on the table, his hand out ready for the bout before Paddy had even sat down. This man was focused and this would be a far sterner test.

Pokou was a big man, even by the standards set in this competition of gargantuan men. Even without his top-tied dreadlocks rising from the crest of his head, he would have been significantly taller than Paddy. The shaved sides of his head only added to the intimidation factor. Pokou wore a brightly coloured, loose-fitting vest, exposing his bulging chest and rippling arms. Paddy was a confident performer, but even he wondered if this might be a bridge he could not cross. Pokou leant forward and tilted his head back, looking at Paddy through his draping dreadlocks.

"Come, boy," he said, quietly, confidently, his deep voice resonating across the stark white expanse between them. "I've been waiting for you."

Paddy sat down slowly, deliberately, recalling previous arm wrestles that he had won. The key to victory was whole body strength. It wasn't really about the arm at all but a complete mastery of the upper body, with the abdominals and obliques playing just as important a part as the deltoid. The referee signalled for Paddy to put his hand up to meet Pokou's and the battle was ready to commence. Just as the two men took the strain of each other and waited for the signal to begin a yell came from the other table and the competitor with his back to Paddy jumped from his seat, clutching his left hand to his right arm, clearly in some distress. A moment of confusion, and then the referee held up the arm of the still seated competitor to signify that he had won by default. All attention now turned to Brazofuerte vs Pokou and the two men resumed the position, shaking the distraction of the other match from their minds.

The referee counted down, and upon his whistle, the bout began. Pokou went hard early on, his biceps bulging as he slowly forced Paddy's hand down onto the table. Paddy gritted his teeth and pushed back hard, doing little to stem the flow of the flood of strength washing over him. It was not in his nature to give in, but he was beginning to think that this was not his competition to win. He closed his eyes and took a deep breath, ready to release himself from this torture, when suddenly, from the back of his mind came a call.

"There can be only one."

The call of the Highlands, memories of home, of Ascension House and Aoife. Of Galloway, and of course, of Claire. Paddy pushed his elbow into the table, cracking the gleaming white veneer and levered his hand back up. Pokou had gone hard early on and was tiring. This wasn't over. Paddy pushed again and let out a deep guttural growl. The crowd around him rose to their feet, yet he was unaware of anything except the need to get his hand down to his left. Pokou was struggling now and brushed his dreadlocks back over his head with his left hand, this manoeuvre being his undoing. The miniscule shift in balance was enough to give Paddy the advantage he needed, and he crashed Pokou's hand onto the table before slumping face first onto his podium of victory.

Chapter 16: The Ukrainian

The final now beckoned. His opponent, he soon learned, would be the three-time and current world champion Mykolayovych Yavorsky. Paddy could not have known, but Yavorsky had suffered from the opposite upbringing to himself. Born to the Ukrainian upper classes, Yavorsky had fallen out of favour following a number of indiscretions of increasingly violent severity, the last of which involved the mutilation of a live goat on the village green. Such a publicly deplorable act could not be hushed up and swept aside as a "boys will be boys" affair amongst Pavel Yavorsky's social circles, and his father was left with little choice but to ostracise his second son and youngest child. This had come as blessed relief to Mykolayovych's elder siblings; his sister Orynko had long worried that her brother's actions would jeopardise her betrothment, and with it, her guaranteed life of luxury, and his brother, Yevhen had long worried for his own safety, despite being three years Myko's senior. And so it was, one bitter November morning, the 22-year-old Mykolayovych Yavorsky was cast out of his family home, never to return.

From his lavish lifestyle in the family estate on the outskirts of Lviv in the west of Ukraine, Mykolayovych headed east to the capital, where he knew there would be many opportunities for a man of his talents, mistakenly confusing the idea of ability with the background of wealth. His father was not so callous as to leave him penniless, and the youngest Yavorsky set out with enough money to see him through a year of living frugally. By the time Myko had reached Kiev, he had burned through three quarters of his allowance, with the majority going up his nose or into his bed. Once in the capital city, Myko avoided the fact that his funds were running low and he needed to find work. Such a concept was alien to a man of his upbringing and was not befitting for a member of the gentry. Delaying the inevitable, he headed into a hotel bar, ordering vodka after vodka, and when the bartender, somewhat bravely, refused to serve him a 12th shot, Yavorsky responded in the only way he knew how, by smashing his latest empty glass into the ear of the poor man.

The bartender was instantly floored, lying behind his bar with shards of glass protruding from his ear, blood slowly seeping onto the floor. Amongst the commotion, Yavorsky climbed over the bar, pulled the remains of the bottle from its optic and calmly left the scene, his bleeding hand dripping a sticky red trail across the floor and out onto the snowy streets outside. When the police arrived, no one present was able to give an accurate description of the man and no one claimed to have ever seen him before. The trail of blood ran outside, but soon disappeared amongst the sludge and grime of the city streets.

Yavorsky walked the streets, swigging from his bottle until he collapsed into a heap in an alleyway, determining to rest for the evening and find work once he awoke. It was then that fate threw him an unexpected and undeserved lifeline in the form of Chaban Rebrov. Chaban had suffered from his own demons – most notably, and thankfully for Yavorsky – alcohol addiction. Unlike Yavorsky, he had battled against the exploits that society deemed debauchery, successfully coming out the other side as, not a good man, but certainly an accepted member of low society. Upon seeing Yavorsky, his instinct was not of disgust, or even of uncaring antipathy, but of piteous protection. The strapping, stocky young man before him, lying prone, unconscious, had clearly fallen on hard times. His clothes betrayed his affluent upbringing, immediately indicating to Rebrov that this was a man who, somewhat like himself, had been abandoned by his own kin. He managed to haul Yavorsky to his feet, waking him from his alcohol-induced slumber, and slowly guided him into his own warm home, and out of the icy reach of the piercing December night.

Over the course of the next few weeks, Rebrov nursed Yavorsky back to some semblance of health and mental stability. For his own part, Yavorsky was happy to be waited upon again, and was not averse to taking advantage of the kind hospitality of his host. As time continued, Rebrov found himself falling for Yavorsky. Love can be cruel, and before long, he was utterly and totally besotted with the man he had saved from an untimely death, the man who could so easily have been just one of many vagrants who perish in Kiev's frozen winters.

Yavorsky settled into his new life happily. Living in a two-bed flat was not as good as the mansion house he had grown up in, but was better, he reasoned, than sleeping rough. Rebrov provided everything he *needed*, but refused to provide him with what he truly wanted, namely vodka and prostitutes. So, for the first time in his life, whilst Rebrov was out at work, Yavorsky took it upon himself to fund his own way, challenging men in bars to an arm-wrestling contest. If he won, they bought him a shot. If he lost, he threatened them until they bought him a shot. He would never ask the same customer twice on the same day, and for the most part, the citizens of the poorer part of Kiev accepted that this was how things were. And then, word got around that there was a hot shot who fancied himself as a hustler, and some of the gangs decided to take him down a peg or two. It was then that Rebrov was first exposed to the darker side of Yavorsky.

Yavorsky had been working his usual ploy of arm-wrestles for drinks when he was approached by a man far larger than he was, a man challenging him, rather than the other way around. Yavorsky accepted, confident of his ability after many drinks already. He duly lost and flew into a drunken fit of rage, taunting his victor and challenging him to a fight out on the street. The man accepted and made his way out, followed by the inebriated Yavorsky who picked up a fork from a table he passed on his way to the door. Although he had the forethought to grab a weapon, he was unable to wield it, and, once his opponent clocked on to this disregard for fighting lore, was handed a severe beating.

Broken and battered to within an inch of his life, Yavorsky crawled his way back to Rebrov's accommodation, passing out on his sofa and awaiting the return of his acquaintance. When Rebrov did return, Yavorsky was a hollow, beaten man and he lay still as Rebrov soothed him, asking no questions and passing no judgement. But when the truth of the matter did out, Rebrov vowed never to let the same thing happen again. Blinded by his love and misguided in his intentions, he foolishly decided that the best thing to do was make sure that Yavorsky wouldn't lose again. After making some calls to men he had not spoken to since his intervention days, he found an ongoing source of anabolic steroids and dedicated his time to making Yavorsky into an unbeatable foe in arm-wrestling circles. When Yavorsky discovered that there were genuine competitions where money could be made, he saw this as his future, and perhaps his way back into his family home.

Taking advantage of Rebrov's unrequited love for him, Mykolayovych sought out contests in which to compete, continually pumping himself with the steroids he felt he needed to improve. He spent minimal time training, and as little time with Rebrov as he could. Their relationship took on one of emotional and psychological neglect, with Yavorsky doing just enough to maintain the status quo as Rebrov's lover, whilst Rebrov refused to accept the truth of the situation, supplying steroids and occasionally urine for samples, allowing Yavorsky to compete at the highest level.

It was well known within arm-wrestling circles the tactics that the Ukrainian pair employed to win, but it seemed that nothing could be done. It was Rebrov's suggestion, much as he hated it, for Yavorsky to hide a vial of urine in his pants for every competition, and with testing procedures nowhere near thorough, the pair continued to get away with their illicit behaviour. Most athletes dreaded facing Yavorsky and would avoid it at all costs, such was his brutality and flagrant disregard for the gentlemanly conduct of the noble sport. Had Paddy have known any of this, he would have realised that Yavorsky's win by default in the semi-final had nothing to do with him being the stronger man (although he probably was), but more to do with his opponent not wanting to face the serial cheat and violent thug that was Mykolayovych Yavorsky.

Paddy was already at the disadvantage of having completed one extra round to his final opponent, and the referees seemed to agree it was only fair to allow a recess before the final bout of the evening. Paddy, having no one to talk to and no idea of particular tactics that might be of use to him sat waiting in the seat in which he had won his previous round, alone, silent and contemplating how the final might end up. Yavorsky, on the other hand, made the most of the delay and, whispering something into the watching Rebrov's ear, marched down the tunnel to the changing rooms with Rebrov scuttling along after him. If any of the officials had followed the two men they would have witnessed a furious argument, Rebrov trying, and ultimately failing, to stand his ground. When threatened with the prospect of Yavorsky leaving him to branch out on his own, he caved, and handed over two syringes, warning Yavorsky against its use, but it was no good. Both syringes went straight into the bulging right bicep, followed shortly by a line of cocaine up the nose. Yavorsky's eyes rolled back in his head, and with a shudder he jumped up and headed back out.

Upon his return, the two men were guided to the centre ring which then rose from its sunken position like a pillar of Atlantis, finally resurfacing after a lifetime of hiding below the foamy waves. By the time that Paddy was facing his opponent the crowd had grown restless. Yavorsky was a pantomime villain to them, with Paddy, mistaken by all for Sergio Brazofuerte, a knight in shining armour, but very much an underdog. The referee signalled for quiet and a hush fell over the stadium. The two men stared into the others' eyes and Paddy could instantly tell that something was not right with his opponent. Rebrov stood at the bottom of the plinth, silently praying for his beloved yet troubled rogue.

"I am going to crush you, leetle man." Yavorsky muttered. Paddy remained silent, focused.

The two men took the strain; the referee counted them in and blew his whistle, a sharp peal to indicate the final round of this test of strength of body and mind. Yavorsky's arm surged forward, using the full power of his chest and shoulders to attempt to force Paddy's hand down, but this time, Paddy was ready. He clenched his teeth and held firm, once again pushing his elbow hard into the table to resist the lateral movement pressing so strongly against him. Yavorsky pushed again, harder, grunting and straining. Paddy, staying silent, eyes gently closed. Holding firm with all his might he focused his mind, employing the visualisation skills that had for so long helped him with his football. Floating above himself he saw his hand slowly inching Yavorsky's hand down, down, down, and serenely watched on as the Ukrainian helplessly floundered and finally collapsed. He saw the referee raise both his arms, the crowd cheering his name, as he was so used to…

"Paddy! Paddy!"

But no. No one here knew he was Paddy. The cries were not of his name, but of another. Snapping back into reality, his eyes now wide, he realised that it was his own hand that was inching towards the table. By now his teeth were clenched so hard he was sure they would shatter under the force of his jaw. Sweat beaded on his forehead and a single vein began to protrude on his temple. The sinew of his muscle screamed, their cries of agony drowning out the sound of the crowd, all desperately urging their mistaken Spanish champion to victory.

And then, the screaming in his body stopped and crowd fell silent. Paddy opened his eyes and looked down at the table in front of him. The match was over.

A snort from across the table was followed by another guttural sound. Paddy looked up from the table where his own hand was lying helplessly under that of his opponent. There were veins popping all across Yavorsky's temple, branching out onto his forehead like unfettered ivy. A trickle of blood seeped from the Ukrainian's nose and across his pursed lips. From far below them, Rebrov began to shout, gesticulating wildly. Paddy could not move his arm, pinned as it was by Yavorsky's hand. Yavorsky released a final grunt before collapsing onto the table, his cheek resting on the glossy white surface next to his victorious hand. The blood from his nose was the only imperfection on the white veneer.

From his left the vast majority of the partisan crowd jeered the defeat of their hero. A small island of cheers erupted amidst the ocean of disappointment. Exhausted, Paddy looked upon his foe; the huge man was yet to move from his resting position, his head still slumped at the effort he had given to his cause. The referee tried, and failed, to raise the man's hand to formally declare him the winner. The thin trail of blood had stopped flowing and a small ochre crust was forming around his right nostril. It was all Paddy could do to wrench his defeated hand out from under his victor. He knew how it felt to give your all and be depleted of all vigour after a hard-fought match, and waited patiently to congratulate his foe.

As the ring was lowered back to its starting position, Rebrov, who had been anxiously waiting at the base of the plinth, rushed on to embrace his champion and lover. As soon as he reached Yavorsky, Paddy could tell there was something amiss. The referee was not so attuned to the plight of Yavorsky and held up a weighty bronze trophy in the shape of a flexed arm with a clenched fist for the crowd to see before thrusting it towards the newly crowned World Champion. When Yavorsky still failed to move even to collect his award, the naïve official instead handed it to Rebrov, plainly failing to see that Rebrov had no desire for a hunk of metal.

Paddy was concerned now, and he bent forward to check the man's breathing. He felt nothing, heard nothing. Reaching forward, he placed two fingers lightly on the oversized neck, desperately trying to find a pulse, but the damp, clammy skin was still and lifeless. Paddy tried to shout out for a medic, but his calls were drowned out by the crowd who had begun to move in to get a closer look at what was going on. This was no longer the fairy-tale story he had hoped to tell at the club Christmas dinner.

From across the table Paddy could see the panic appear in Rebrov's eyes as Rebrov shoved the trophy towards him. For a moment the two men's gazes met. No words were spoken, no language was shared between the two of them, but Paddy could tell what Rebrov was saying to him – get away from here, take this cursed trophy and get away.

As Paddy received the trophy that he had not earnt Rebrov began to scream: a soul-piercing, anguished sound that Paddy would never forget escaped Rebrov and in a moment that still shames him to this day, he stepped out of the ring and fled the scene, back into the tunnel, away from the swelling crowd, away from the competition he had so nearly won, away from the man mourning his lover and away from the madness.

Although Paddy never did find out what had happened at the end of that competition it was later announced that Mykolayovych Yavorsky had suffered a massive coronary failure, the combination of steroids and cocaine proving fatal. He was taken back to Kiev by Chaban Rebrov and buried in an unmarked grave. Other than Rebrov himself, no one attended the funeral, and no one mourned. In time, Rebrov was surprised to feel no sadness at his loss. Instead, he found a freedom that he had not enjoyed since before the sadistic but handsome man that he found on the streets had come into his life.

Chapter 17: The Day The Crowd Gasped

One of Paddy's earliest memories was advice, somewhat inappropriate considering his age, given to him by his father: "Son, if ye're ever threatened by a group of guys then there is only one thing tae do. Turn tae the biggest of the group and tell him that, whatever happens next, ye're going tae break him. Once ye have him on the ground then go for the next biggest. Repeat. Repeat. Repeat. Once the dust settles, only the strong remain." Paddy always remembered this.

Growing up on Ascension House was both a gift and a curse: during his formative years he was challenged early and challenged often, and he had taken more than a few beatings. Once he had dished out a particularly savage kicking to Bobby McAlister though, he was never challenged again. It's not that he was a "hard man" or a "nut" – he was just relentless, and his workout regime in his youth focused primarily on power; something that probably accounts for his preternaturally large frame and renowned upper body strength.

Indeed, the thrashing he'd dished out to Bobby had been passed from generation to generation and was known locally as *The Day The Crowd Gasped*.

If you utter those words to anyone walking the streets of Ascension House everyone will stop to regale you with their version of events. There is an identifiable coherence to everyone's tale, even if the importance of each different narrator's part of the event is often eulogised.

Unlike Paddy, Bobby was a "hard man" and a "nut". There were rumours that as a wee bairn he'd beaten his Irish Wolfhound to death with his bare hands because it bit his little sister. Others still suggested the reason had little to do with his sister and more to do with Bobby not liking the way it had looked at him. By the age of eleven, Bobby already had a reputation as a serious guy, someone that you don't cross. He was part of The Ghost Mob: a group of twenty-strong youths that would descend upon their enemies without warning, provocation or mercy.

The Ghost Mob was founded and ruled by Shaun O'Neill – a terrifying, imposing man who grew up in the shadow of The Troubles. Born in Derry, late in 1957, Shaun cut his teeth in a life of violence fighting firstly with his brothers, whom he lived with in an overcrowded house that overflowed with family members, disease and vermin, and then with strangers as he took to the streets, using violence for money, status and power. The biggest marker that he laid down for the people of Derry was his role in the Battle of the Bannmouth. His family were staunch Catholics and well-known in the area as a source of violence and danger. Over the three days: 13 to 15 August, 1968, Shaun and his older brothers (as well as a supporting cast of local Catholics) took part in a pitched battle with the RUC and local Unionists. Each of them kept their tally of men that they had battered; his brothers managed a creditable number, but Shaun bettered them all, displaying callousness and savagery in dishing out his beatings. Despite being only ten years old, Shaun's reputation was cemented, and he spent the next thirty years fighting for Irish independence from the United Kingdom. On the 10th of April, 1998: the day the Good Friday Agreement was signed, Shaun boarded a ferry from Larne to Cairnryan, seeing that the battle was lost and fearing greater persecution than he had ever experienced before. He found his new home in Claston – using his ill-gotten funds to purchase a penthouse apartment in Ascension House council estate, where he established his new criminal enterprise.

Shaun, known as IRA Shaun throughout Ascension, oversaw all initiations, delegated crimes and schemes, appointed lieutenants and organised his forces. He liked to keep full-time members limited to people that he knew and could trust, hiring young, desperate boys and girls to act as lookout and signalmen. Shaun led through fear and was ruthlessly efficient. He allowed no errors and was proficient in making those people who disappointed him disappear. He used his penthouse as a base, and surveyed his territory day and night, missing nothing.

One of the initiation rituals of The Ghost Mob was said to be the running of The Gauntlet. The premise was simple: the names of all the gang's members are placed into a sock, the inductee choses five at random. The clock starts when the fifth name is drawn and all this person must do is survive for six minutes. Some people run. Some people choose to fight. Some try a mixture of the two. Most people fail. Ascension House was abuzz whenever an inductee was slated to attempt The Gauntlet; crowds would gather to watch, eager to sate the bloodlust that IRA Shaun had brought to the area and from his arrival seemed to go hand in hand with the deprivation of Ascension House. Sometimes people would come from afar; men and women who were clearly from the other side of the great divide (the vast tract of railway tracks that separate the gentrified centre from the desolate east) to sample a little taste of slum life. More often than not they left with a story to tell, albeit a frightening one, and very little money. Sometimes they didn't get to leave at all; the rivers that skirt the edge of the city had been used for more than shipping.

Bobby's initiation though, happened when he was nine; some may think that's a ludicrously young age to join a gang, but in Ascension, there are few options and even less freedom. Those who aren't academic, or haven't been born into a family that can help them to find a trade to ply are often sucked into the underbelly of the city, eagerly signing up as cannon fodder in the frequent turf wars that blighted the city, following the gilded false promise of a better life.

Paddy, in the first few weeks at Thistledown College, once the more well-to-do boys in his form had learnt where he was from, overheard one of the merry little rakes of the Oxdown Club (a club for rich boys to do posh things) opine, wittily (in his opinion): Dulce et decorum est mori pro acervo lutum." (It is sweet and fitting to die for your pile of dirt). Paddy failed to see the humour; he had seen it happen.

Bobby did not have to face The Gauntlet and was instead inducted into the gang after he took part in what is known in Ascension as a "Slash Off". Two gang members, both armed with Stanley knives face each other, surrounded by a ring of men. The only way to win is to draw blood from your opponent's face before they do the same to you. Bobby's opponent in the slash off was Jamie McGowan, his older cousin, who had been with the gang for six years previous. He was a towering hulk of a boy, and at fourteen years old had five more years of hardening on the streets than Bobby did. Other gang members thought that because Jamie was Bobby's cousin, he'd take it easy on him but if they thought that then they didn't really know Jamie. Jamie would punch his own mother to move up the ranks in The Ghost Mob and he had already taken part in multiple stabbings, muggings, armed robberies and car thefts before Bobby had even thought of joining.

Typically, a "Slash Off" will last between two and three minutes. The participants will circle each other, cagily at first, with the occasional hopeful slash easily parried by the more experienced fighter before a close-range scuffle breaks out, one of the two is caught with a punch they didn't see coming and the victor slashes the face of his opponent while he is reeling. The larger man generally wins.

Bobby's "Slash Off" with Jamie lasted for eight minutes. None had ever lasted longer. It began with circling, feeling each other out, but Bobby had another strategy: he was not interested in slashing, no – he wanted to hurt Jamie. He grappled with him, stabbing at Jamie with his free hand. This strategy seemed a foolish one for the smaller man to adopt, but Jamie wasn't expecting Bobby's pent-up rage, his angst, his feeling of abandonment to come out in this volcanic blast. Bobby stabbed Jamie in the arms, in the hands, anywhere to weaken him. Jamie, in turn, landed blow after blow on Bobby's face and though Bobby was bleeding profusely, simply bleeding didn't end the contest – it must be the cut of a blade. Weakened through the loss of blood and the constant grappling of his cousin, Jamie made a wild lunge for Bobby's blade; a serious error. Bobby took one step back, forcing Jamie off balance and floundering forward, plunged his Stanley knife directly into the eye of his cousin, permanently blinding him on his left side. There were no cheers that day. No handshakes or fist bumps. No hugs. Just silence. Awe.

In the intervening years, Bobby had had six more "Slash Offs," each one ending in victory and costing the gang a potential member. "Nae matter. We dinnae need any fuckin' pussies in our group; we're Th' Ghost Mob 'n' we dinnae gi' a shite." Most of the members of The Ghost Mob had a healthy fear of Bobby, but they reasoned that it was better to have him around than not, and he mostly kept his violence in check, or rather, they did, with sufficient numbers at hand.

Though Paddy was aware of Bobby's existence, and vice versa, they had never crossed paths; Paddy's focus on, and popularity from, football kept him insulated from the darker elements of Ascension and though he had fights with regularity, often he was exposed to the young louts who had something to prove, not those who had already proven themselves worthy.

On *The Day The Crowd Gasped*, Paddy had spent the day in school: in those early days at Thistledown College Paddy was more focused on establishing himself as someone to take seriously: most days he was referred to as "Scholly" (mockingly referring to his tuition fees being paid for by the Celts, not by his family), and it took all of his self-control to not lash out physically. He knew that if he couldn't control himself though, he would have no chance of making it with his beloved club. He made his way home in the normal way: his driver took him to the edge of Ascension, leaving him to walk the rest of the way (it was better not to draw attention to his new-found comfort and his driver preferred not to enter the infamous territory) when he was invited to join a game of football by some of his old friends from primary school. Paddy was twelve years old then and was just beginning to develop his muscular strength; his shoulders were beginning to fill out, he already had some definition across his chest and his six pack had begun to show through his lean torso. In fact, the (legal) supplements that his coaches had given him, alongside his daily regime of four to six hundred press ups had given him a pleasing triangular shape. He was popular on Ascension, but not feared yet.

He shouldn't have joined the game; it wasn't permitted by his team. He couldn't play for the school team and the only time he should kick a ball was at a scheduled training session with the Celts. A love of the beautiful game coursed through his veins though; sometimes Paddy just couldn't help himself. He trotted over to the pitch, neatly skirting the unidentifiable animal carcass that lay across his path, and put his boots on, joining the losing team.

Not much is remembered about the game itself, it is the aftermath that is spoken about. A younger acquaintance of Paddy's, Martin Proctor, had been attempting worldies all the way through the game – missing every time, but some of the balls had bounced perilously close to where a small company of The Ghost Mob members were congregating, playing cards, drinking and smoking on a step. Bobby, sixteen by this time and already one of the more senior members of the gang, had been drinking heavily all afternoon, and was shouting disparaging words at Martin. Paddy, who was becoming used to suppressing his frustration when his performance did not meet his expectations, took Martin around the shoulder and shared some of the tricks with him that he had learnt: "Focus on yer breathing, nice and slow. In through the nose, out through the mouth. Ignore all that noise and see the ball going intae the net just as ye're preparing tae strike it. Positive mind frame, that's all ye'll need."

It didn't work. The next shot that Martin took ballooned up into the air, striking one of the tower blocks and inciting hoots of laughter from The Ghost Mob members. Paddy sensed that something was about to happen. People began to gather; he could feel the crowd forming. The ball, having bounced back down to the ground sat mere feet from the edge of the gang; none of the boys wanted to retrieve it. Paddy was a hero to them: they all looked in his direction for guidance. "Head up, Paddy," he whispered to himself, trotting over to collect the ball. Uncouthly, and lacking balance, Bobby stepped out of the circle of his cronies, booting the ball as hard as he could onto a nearby building site. And then a plank in reason broke.

"Whatever happens next, Bobby fuckin' McAlister, Ah'm going tae break ye."

Silence.

Then the crowd swarmed. Paddy found himself alone, deserted by his teammates, though Martin at least had the decency to look over his shoulder at Paddy as he fled. A large ring formed around them: one of the most feared and dangerous men, for Bobby was undoubtedly a man now, in Ascension and a fledgling young sports star, ripe now for plucking.

Bobby's drinking did him no favours, Paddy could see he was off balance. He mastered his nerves – he'd fought before – and lanced out his left hand, landing cleanly on Bobby's nose. Blood. Bobby didn't flinch, didn't even take a backward step. On he lumbered, closing the distance. He hadn't so much as thrown a punch yet and Paddy could feel the menace that he brought. Wildly, Bobby swung his right at Paddy's head, though Paddy – ever the balletic mover – rolled to his right, dancing out of the way. At that, Bobby paused. He had all the advantages: he was bigger, stronger, more experienced and far,

far more ruthless. Silver spoon boy here with his scholarship and his driver should be a pushover. The fight should already be done.

Paddy continued to circle: he knew he had to be patient. He also knew that Bobby was reckless and easy to anger. "C'mon, Bobby. Ah thought ye were solid?" Bobby lunged again; Paddy once again circled and ducked under the punch. Bobby now took it to the dirt, reaching for Paddy with both hands, grabbing the collar of his shirt and using his bulk to press him to the ground. As far as the crowd were concerned, the bloodbath was about to begin. Paddy was focused, though: he had fallen near a small pile of stones and glass and grabbed a handful, much like his mother had on the day of his birth. He waited for Bobby to lean back, exerting all of his strength into a blow that would undoubtedly have ended Paddy there and then and, choosing the moment where Bobby's fist reached its peak, flung them into his eyes, causing deep lacerations in his face. Bobby rolled off, holding his face: he was all but blind now and blood flowed freely over his fingers. The crowd had quietened, not yet ready to throw their lot in with Paddy: they knew the danger that that kind of act could bring.

Paddy now attacked, throwing a right and a left at each temple, landing both times. Bobby screamed in rage and pain. Charging forward like a matador, Paddy rebuffed him, spinning to the side and landing a huge punch to his kidney. Bobby, drunk, blinded and exhausted, fell to his knees. Paddy couldn't leave it like this – he couldn't risk retribution: he had to send a message.

Taking five steps back, Paddy created some space to run. He shot a look at The Ghost Mob. The message was clear: stay out of this. They looked to each other, leaderless. No movement.

Paddy accelerated, strides lengthening as he closed in on Bobby's prone form. Paddy swung his prodigious right boot at Bobby's face, catching him sweetly on the cheekbone, shattering it, utterly. Blood and gore shot across the crowd, who observed, still silent. Paddy reached for Bobby's broken face, pulling it up towards him. "Ye had enough, fucker?" Bobby, choking, managed a nod before Paddy thrust his face back into the dirt and strode away home, leaving the Ghost Mob without a second glance.

In his tower block, alone, Shaun O'Neill shook his head. His gang was done and he knew it.

Below, seeing Bobby's total destruction, the crowd gasped.

Chapter 18: The Documents

Paddy had to get away from that stadium. He had seen almost every sport in various capacities and contexts: he had watched Darts at The Alexandra Palace (in fact, it was he who first began to sing Chase The Sun during the breaks between matches), seen the Silverstone Grand Prix from Becketts, spent a day at Lords watching a late collapse for England's batters (not exactly a collector's item) and had been present for numerous boxing matches, big and small in stature, yet he had never seen anything as intense and borderline insane as the scenes at the arm-wrestling world championships. The intensity in the Ukrainian's eyes (Paddy was unaware of this man's history) terrified him: he had never seen anything like it before and was desperate to put as many miles between himself and that crowd as possible.

However, Paddy was here for a reason and he had already been too long away from Claston and the training sessions that were clocking up without him. He didn't want to be excluded by his club and he needed to be available for the final so had to return, and quickly.

His next destination was the offices of Ordenadex: the company that had bought up huge quantities of thalelamide – the compound that had coursed through his, and poor Claire's, body and wrought such horrendous chaos. He was convinced that there was a link between this company and what had happened to him and Claire. Whatever it was, he needed to find out, quickly and quietly.

Holding the unearned trophy in his left hand, leaving his right free in case of mayhem, Paddy snuck through the labyrinth of corridors, using the surging crowd that the security crew had been unable to hold back as a smokescreen to aid his escape.

Paddy followed one generic corridor after another, choosing his directions by using his intuition (all signs being in Spanish) as his compass. All he wanted was to feel Bilbao's fresh air on his skin, rather than the choking humidity of the stadium.

After what seemed like an interminable bid for freedom, Paddy felt a breeze running through the corridor, its origin to his right. He followed the breeze, hoping it would lead him outside, and to safety.

He made his way towards the river, confident that the cooler air down by the water would help him to regain some semblance of calm after the adrenaline-filled experience of the crazy championship he had just been in. He felt a pang of remorse at his actions, his simple curiosity having ultimately been the fatal undoing of that man they called Mykolayovych Yavorsky. He still could not get his head around the fact that he looked so alike to this total stranger they called Sergio Brazofuerte.

On the wall that led down to the riverside, Paddy spied another poster, identical in image, but significantly smaller than the one that had so shocked him earlier that day, the one that had led him to take part in this championship. The resemblance really was uncanny; it was as if this man were his twin... or his clone. Pulling himself away from this image, Paddy opened the door and to his relief saw the meeting of navy and pink painted across the sky above him, the sun having passed the horizon, beginning its long descent through night to reappear again for another day.

Paddy's intuition tingled again, warning him of the impending danger that he was facing. He hurried along the river path, heading east along the boardwalk. It was quiet down here, far quieter than the streets that headed back towards his hotel. In the distance he could see the rising tower that was his goal, the beautiful and imposing Torre Iberdrola, lit like a beacon in the fading twilight. And then, to his left he noticed what at first glance seemed to be a sleeping otter. Paddy turned to take a closer look and, in the darkness, noticed that it was a man, lying facing up, a vacant look in his glassy eyes.

The body floated slowly towards him and Paddy stood still in horror as the head bumped against the boardwalk. The face was his own and eventually Paddy realised that this must be the real Sergio Brazofuerte. And if Paddy had been mistaken for Sergio, had Sergio been mistaken for Paddy? Why anyone would expect to find Paddy McAlpin in the centre of Bilbao in the middle of April, when he had told no one of his plans, was beyond Paddy's comprehension, but that thought was inescapable. The one constant thing that echoed in Paddy's mind though, was that in Scotland, in England and in Spain, someone wanted him dead. He had to find the Ordenadex building, get some information that would lead him to his pursuer and get the hell out of Bilbao, and fast. He let his lifeless body double continue to drift away, hoping that it would be spotted before it was lost to sea, hoping that the man's family would know the truth and get justice.

With adrenaline coursing through him like a river ready to burst its banks following incessant rain, Paddy had a decision to make on how to best approach his destination; although not the most direct route, the one he chose was simple and wound along the river, through the quieter park that sat on the banks of this once-crucial waterway. He wanted to get to his destination fast, but on this day his paranoia outweighed his urgency and a quieter, more circuitous route seemed prudent.

Paddy broke into a jog, aware that he was nearing his destination, the huge glass monolith rising from the ground just beyond his eyeline, guiding him to the smaller and more modest office he had to visit: the Ordenadex building stood in the shadow (at least during the day) of the Torre Iberdrola. Ten floors of red brick and glass, incongruous in its contrast to the beautiful, if unorthodox collections of buildings around it. At this time in the evening it lay empty, with two guards at the entrance to deter any random acts of vandalism by those who celebrated with too much vigour in the city centre.

Paddy was not confident enough in his Spanish abilities, indeed he knew next to none, to charm the guards and he didn't want to draw any attention to himself in such a public forum, so he opted a stealthy, ghost-like approach. He couldn't interrogate anyone – he didn't know how much English they would speak – so he had to try and get some sales records to see what was happening with the surplus (for there must be a surplus) of thalelamide. Circling the building, Paddy's keen eyes saw multiple possible entry points into the building: it was shockingly under-guarded for one of Spain's foremost computer hardware suppliers. The most obviously quiet route though, required Paddy to ascend a drainpipe and gain entry through a second storey window, via a small balcony. His agility and upper body strength were unquestioned, so Paddy had very few concerns about his ability to do this; his black leather jacket was dark enough to ensure that he wasn't spotted during his quick ascent up the unlit side of the building.

Shimmying up the pipe, Paddy was struck by how easily this was working: the construction was strong enough to maintain his bulk without making enough noise to alert nearby pedestrians, yet the window, when he reached it, was not strong enough to resist a perfunctory kick with the heel before it shattered. Paddy had covered the glass with his jacket, thereby minimising the sound that would normally have betrayed his presence, hoping that the silencing effect would be enough and that no alarm would sound. He waited patiently, yet no obvious siren rang out, and he seemed to be in the clear.

Once inside, Paddy found the nearest floor plan. Having a good, if somewhat rusty, understanding of Latin, he reasoned that "registros" meant something like "registration documents" or "sales" and followed the map to his destination. He saw no one on the corridors, no cleaners, no one working late – no one at all. Again, he was struck by how smoothly this process was going and chuckled lightly to himself, muttering "Mebbe ye coulda been a spy, eh Paddy," underneath his breath. The door too, was unlocked and the room was filled, wall to wall, floor to ceiling with cabinets containing files. Thousands and thousands of them. Again, Paddy deduced, there must be some sort of link between the Spanish and Italian languages, so he looked for transazioni (transactions). Nothing. I saldi (sales). Nothing. Finally, Paddy scanned the labels on the cabinets realising that "Enero, Febrero, Marzo, Abril, Mayo, Junio..." must be months of the year.

These cabinets contained all of the company's transactions for the last... five years! Opening the nearest one, he saw the year inside: two years previous and he opened three more cabinets marked "Febrero" before he found the right year. Then it was just a case of finding a file, or anything, marked with thalelamide or OptimoPharm.

It didn't take long: the thalelamide file was the thickest and most prominent one there – there must be three hundred pages in the file. Paddy took them all; his need was greater than Ordenadex's, or so he reasoned, and they must surely have electronic copies too.

Going back out the way he came, Paddy descended the pipe and, head down, collar up, fled the scene of his most recent criminal activity. This time though, Paddy was enjoying himself. He was getting used to the adrenaline that came with this kind of act: maybe this was his future, he thought to himself. Football can't last forever, after all.

He needed to get back to the relative safety of his hotel, and headed east toward the river, following it northward. He passed three bridges and recognised the striking Guggenheim museum to his right, with its dashing curved edges and reflective surfaces. He curved away from the river at the Paseo de la Memoria and, mastering his suspicions, took the back streets back to his bed for the night, storing the documents in his room's safe, aware that he would need to find a translator to help him.

He passed the remaining hours of darkness in his hotel room, too exhausted to flee that night and unsure of what to do with the growing pile of illicit documents in his possession.

Awakening early the following morning, Paddy spoke with the concierge about his need for someone who reads Spanish and speaks perfect English; the concierge was a well-meaning chap, but his English left a lot to be desired and Paddy was reluctant to trust such an important task to someone he couldn't understand with perfect clarity. The concierge though, suggested his cousin, Lucia Fernandez, as a perfect candidate (that was, at least, what Paddy assumed he had said, his thick accent and poor grasp of English preventing a full understanding) and scribbled an address on a piece of paper, thrusting it into Paddy's hands, smiling obsequiously all the while. Paddy looked at the address: Plaza Cantera – just a short walk from the hotel.

Peering at this man's face, Paddy's instincts for an impending threat, which had been sharpened by his experience, honed by his ability to read a crowd and anticipate problems, tingled: he felt trouble brewing now. He had though, no other option – he had to get these documents translated. Rather than take the packet with him though, he chose to go and meet this Lucia in person, leaving his important cargo in the hotel's safe. At the last moment, he picked up his newly-received (not won) trophy. Although he a sense of guilt carrying around something he had not deserved, he loved the feel of it, the solid heft in his hand bringing an air of quality to the object, not to mention the cover that it would bring him should someone see him. Here, he was not Paddy McAlpin, but defeated World Arm Wrestling Championship finalist Sergio Brazofuerte – assuming that no one had found his corpse yet, he could continue to steal his identity.

He had a good sense of direction, and before long was only streets away. Nearing his destination, he turned onto Las Cortes and stopped.

Chapter 19: The Kidnapping

Before him stood a large group of men; maybe ten, maybe twelve. Far more men than even Paddy could realistically consider challenging. Each of them wore a balaclava, obscuring their identify and marking each as the threat that they were. None seemed remotely perturbed by their presence on this city centre street in mid-morning. Paddy looked around and noticed that there was no one else around. It seemed he had walked into a well-planned ambush.

Doing what he knew, Paddy stepped forward, pointing at the man at the head of the group, the largest and most dangerous.

"Alrigh', lad: I'm going tae break ye."

The group now began to reconfigure, spreading in a circle around him, surrounding Paddy on all sides. He was vulnerable and he knew it.

"Paddy McAlpin, Hemen nago zuretzat. Ez da ezer pertsonalik: futbolari zoragarria zara, baina negozioa gogorra da ... " (I'm here for you. It's nothing personal: you are a wonderful footballer, but business is tough...)

Paddy shrugged. "Ah dinnae speak Spanish, sonny. Let's go."

Paddy aimed a double-handed blow at the leader's head using the trophy as a bludgeon. This gargantuan man, clearly used to violence stepped back, avoiding the blow by an inch. Fortuity, however briefly, was on Paddy's side and the blow struck one of his nemeses on the shoulder. The screams that accompanied the crunching blow confirmed Paddy's diagnosis of a dislocation, possibly even a broken collarbone; this man wouldn't fight again, at least not tonight. For the rest of the fight the only noise that registered in Paddy's mind was the screams of this man, who sat on the floor, cradling his obliterated arm in his lap and making an unholy racket.

This gang was more organised and well-drilled than his old foes on Ascension: they didn't come forward blindly, nor were they interested in the glory of a one-on-one confrontation. This fight was not about honour for them, they were in this for the money and efficiency was key. Moreover, Paddy was clearly a dangerous target. They continued to rotate, to swarm him in twos and threes, changing their attack patterns while Paddy continued to lash out with his trophy. Occasionally, he had successes: he shattered the forearm of the next man that came too close and beat a hasty retreat to the edge of the ever-tightening ring.

By now, Paddy was bordering on exhaustion. He had taken part in a world championship of strongmen and was now faced with a well-organised crew, with utterly overwhelming odds. This sure would make a good story back at the club, should he ever make it there. Bizarrely, Paddy's mind turned briefly to his next club Christmas meal speech, thinking how he could regale this crazy trip to Bilbao to anyone who would listen. When the moment came, he was a story-teller.

Paddy was quickly brought back to reality when he was struck from behind with a piercing blow; a small knife had been thrust into his back, just to the right of his spine. Lucky me, he thought, wincing at the pain of the blade in his flesh. He launched the trophy (its weight was slowing him down) at the nearest cluster of enemies, incapacitating one more with a clout to the skull; the balaclava clad man lay on his back, unmoving. Paddy cast his eyes around at the group: only six remained and Paddy began to hope. As every football fan knows though, it is the hope that kills you.

The leader, whom one of his subordinates had called Gorka, now signalled to his two most well-armed men to come forward. These men were carrying baseball bats and wearing military-issue (to Paddy's eye) combat gear. The pair attacked him simultaneously, and as Paddy blocked the blow from his left, which was aimed into his ribs, the other's blow caught him on the hip, knocking him off balance. Then, the swarm began. The baseball bats were dropped in favour of the more close-combat friendly fist. Blow after blow rained down on Paddy's head, neck and torso – they were conspicuously avoiding his legs, perhaps knowing that they required him to walk, perhaps valuing him as a captive that they could hold ransom. That was Paddy's last thought before a blow, the like of which he'd never felt before, crashed into his temple and thrust his head into the pavement.

When Paddy awoke, his head throbbed. Any movement almost made him scream. The world was dark, but faint slivers of light permeated the edges of the cloth across his eyes. In the pit of his stomach a thousand snakes churned, dancing to an unheard tune. With great effort, Paddy prevented the bile from rising in his throat and attempted to assess the situation.

He was gagged, as well as blindfolded – the disorientation was maddening for someone who is usually so balanced. He was moving, of that much he could be sure. The floor beneath him was metal and he could feel every bump and turn. He was no longer wearing any clothes, except for his underwear – Paddy thanked fate for that small mercy at least. He felt the coolness of the dirt-covered, rusted floor and surmised that it must be a van, or at least a people carrier with the seats removed. Though he was bound – wrists, ankles, mouth and eyes – he was not secured, so he was thankful that the driver seemed to have been taking it easy. Any sudden moves would mean that he was propelled across the floor of the van, and, in his state, he was worried that that might kill him.

He felt every bruise. He tasted the blood in his mouth. He imagined that he could feel his lungs struggling and his nose splintering, but the swelling on his face meant that he couldn't assess the damage with any degree of accuracy. He ran his tongue around his mouth; despite his fears, he counted a full set of teeth still, although he did think he could detect several chips and cracks. With the pain overcoming him, he couldn't be sure of anything though. His lips were dry, cracked and swollen and he winced in pain at every attempt to swallow.

The drive lasted for a long time; at least an hour passed while he was conscious and he couldn't tell how long he had been out for. What Paddy knew for certain was that he was no longer in the city; the quality of the roads they were travelling on had degraded hugely during the journey and he felt the potholes increase in regularity, much to his chagrin, but to the single advantage of causing the loosely-tied blindfold to slip down his face.

Eventually, the van stopped moving and a group of men exited the vehicle. Paddy counted 6 – probably the remaining men that he hadn't managed to take down. His pride burned at that, even though he knew that the odds were hopeless from the beginning. One on one, Paddy felt that he could have taken them all. The rear door of the van was pulled open, creaking loudly. His slipped blindfold was duly noted, roughly pulled back into position and tightened carefully. Darkness fell upon him once more.

He was yanked hard by his shoulder – pain flooded his body and he couldn't suppress the scream that shot out of him – and dumped onto the dusty ground beneath. Small particles found their way into his nose and mouth despite the gag and he couldn't suppress his natural reaction to cough. With each cough though, the pain began anew. Each contraction of the muscles landed like a fresh blow to his sternum and wracked his body with suffering. He felt that no one could ever have taken that heavy a beating and lived to tell the tale.

He was hauled to his feet. Before he could gain any sense of balance he was being dragged and stumbled along. I guess that answers my theory about them avoiding my legs, he thought to himself. The pain coursing through his delicate body as these men manhandled him with no consideration for what he had just been through was like sharp needles pressing down on him from every angle. He struggled to keep pace but refused to make a sound, clamping his lips tightly shut, forcing air through his nose as slowly as he could manage. As far as was possible, he would not let his captors know the pain he felt. He couldn't say how long, or how far he was transported in this way, and on many occasions sought to gain a foothold, but the speed and angle at which he was held made this impossible. Eventually he was placed, more gently than before, into a chair – leather upholstered, with wooden arms and legs, Paddy surmised. Fools, he thought.

If you've ever been blindfolded with no regard for your pleasure, you will know the disorientating effect that it has on you. Your eyes do not believe the absence of light and your brain tries to make patterns from everything it thinks that you see. Even the smallest beam or fleck of light creates images and you must master your mind or become overwhelmed. When the blindfold comes off, though, that is an exquisite torture all by itself. The too-bright light sears your retinas, and Paddy – the binds on his wrists and ankles now being used to secure him to the chair – could not protect himself from this new sensory punishment. The gag, unfortunately, remained secure.

Paddy heard shutters being pushed closed and his thirsty eyes were quenched by the comparatively dim light. In front of him stood a large man whose gait and stature indicated that he was the leader of this band of kidnappers, the one they referred to as Gorka. Paddy knew how to get under people's skin and he wondered what Gorka's reaction would be if he were made angry. In the fight, or more accurately, the beating, Paddy noticed that Gorka moved quickly but wasted no energy in doing so. He was calm, measured; but in life, as in fighting, different situations lead to different reactions.

Paddy needed to get that gag out of his mouth.

He considered trying to shout through the gag, but felt it best to preserve his efforts, refusing to waste any energy on fruitless labours. He would need it soon enough.

Passively, Gorka waited. His eyed betrayed no emotion, except, perhaps boredom, ennui, insouciance. Gorka peered now at Paddy, who knew that he couldn't show any weakness here. Gorka held all the cards.

Gorka grunted and barked an order in Basque, unbeknownst to Paddy, who couldn't discern the difference from Spanish. One of his underlings brought him a chair, another one brought two beers, handing them both to Gorka. Paddy watched the condensation run down the outside of the bottle, the bubbles making their way through the liquid before bursting onto the surface. Paddy wanted that beer more than anything else in the world. He needed hydration: it was now morning and the building was warming up; it had been many hours since he had had the pre-competition beer and Spain in April is tropical, at least for a man more used to the chilly climes of Claston all year round. He also harboured a hope that the beer would be strong enough that it might dull some of the excruciating pain that coursed through his body.

Gorka had the sun at his back as it poured in through the window, past the resistance of the shutters and onto Paddy's face, rendering Paddy's new foe little more than a silhouette. Perhaps that was intentional, perhaps not, but it certainly added to the man's stature. Paddy could make out few details. He could discern the man's huge frame, his close-cropped, almost bald pate and a slight favouring of his left leg. An injury perhaps. Paddy made a mental note of that: you must always look to exploit your enemy's weaknesses – a valuable lesson that he learnt from the fitness and conditioning coach during his time at Hamburg: Erna Schuster. He was an articulate, intelligent man, fluent in German, English and French who often quoted Sun Tzu, Machiavelli, Proust and Mao. His best phrases, though, were the observations that he made himself about life. And the observations that he made about football, such as the aforementioned one, were often true in myriad other scenarios.

Still they waited, locked in a battle of will. Gorka opened the bottle using a nearby wall and his open palm, bringing it down upon the top of the bottle with swiftness and accuracy. The sound, that heavenly hiss of gas escaping from the bottle, made Paddy salivate, driving him mad with desire. All these years of success had made him unused to deprivation. No matter what his nutritionist said, if Paddy wanted a beer, a burger or any other damn thing, he would have it and woe betide anyone that stood in his way. Except that Gorka now stood in his way, and Gorka was a good six inches taller than Paddy, barrel-chested and with arms that looked like they could manhandle a bull, should he wish. Intentionally or not, Gorka lifted the bottle to his mouth, pouring in so much beer that much of it spilled over his lips and ran down his face, splashing onto the floor. Paddy's eyes betrayed him: his hunger, his desire, was there for all to see and Gorka relished seeing this weakness.

Gorka laughed then. It was a laugh devoid of joy or humour, like an alien approximating happiness based on a book that it had read. The sound reminded Paddy of the slow cracking of cement in the intense heat of the German summers. Gorka watched him wriggle, exploring his captivity with his hands and feet, looking for weaknesses in the bindings or the chair. There were none: this gang had been through this before.

"Beer, Paddy?" Gorka's voice was worse than his laugh; a voice that was lightly accented, one that betrayed nothing of its origins. It was deep, filled with malice and contempt. He stepped towards Paddy, beer outstretched and pointed towards his hand. At the last moment he paused, raised the bottle and unleashed a tide of cold beer onto Paddy's lap. "Oh, excuse me my friend. What a terrible accident." That laugh again. It was haunting, powerful, intimidating. Paddy sat, wearing only his sopping wet underpants, refusing to squirm. Gorka wanted a reaction – he wouldn't get one.

"This is my favourite part, Paddy. You see, you are not here to be ransomed. You have no one to come and rescue you: no one knows where you are – Fergie told me that much." Again, Paddy's face betrayed him. That laugh again. "Paddy, surely you knew that you couldn't trust him? After how you treated him? Paddy...so naïve? So sad. Your Fergie has made some powerful friends since his school days. Not necessarily good friends, but powerful ones. He knew that there might be something in it for him if he told a certain someone about you coming this way. There isn't, but he thought there might be. Obviously he has no idea who his friend is friends with... So sad.

"We have already been paid, Paddy. The money changed hands from the minute you got here: we're professionals, you see. We don't miss, we don't fail and we don't take partial payments. We get results and we do things quietly. We were paid for one thing, Paddy: to end your life. Ez da ezer pertsonalik, but I can't help but love to take my time, to enjoy the delicious beauty of a man choking on his own blood, watching his own body fail piece by piece." At that, Gorka reached across and grasped Paddy's left thumb, snapping it, and tearing the tendons. Every living soul within a mile heard Paddy's scream of pain, a howl that reverberated through heads and hearts of those within earshot. All four of Gorka's gang still on site shuddered involuntarily. No one else would ever know the depths of the sound that Paddy had made.

"I'll see you in a short while, Paddy McAlpin." That laugh, again. The sound faded, leaving only footsteps. Then Paddy's gentle sobbing.

When he resurfaced from his latest dip into unconsciousness, he found that he had a new companion. This one was less large and kept his back to the rays of the sun. Clearly this group had been trained to act this way. Where there is rigidity, Paddy thought: there is weakness. This one paused to look at Paddy's hand whenever he walked by, and Paddy saw the lump in his throat rise. Eh, not as bloodthirsty as the other, he reasoned.

Now that the pain had receded somewhat, Paddy took some time to acclimatise himself: "He will win who knows when to fight and when not to fight," he recalled Herr Schuster saying once, and Paddy committed it to memory. He used it in football contests often, knowing who to dribble past, who to nutmeg and who he could challenge in a 50/50, or more often a 40/60, and come away victorious, but the same principle applied here. If he chose the right man, at the right time, Paddy could do this.

He was tied to a wooden chair in the centre of a medium-sized warehouse, well outside the city. The building was on at least two floors, with the upper floor presumably serving as some form of sleeping quarters, hence Gorka's lengthy disappearance upstairs. The ground floor was sparse. The room to his left was a makeshift kitchen, though it only appeared to contain a gas stove and a length of rubber hose, which was attached to a pipe fitting in the wall. Other than that, there were various cupboards and cabinets, chairs and sofas. If this were this group's headquarters, clearly they were idealists and not interested in capitalism in the least.

After some time passed, this new guard poured himself a glass of water from the hose. Paddy, sensing opportunity, began to cough, startling him. He paused, looking, pondering. He sighed. Reaching for another glass, he poured again, and again paused, suspicious. Finally, it seemed that he decided that a man who had been beaten, stabbed, was clearly concussed and had a broken thumb, as well as being bound hand and foot, could be of no danger to him. Approaching Paddy, he declared: "No trouble." His tone betrayed his words: this man was nervous. Look at the beads of sweat, Paddy – he's not struggling with the heat – this is his land, those are beads of remorse. He walked behind Paddy, gently loosening his gag, letting it fall onto his shoulders. Rather than free his hands as well – he was too wise for that – he simply raised the glass to Paddy's mouth and began to pour. Like a dog, Paddy lapped at the water, gulping and guzzling that lukewarm elixir. Briefly, for just a sliver of a moment, Paddy's pain receded.

"I am Unai. I know you. Great Paddy McAlpin. Win all Ballon D'ors, best player. We want you in Athletic. With you we win league. We have no money for you though. In my dreams, only. Paddy McAlpin at San Mamés! You know why you are here? You know who we are?"

Paddy shook his head. "Nae son, but if ye ken who Ah am, ye ken what kind of shit will follow ye when Ah'm found."

Unai smiled, hopelessly. "You no be found, Paddy. You know who we are – you just need to think a little. We use bombs. Someone find part of you, but not you."

Shite, Paddy thought. He did know who they were – he didn't want to mess with a violent paramilitary group; and why the hell were they after him? It's not like he was representing the Spanish government, he'd never said or done anything against them.

Then he remembered what Gorka said: "We were paid for one thing, Paddy: to end your life."

So, he thought – this is another attempt on my life. I don't know who's after me, but whoever it is has deep pockets; very deep.

That laugh returned again, reverberating around the deserted building. The footsteps came closer, never rushing; measured. "Arra, zergatik da jodea bere mordoa?" This one was not aimed at him though – this was spat at the younger, smaller Unai. He heard the unmistakable sound of a smack and saw Unai stagger back across the room, losing his balance and falling over a chair, crashing into the floor. That laugh again. That slap and Fergie's were worlds apart, Paddy thought. Fucking Fergie, the turncoat. How is he involved? Was this all because of some silliness at school? How did he even have the contacts to do this? He must be a part of the plot, but how? Did he contact these hooligans directly, or was there a middle man? Surely the latter, but who?

"Get comfortable, Paddy. You're going to be here for a while: I want to have a little fun with you." That laugh. That fucking laugh.

At that, Gorka jabbed, lightning fast, with his right fist crashing into Paddy's left eye. He flew backwards, the chair toppling beneath him, leaving him lying on his back unable to move. Out of sheer joy, Gorka laughed again, kicking him hard in his back. "Fun, Paddy, eh? Fun."

That laugh.

Chapter 20: Vienna

The world swirled around him, the light intermittent as he struggled to keep his eyes open. He had experienced pain before, but not like this, not this overwhelming, all-encompassing torture that had taken hold of every fibre of his being. Somewhere in the back of his mind he was thankful for his previous experiences of what he had, until now, thought of as suffering.

Paddy had enjoyed more post-match victory celebrations than he cared to remember; more post-match defeat commiserations than he cared to forget, in many cities across many countries throughout Europe. And now, as he lay beaten and bruised somewhere outside Bilbao, his semi-conscious mind flickered back to one of the most memorable. He did not try to stop it, happy to drift away from the here and now, and welcomed the vivid recollection like the old friend it was, guiding him by the hand into a pain-numbing slumber.

Paddy had made an impact with Claston Celts at the back end of the previous season, initially making a few substitute appearances before starting the final three games of the season once the league was already won. He was disappointed to miss out on a debut goal, but had found the net on his second start, playing that day as a centre-forward. Fans were excited about the prospect, as they always were with young players that had been developed by their own academy. His first goal was greeted with choruses of "He's one of our own, he's one of our own! Paddy McAlpin! He's one of our own!" and only added to the anticipation of what this teenager could bring to the team. In those final few games of the season, Paddy played without fear, scoring two goals in his three starts and beaming like the schoolboy he still was on both occasions, running wildly around the pitch, unsure what to do with himself. His performances had caught the eye of the fans and suggested to, if not the world, then at least Scotland, that this 17-year-old boy in a Greek god's body, born and raised in Ascension, was ready for the real thing. When the new season began though, Paddy, as is often the case with young players, was no longer in the first team squad and had to watch on as Claston Celts progressed through the first and second rounds of Champions League Qualification. An injury to veteran centre-forward Colin Wriggles, just moments from the end of the second round, brought him into the squad, and it was that twist of fate, so cruel on the long-serving and beloved Wriggles, that played such a crucial hand in bringing McAlpin to the attention of Europe's elite.

The third and final round of the qualification pitted Claston Celts against SK Rapid Wien: the first leg was to be played in Scotland, the second in Austria. Paddy had to watch on for the full ninety minutes of the first match, heading every high ball, playing every pass and crunching into every tackle from the comfort of his seat on the bench in the Scottish sun that July evening. The game started well, with Claston taking an early lead, only to be pegged back on the stroke of half time. The second half proved to be an almost carbon copy of the first, with Celts going ahead, only to see their opponents once again score deep into injury time to snatch a draw, and more importantly, two away goals. Going away to Rapid Wien and winning would be a tough ask for the Celts. They had failed at this final qualification hurdle for the past seven seasons and hope was not high that this season would be any better.

Paddy was not expecting to travel to Vienna that fateful day, but a recurrence of his injury the day before travel meant Wriggles would once again be unable to play, resulting in an unchanged squad flying out for the second leg. A man (or boy, really, at this young stage) already ahead of his time, Paddy had employed his own personal sports psychologist as soon as he broke into the first team, convinced of the good work they could do with him. In preparation for this game, he had been visualising what it would be like to play in the intensity of a Champions League fixture, to score a goal, perhaps even the winning goal. He pictured himself outpacing a tired defender onto a through ball, remaining calm in the one-on-one situation, rolling the ball gently into the corner of the goal, out of reach of the stretching fingers of the goalkeeper. He knew that the scenario he thought back to time and again was highly unlikely, but he kept playing it through in his mind, almost to the point of obsession, desperate for it to come true, knowing that having experienced it once, he would not fail should it come round again.

He sat in the changing room before the match, thinking this dream play through again and again, barely listening to his manager as he tried to drill his message into the minds of his teammates. He looked around at the vacant eyes of the Celts team, wondering if they cared what was being said. Paddy hadn't come this far by following instructions: for him instinct was everything, not the carefully laid out plans of a man who could no more tell what was going to happen on that field of dreams than he could tell a penguin how to fly.

The game started, and Paddy watched on as a fan, not as a substitute. And as a fan he grimaced when Rapid Wien scored after 17 minutes of domination. In order to progress, a minimum of two goals were needed from a team who had hardly touched the ball. The seconds ticked on into minutes, the minutes soon became an hour, and with fifteen minutes to go, the score still at 1-0 to the comfortable and cruising home side, Paddy was asked to get warmed up.

To his right he could hear as the Celts fans sang in unison. So used to exiting at this stage, and yet so desperate to reach the group stages of Europe's biggest club competition they sang a self-deprecating song, regaling the chorus to Ultravox's Vienna. As a fellow fan, Paddy knew that an exit at this stage would mean everything; the longer the wait, the more it meant. Another year of missing out would be painful beyond measure for those fans who had made the trip to Austria as well as those watching or listening intently at home.

Barely had he removed his tracksuit and he was on, playing centre forward for his boyhood club in Europe's biggest club competition. Overawed, Paddy struggled to exert any influence on the game, his mental coaching seemingly redundant once he was faced with the reality of the task that lay in front of him. For the first six minutes of his time on the pitch he stood motionless, helpless and hapless until, trotting over to take a throw in, he happened to be handed the ball by his father. Unbeknownst to Paddy, Matthew McAlpin had flown out in the hope of watching his son make his European debut; now he had been granted the unlikely chance of speaking to him he was not going to waste his time on congratulations for what had, thus far, been an incredible disappointment.

"What the bloody hell are ye playing at, son?" Paddy blinked and looked up, ready to fight his corner with this aggravated fan and was shocked to see his old man was the one remonstrating with him as he handed him the ball from the side of the pitch. He tried to offer a reply but found his tongue shrivelled and dry in his mouth, unable to articulate anything of sense. Not receiving a reply, his father continued. "Ah've flown all the way out here tae watch mah son play like a streak o' pish? What'll Ah say tae yer maw when she asks me how ye did? Get yer head out yer arse and play like ye always have – with confidence!" Matthew McAlpin thrust the ball towards his son and returned to his seat, scowling.

The thought of disappointing his father – and of picturing his mother's disappointed face – was all that was needed, and finally Paddy could feel the adrenaline starting to pump through him without the fear of mistake. He embraced it, knowing it meant he was ready to perform, no longer worrying that it would hinder him. He felt a sense of urgency that, when combined with the invincibility of youth, told him that this game far from over. He wasn't here for experience: he was here to change things.

He took the throw in quickly, receiving the ball back to his feet and surged forward along the left wing, chased by a tiring full-back. His opponent had nothing on him for pace, and soon Paddy was free and in space. He turned sharply as he was approached by the on-rushing centre-back and cut inside, tiptoeing lightly past one cumbersome challenge after another. The remaining defence in front of him closed ranks, blocking his way to the goal as he reached the corner of the penalty area. Slowing his run, he drew the two defenders to him, feigning left, right, left again, before looking at the overlap on his left and lifting his right foot to play the ball into the space behind the defence. Both defenders fell for his dummy, with the nearest following the overlapping runner, the one just the other side stepping across to cover Paddy, who delicately rolled the ball to his right, sending club captain Henry Alexander through on goal. Alexander made no mistake with his finish, taking a single touch to steady himself before blasting the ball beyond the keeper and setting the game up for a nervy finish for the home fans.

With only minutes to go, and leading the tie on away goals, it was clear that Rapid Wien would sit back and defend their slender lead.

From kick-off the ball made it all the way back to the goalkeeper and across the back four, left to right to left to right. Paddy was energised now though, and he chased and chased, his enthusiasm inspiring his team to do the same. Facing increasing pressure, the ball was cleared long and into the arms of the Celts 'keeper. By now the clock had ticked over the 90-minute mark and the fourth official's board showed the ground there would be only one minute of additional time. There was no time for anything else, so the ball was once again launched forward in the hope that something would come of it. As it plummeted from the sky like a cannonball fired into enemy territory, Alexander found himself underneath it. He forced his tiring legs into one final leap, outjumping his opponent and flicking the ball forward, directly between the two central-defenders. Paddy was onto it like a flash, sprinting round the back of the pair to reach the still bouncing ball first. One touch with his chest allowed him to keep his momentum, a second with his right foot across the nearest defender gave him space and a third with his left sent the ball rolling into the bottom corner of the goal, just as he had known it would.

The Rapid Wien players slumped to the floor, unable to comprehend how this unknown 17-year-old boy had undone them so easily in the final moments of the match. The Claston Celts players and management jumped and screamed and cheered, pumping fists, dancing with joy, and to a man, rushing towards the hero of the hour. After watching the ball roll into the net, Paddy had slowed his sprint to a jog, and then a walk until he stood behind the goal in front of his fans. He did not raise his hands; he didn't even look up. This moment had happened so many times for him in his head that it had been inevitable. From the depths of the crowd, the birth of a legend began as a single man began to sing, soon joined by those around him, until the whole collective were bellowing in unison.

"This means nothing to me!
"Oh! Vienna!"

Not long after the game, the players had gathered together in the hotel bar in high spirits to celebrate their victory and the prospect of welcoming Europe's best teams to their home over the coming months. Beers were drunk – songs were sung. At 17, Paddy was permitted to consume alcohol, being as they were in Austria, yet he chose not to, wishing to preserve this night in his memory for eternity. When Alexander suggested they move on to enjoy some of the sights of night-time Vienna, Paddy was only too pleased to suggest the karaoke bar he had seen on their way in. For many players, singing in front of their team was a dreaded exercise, completed only on first team initiation day when their acapella efforts saw them accepted into the fold with laughter from their senior peers. Not so for Paddy, who had grown up singing with his mother in Ascension, unknowing at the time, that she had done so to drown out the less-salubrious sounds of the goings-on of that bleak abode. Captain Alexander felt he could hardly refuse the young star his moment, and soon the team were sat around a large table, watching on as locals and tourists alike belted out hit after hit with varying success.

Paddy put his name down as soon as the team had entered and kept his song choice a closely guarded secret. When his name was called to perform, he made his way unhurriedly to the stage and onto the single black leather-topped stool that sat there. Perching himself on the front of the seat, he held the microphone to his lips with his right hand, allowing his left hand to rest on his left knee. His head bowed, his eyes shut, he took a deep breath as he waited for the backing track to begin. A number of his team laughed and whooped, but were soon hushed as the deep synth buzzed, followed by the unmistakable beat and haunting strings of the song's introduction. Paddy opened his eyes and stared at the floor, his body still, not looking at the screen. He knew the song, had sung it a hundred times in the desolation of Ascension House with his mother. He needed no prompts.

"We walked in the cold air…" His voice echoed around the room, softly but with unmistakable power.

"Freezing breath on the window pane, lying, waiting." The soothing tones that escaped the lips of this confident teenager held the whole team and everyone else present in a trance as they waited in anticipation for the next line.

Still Paddy sat, his feet just touching the floor, his back slumped, his head gently bobbing to the slow, prominent beat, never looking up, appearing to all to be in deep contemplation.

"A man in the dark in a picture frame.

"So mystic and soulful." Another pause as the echoing beat thudded on. And still Paddy sat.

"A voice reaching out in a piercing cry.

"It stays with you until." And as the strings rose, bringing life to the song, so Paddy rose, bringing life to the bar as the song reached its chorus. He held out a clenched fist in front of him as he sang, slowly raising it until it was above his head in a salute, coordinated perfectly with the power projected from his voice.

"The feeling is gone, only you and I, it means nothing to meeee!" Paddy sang this final word with the intensity that was meant for such a crescendo, holding his fist aloft for the duration of the pitch-perfect note, his head now raised, staring into the distance beyond the mesmerised onlookers. In the short gap between lines, Paddy dropped his fist to his side and stepped forward to the front of the stage, bringing his eyes down to meet the crowd and now sweeping his left arm across his body from right to left, indicating everyone in front of him as he sang the final line of the chorus.

"This means nothing to meeee – OOOH! VIENNA!" Cheers flooded the small cavern as Paddy turned to face away from the crowd. He wasn't finished yet and ignored the noise around him, little more than an unnecessary distraction to his art.

The second verse was completed with Paddy looking away from the crowd who had once again been silenced by the poignant lyrics and quietly powerful delivery. At the second chorus Paddy stepped off the stage, walking amongst the crowd, serenading strangers with his voice and bringing the bar to its feet. In the interluding instrumental, Paddy made his way back to the stage. As the strings rose to the fore, the piano thronged and the tempo quickened, Paddy stood still in contrast to the direction the song wanted to take him. He was in charge of this moment, and, as if bending to his will, the backing track slowed, ready for the final delivery. Paddy dropped to his knees and threw his head back, singing with all his might. He was not alone, with his whole team, the whole bar, seemingly the whole city taking up the song in unison:

128

"This means nothing to me!

"This means nothing to me!

"OOOOH! VIENNA!"

That world away from where Paddy lay was what echoed through his mind as he lay battered and broken on the floor of an anonymous warehouse, somewhere outside Bilbao. Having come to hate the song, seeing it as an arrogance expressed by the Celts fans, he could not help but soften toward it in his time of painful reflection, realising that it wasn't borne from arrogance, but from affection. For him.

Despite his pain a faint smile crossed his lips as he considered that no matter what happened to him in this ever-darkening nightmare, he had made his mark on the world, had experienced the highest of highs in the face of this lowest of lows. As he drifted back into sleep, desperate to relive that night in Vienna again and again, he found himself comparing his current plight to those thousand memories he had been fortunate to experience throughout his career, those memories that millions of football fans across the world would do anything to experience. And as he suffered, his mind also broken beyond repair, he could not help but think those immortal, haunting words: This means nothing to me.

Chapter 21: The Awakening

Paddy awoke suddenly, trying to cling to the dream that was vanishing like smoke into the wind. Laying still, he had almost forgotten about the pain that was pulsing through his body, though it did not take long for everything to come flooding back to him. Legs and groin sticky from the beer, his eye socket bruised and bloodied, severely blurred vision. His eye had almost swollen shut within the past hour. No one had looked at the wound on his back but in these filthy conditions it must surely be infected and his body: *ugh*. It was a patchwork of black and purple marks, boot prints and fist outlines peppered his flesh. Paddy had never experienced anything like it; he wasn't used to pain like this – his talent meant that his struggles were usually emotional ones: losing his father, not being able to convince his mourning mother to leave Ascension House and having to watch her degenerate and fester in that tiny hellhole; rejection from teammates and poor press coverage. Nothing in his life had prepared Paddy for a hellacious beating and the torment of the aftermath.

Just after dawn on the following day, Paddy was awoken by gentle footsteps: he had only had interactions with two of the guards and this was certainly not the sadistic Gorka. He hoped that it was Unai. He may not be innocent, but at least he had been gentle.

The footfalls came closer and Paddy heard the running of water and an accompanying splashing sound. Closer they came. "Shhh. No talk." Paddy felt a surge of relief on his eye as Unai placed a cool, wet cloth across it, holding it in place, gently. He pulled the chair upright, though Paddy could only feel the pain of his bonds and a harrowing tingling sensation in his hands and feet. "Gorka no let me help you. He say leave you, but I cannot. You okay?"

Paddy suppressed a laugh – that hurt too. "Aye, Unai, Aye." Unai, unversed in Scottish colloquialisms, had no idea what this meant and waited for confirmation from Paddy that he meant yes. Paddy nodded, much to Unai's relief.

"You not survive, Paddy. You die today. I am sorry." He cast his eyes downwards.

With his unbroken hand, Paddy began to flex.

All warfare is based on deception – another wise set of words that Schuster had said to him during training, though now that Paddy thought about it, it seemed that these sessions were mostly just lots of sprinting and quotes about fighting. Paddy locked that away for later, wondering if old Erna Schuster were actually an intelligent and experienced coach or just a madman in a tracksuit; then again, he knew plenty of coaches who were both.

Paddy began to flex his right arm, testing the strength of his bonds. When he was prone, the pressure on his body, matched with his exhaustion meant that he couldn't muster any momentum or movement; now, after a day's rest (though little water) and more freedom of movement, it appeared that there was scope for an opportunity.

Unai turned away from Paddy, clearly guilty about what was to come. He picked up a satchel, something that Paddy had not noticed him bring into the room, and pulled out a small box with wires protruding from the sides. "Sorry, Paddy," he whispered. He began to tinker with the box, engrossed in his task.

A new plan began to form in Paddy's mind. He thought back to his early days at the Claston Celts; they were dark days, in footballing terms, where the side would routinely sound the route one klaxon and ping the ball up to the big men. Set pieces were the most prolific route to goals in the league at that time and each team had a designated free kick taker, corner man and long-throw merchant, whose most important role was the delivery of fast, drilled balls into the penalty area for the big men to attack.

Paddy's proficiency with the ball at his feet in any scenario made him the obvious choice to take free kicks and corners, but it was his throw ins that were his speciality. His teammates nicknamed him The Trebuchet, such was the devastation that his delivery wrought. His nickname had initially been The Catapult, until he pointed out in his player of the season speech at the club Christmas dinner that the trebuchet is by far the superior siege engine in terms of craftsmanship, accuracy and range. How they laughed at that anecdote. Or was it him they laughed at. The attempts on his life had seemingly changed him, made him think about the wider world. He was sure of nothing about his past any longer, only his present, only of escaping.

Paddy's training regime was implemented by Vitor "Man O' War" Santos, the legendary Portuguese trainer who oversaw all of the Celts' set piece design and implementation for a forty-year period – their Golden Period. It was simple: one hour per day on the rowing machine, two hours of weight training and one hour of throwing technique, which Vitor filmed and played back to Paddy, critiquing each separate throw-in and eradicating any inconsistency he found within. It was a gruelling process, but over a four-year period, Paddy's assist record spoke for itself: near 20% of his assists and created chances came from his throw ins. A perfectly-performed throw in, Vitor told him, had "pace, power and, most importantly, precision; if you only have the first two there is no point in trying as you'd be relying on luck, and Paddy: Lady Luck is a fickle mistress."

And so, Paddy practised. Even when his throw ins were perfect, Paddy practised. He wouldn't allow this huge asset to slip away, and like the rest of his training, he dedicated his art in order to gain any edge he could over his opponents.

Paddy's plan relied on his hope that Gorka hadn't seen him delivering his special throws. Now, he hoped, he had a secret weapon.

Unai continued to tinker with the device, keeping his back to Paddy; unwilling, it seemed, to meet his eye. His nervousness was betrayed by his trembling shoulders and beads of sweat that Paddy could discern though his threadbare shirt. Paddy felt guilty about what he knew he had to do, but in this situation, it was very much him or me.

Paddy began to lever his right arm back and forth, weakening the bindings and the arms of the chair. His muscles beneath his shirt, despite the soreness from his beating, strained against their confinement, but years of living at peak physical fitness, eating well (within reason) and developing his muscular strength meant that even Paddy's most ardent fans were unaware of the true depths of his power. In these types of situations (this was not the first time he had been constrained in this manner, even if it was the first time he had been wholly unwilling) bicep and tricep strength is not the only important factor: full body power would be his route to escape. Paddy knew how to exert force in the right way, but he knew that once he freed his right arm, he would have mere moments before Unai turned and was upon him. If he wanted to gain the upper hand he would have to be quick; he would have to be quiet. He knew that there were only two guards by now. He had been in this warehouse for over 20 hours and had only seen Unai and Gorka: clearly this band were confident that they were safe – another mistake. Paddy had exploited other's hubris on many occasions, and he felt it, tasted it in the air here.

Paddy cast about for a projectile: on the table in front of him was an untouched bottle of beer, opened by Unai minutes earlier. That would do, Paddy mused, but he knew that the noise of the smashing bottle would attract Gorka: Paddy's real concern was how he would deal with that man mountain, Unai would be merely an aperitif. Gorka hadn't struck him during the fight: he hadn't felt the need to, simply orchestrating his gang of followers to take Paddy down, but Paddy was concerned that Gorka's blows may be more dangerous than his own – he was clearly an expert in violence and Paddy was badly weakened.

Paddy did some quick calculations: the distance from the top of the stairs to the bottom was around forty feet, meaning that once he had taken Unai down he had around thirty seconds to make his move before Gorka was on him. He was unsure whether he would be able to free his other hand, useless by now, or his legs in this time. No matter what he did, Paddy would face a major disadvantage once Gorka descended the stairs. He had to time this well and he would have to be lucky.

His focus was broken by a firm beeping from the device that Unai was focused on. It finally dawned on Paddy how Unai was planning on dispatching him. He hadn't heeded the hints or clues that surrounded him, but now he knew. This device that Unai had been so closely monitoring was an explosive device.

Paddy had lost the opportunity to choose his timing, he had to act swiftly: the long, sonorous beep that he could hear was familiar to him from the films of Arnold Schwarzenegger: the device was armed.

Paddy jerked his right arm forward, decimating the bond holding him there; Unai span to face him, still holding the device, his face contorted with shock and fear. In one swift motion, Paddy reached down with his free arm and seized the beer bottle, bringing his arm back over his head, using his well-honed throwing technique to launch the projectile as hard and as straight as he could. The bottle caught Unai sweetly, striking him on the bridge of his nose, which exploded with a discernible popping sound. Unai crumpled to the floor, dropping the device onto the ground beneath him. Fortuitously, it bounced away from him, well out of his reach. Paddy held his breath, awaiting any noise from overhead. Nothing. He worked to free his legs, managing to loosen the knot around his left ankle when he heard a shout: "UNAI?"

Time was of the essence; Gorka would come and investigate the noise and the lack of response. His haste meant he struggled to undo the cloth ties that secured his devastated left hand, and he was still struggling when Gorka appeared at the top of the stairs, screaming: "Unai you fucking tonto! What was that?"

Then he realised and careened down the stairs, taking them two at a time. Paddy, now with only one binding to go, realised that Gorka was moving more awkwardly than he expected, clearly the leg that he was favouring on the previous day was a more pronounced injury than he had initially thought.

"Paddy McAlpin! Stop there!" Paddy ignored him and tore his left leg free and, finally able to move for the first time in almost 24 hours, he realised the toll that this experience had taken on his body. On a good day, maybe Paddy would have been able to take Gorka in a fight, man to man; maybe he could have exploited his lack of agility with his injured leg and outlasted him, wearing him down with well-placed blows until Gorka collapsed under his own bulk, just like Bobby had done all those years before. After all the punishment and deprivation he had suffered though, Paddy had no chance in a fair fight and Gorka was now closer to the only other remaining projectile in the room: the device that Unai had been working on. Gorka

134

stopped and stooped to retrieve it as he moved inexorably towards Paddy.

Casting around for another option, Paddy's eyes alighted on the makeshift kitchen that lay to his left. The hose! Paddy staggered in its direction as Gorka came closer; he could hear his ragged breathing from the exertion of the chase.

Wrenching the hose from the wall, he now had eight feet of rubber pain to inflict upon his sadistic foe. The makeshift whip felt joyous in his hand and with his opening salvo: a mere warning shot across Gorka's brow, screamed out a foreboding message.

Gorka, though, was unafraid. He was a veteran, used to combat and he had been in this situation many times before. He raised his left hand: "Paddy, you know what this is, yes?" Nodding towards the bomb, which looked insignificant and this man's mammoth paw, his smile sent a message that Paddy couldn't fail to understand. "Look at the number on it, Paddy."

1:35...1:34

"Shite."

"Exactly, boy. I don't need to beat you; I just need to be near you when this baby goes off." That laugh. "We have been paid for your death; my demise will be a sweet one. I've always thought about dying amid the flames. There's something poetic about it."

1:14

Paddy, with resolve hardened by urgency, leaned back, ready to compel his weapon into Gorka's mass and then catapulted it forward, cobra-like across Gorka's arms. The scream that emitted from this beast was unholy. Again, he laughed.

Paddy couldn't contain his rage, he launched his whip into Gorka's body again and again, staggering him back, drawing bloody streams from a dozen different injuries. Gorka, staggering from the savagery of his beating, reeled. Paddy drew a deep lungful of air and raised the hose for one more strike: with his legendary precision and all his might, he struck directly onto Gorka's damaged left calf, dropping him to one knee.

0:48

Paddy couldn't wait any longer: his body screaming at him to stop, his mind screaming the opposite, he leapt forward and aimed his knee at Gorka's jaw, when bone met bone the mandible shattered. Both men collapsed to the ground in exhaustion and agony.

0:35

Despite all he had been through, Paddy couldn't stay still. His years of mental training, of determined resolve, of continuing when all seemed lost, came to the forefront of his mind. He had to keep struggling. Seizing the bomb from Gorka's outstretched hand, prying it from his knotted fingers, Paddy sprinted to the door. Even after all the pain he had been through and the knowledge that this bomb was made for him, Paddy was unwilling to take these men's lives. He wouldn't accept that on his conscience.

Barrelling through the door, the bomb read 0:14. Paddy leaned back, holding the device over his head, trebucheting this handful of death into the distance, towards what looked like an abandoned scrap yard. The bomb landed far off in the distance. Paddy waited. And waited. After all that – a false alarm, a decoy. Nothing.

And then a deep boom.

Its timer having finally counted to zero, the device exploded amid a large, rickety construction which was engulfed by the force of the combustion and utterly demolished. The shockwaves knocked Paddy off his feet, where he lay for a few moments, recovering from his exertions.

He still had to act though. He'd been stabbed, beaten, bound, tortured and almost murdered (and his right knee was severely chafed from the binding), but Paddy couldn't waste time: these men still meant to kill him.

He limped heavily back into the room, swaying with exhaustion. He could hear Gorka's miserable, hacking breaths, the knee to the face had damaged his visage irreparably and rendered him unconscious.

Taking the hose, he tied Gorka's arms together and dragged him outside to dehydrate in the sun. Unai received gentler treatment: Paddy used his earlier bindings to secure him to the chair of his own confinement.

Reasoning that someone must have heard the explosion and that the police must be on their way, Paddy needed to get out of there. He couldn't be detained by Spanish police: Fallanks would end his career, providing he hadn't already. He

136

entered the black van that was parked in front of his warehouse-prison, spluttering a laugh at his only moment of good fortune in finding the keys in the ignition and his possessions tossed into the back of the van. He pulled on his clothes; how naive, he thought, and as the engine coughed into life, he heard Gorka's latest ejaculation. Not a laugh this time, more a rueful sob. He had regained consciousness just in time to see his quarry escape.

Paddy pulled out of the warehouse's driveway and pointed in the direction of – he hoped – Bilbao.

Before long, the donkeys and farming vehicles thinned out and Paddy found a road worthy of cars, following signs to Bilbao. It wasn't the quality of ride he was used to – in his eyes there was very little that could match The Jag – but it was faster and safer than walking or hitch-hiking.

Looking around the van's interior, Paddy discovered an unmarked cassette tape in the glove compartment; it was going to be a reasonably-long journey and Spanish radio stations weren't stimulating Paddy's enthusiasm. When he pressed the cassette in and it began to play, he was stunned by an instantly-recognisable voice reading those famous words: "Out of Austria. I was born into a year of famine. It was 1947, and Austria was occupied by the Allied armies that had defeated Hitler's Third Reich..." It appeared that he had more in common with Unai and Gorka than he had ever thought possible – it seemed that they were Arnie fans too!

It was an enjoyable drive for Paddy; despite all the pain he was feeling it was a huge relief to be free again and to be hearing the life-affirming words of his hero during the drive. "From the bodybuilding days on, I learned that everything is reps and mileage. The more miles you ski, the better a skier you become; the more reps you do, the better your body." Damn right, thought Paddy, nodding his head in approval of the mantra he had lived by.

He sped back to the city, though his phone had died and he had no map: it was the epicentre of this region and Paddy couldn't fail to return to the place of his most recent double-cross. He suspected that the concierge had been in cahoots with Gorka all along and had called him the moment Paddy had left. He wondered if Lucia even existed at all.

Pulling into the hotel's car park, Paddy didn't bother to lock the van. In its current condition you would have to be desperate to steal it, and if that were the case Paddy was happy for that person to risk their lives in such a vehicle. He entered the lobby of the hotel, pausing only a moment to give a death stare to the concierge, who paled upon the realisation that not only was Paddy still alive, he was aware of his role in his abduction. Paddy though, had no intention of wasting his time on more underlings: he had to find out who was behind these repeated attempts on his life; the power behind all the violence.

He collected the ever-expanding pile of documents from his safe, as well as the meagre belongings that he had brought with him from Claston two (? Three?) days ago – Paddy could no longer tell how long this adventure had been going on for: he just wanted it to end – and headed back to the lobby. Walking past the service desk, he pointed to the concierge and informed them that "that shaking little man over there" would be footing his bill for his stay. The concierge nodded, palely, and spoke quietly in Spanish to his colleague, who took Paddy's key and smiled. "Gracias senõr."

With that, Paddy was gone. He returned to the van and headed to the airport, vowing never to return to Spain unless it were for a big European tie for his beloved Celts. He only hoped that he would get to play for them again.

Chapter 22: The Return

Paddy threw his credit card on the customer service desk and smiled at the dusky, gorgeous woman behind the counter. "Get me tae London, please beautiful." Clearly used to English in a variety of accents, the assistant wasn't fazed by Paddy's usual voice: his thick Claston brogue had resurfaced after the suffering of his time in Spain; she gazed at him though: obviously with admiration at his frame, but also with concern at the cuts and bruises on his face and knuckles. He noticed the look and chuckled, suddenly aware of his appearance: "Ye should see the rest o' me. It isnae a pretty sight! Where can Ah get a Cerveza?" The assistant gestured behind him to a quaint café only twenty metres away and he smiled. "First class, Heathrow, as quickly as ye can. Can ye bring mah ticket over? Ah'm thirsty." He winked, turned and limped awkwardly towards the café; she noted the blood seeping from a wound on his back and reached for her phone.

Sitting at the café, Paddy realised that he would need to have his back looked at to make sure his wound wasn't infected. That sort of thing could kill you, he thought, unable to suppress a snort of laughter as he struggled to swallow his beer.

The flight was a simple one: first class passengers rarely get any hassle on such journeys and Paddy took time on the flight to come up with a plan. He thought through all of his former teammates and couldn't think of a single Spaniard that he could trust to translate such an important document (and to keep the findings safe). He made a mental note to visit Fergus again when he was next in London, whenever that would be.

That thought of his old schoolmate (if such a term could be applied to Fergus after his treachery) got Paddy thinking about any contacts he could make use of, and, once again it was Thistledown College that brought the result that he needed. There was a young languages teacher there that had been offered a job at Eton College towards the end of his time in the prestigious Scottish establishment. Paddy remembered Ms. Beard fondly: she taught him Latin, but he remembered her being fluent in Spanish, Russian and French too. More importantly, he had disclosed a secret to her once (just as a test: Paddy used to do that regularly as a young man, just to see if his secret was ever passed on – that was how he knew who he could, and who he could not talk to) and he never heard anything further from it, so he felt that this was someone that he could turn to at this time.

Having charged his phone on the flight, a quick search online told Paddy that she still held a post at Eton, which was a short drive from Heathrow. He only wished he had taken that tape with him: he could do with some words of wisdom from the man himself right now.

Arriving at the college in the late afternoon, Paddy hoped that he would be able to see his former guide. Not only could she help him, he wanted to show her that her hard work as his teacher had not gone to waste. He practised some of the key welcoming phrases that he could remember from his Latin classes, hoping that his pronunciation wasn't too rusty. He asked at the office for Ms. Beard, explaining that he was a former student, though he gave the name as Killian MacPherson – an old school acquaintance – and without too much effort she was contacted, appearing a few minutes later. Smiling, her enthusiasm and happiness to see Paddy was tempered by the confusion of his pseudonym, though she made an obvious effort to conceal this. She walked towards him, arms outstretched: "MacPherson – how lovely to see you." "Et voluptatem ad vos," he said, uncertainly. She smiled, though her eyes betrayed an infinitesimal tinge of disappointment. Paddy's accent always hampered his pronunciation of the classical languages.

"Ms. Beard – "

"No, *Killian*. You are a grown man now; we don't need to rely on outdated titles. You can call me Sam." Her voice was an octave lower than he remembered, her posture more assured: she always had a look of nervousness during their time together. She had aged well: her light umber skin, with tightly-curled, short locks at her temples accentuated her beauty. The lines around her eyes were more pronounced, he thought, as were the furrows across her brow, but she was still a handsome woman, comfortable in her skin.

140

"Alright, if ye insist, Sam – Ah need yer help with some translation work. This isnae something Ah'm wanting tae share with just anybody, ye ken? Ye're the only person Ah can think of that Ah might be able tae trust."

"Paddy, I've missed that accent," she smiled. "You might want to cover your face, though, at least a little: you know you're a national news item right now, don't you? I'm happy to see that you're safe: you had me worried. I assume that this is the reason for the deception at the office?" Paddy nodded.

He was surprised at the idea that he was national news: he thought he had managed to keep a low profile, but he reasoned that if Fergie had betrayed him once, he could have sold the story to the press as well: he needed the money for coffee capsules after all. Paddy had more than one reason to have a little chat with Doctor Wyatt...

"Ah'm happy tae *be* safe – thanks for yer concern. Ah have some documents that Ah'd like ye tae look at fer me, quietly. Do ye have a place where we willnae be disturbed?"

With a nod of her head, Sam Beard walked past Paddy and led him through the grand halls and corridors of Eton College until they came to a huge oaken door with an ornately carved sign that read "Block F: MFL and The Classics". Walking inside, Sam gestured to her colleagues, speaking with a heavy Scottish accent that Paddy had never heard her use before – a curious affectation, he thought. There was a firmness in her voice that he recognised from his school days, an edge that would tolerate no dissent or timewasting; she was a formidable woman, no doubt. "Thanks ever'body: Ah'm needin' th' room. Please make sure that mah friend 'n' Ah are nae disturbed." The room emptied without pause and Paddy looked quizzically at his former mentor. "Our common history, Paddy, has to be useful for something," and with that she smiled and outstretched her hands, expectantly.

"These are the documents then? What are they?"

"Ah'd rather nae explain everything, Ms... Ah mean, Sam, if ye dinnae mind. It's a... delicate situation. There are some sales records, can ye just let me know what they say?" Aware that he was putting her in the very same delicate situation he had just outlined, Paddy smiled at her, briefly and looked to the ground, unwilling to meet her gaze for too long.

"Okay, Paddy. Let me look." And so she did. Paddy was hoping for a quick scan and to be on his way, but Sam was thorough; she perused each page slowly, making annotations on a small pad that she had taken from her bag. Every now and then she grunted or murmured quietly; each time, Paddy stared, alert, but was met with no further information.

Sam's reverie was broken by the booming of a bell, striking out its message four times: Lupton's Tower housed an immense clock that signalled the passing of the hours and shook Sam's concentration. "Okay, Paddy: I think I have what you need. On this pad are written the names of this company's biggest customers – those five are buying various computer parts, those five are the ones paying the highest consultancy costs. The remaining two names are the ones in which you will be the most interested, I would imagine: they are paying huge amounts of money to whomever this company is in '*miscellaneous* fees' – a rather unusual practice, I would imagine. What is this about, McAlpin?" Concern had crept into her voice now; all of her commanding tones had slipped off quietly into the afternoon sun.

"Ah cannae tell ye, Sam: it's nae safe for ye tae ken. Thank ye so much for doing this and, please – nae one can ever ken that Ah was here." He reached out and took the pad proffered to him and gathered up the now-loose pile of papers that he had taken from the offices of Ordenadex – he had got her into enough trouble and couldn't leave her with the evidence that he had gathered: he would need this for his next move. Kissing her on the cheek, Paddy turned and shuffled back towards the main entrance hall, his body was slowly recovering but still shimmering with pain from the week's exertions. As he was signing out at the school reception he asked if there was a first aid kit that he could make use of. Paddy's ability to keep a low profile occasionally left a little to be desired: he wasn't aware of what a strange request this was. After furrowing her brow at Paddy, the receptionist duly obliged, asking him politely to hold on a moment.

As he waited, Paddy heard his own name being spoken in the otherwise empty room, realising that a radio was playing from behind the reception desk. Clearly, Ms. Beard's statement about him being national news was accurate. The English news did not often mention Scottish football, but here was a headline news story about him, or specifically, about how he had disappeared. Paddy listened intently, wondering how true the account would be.

"It has now been three days since Scottish superstar and five-time Ballon d'Or winner Paddy McAlpin was last seen, prompting speculation that he has had a falling out with his confrontational manager Jim Fallanks. It is often reported that no one man is bigger than the club, but in McAlpin's case, that old adage might not be quite so cut and dried. McAlpin revolutionised Claston Celts as a young academy graduate and set them on their way to the success they are currently still enjoying, prior to his departure for the continent. Whilst abroad he spent six glorious years playing for German side Hamburg, establishing himself as the finest footballer on the planet with his five consecutive Ballon d'Or wins and his many domestic and European trophies. His recapture by his hometown club was seen as something of a coup, with most spectators expecting a move to one of Real Madrid, Barcelona or Juventus to follow. Yet McAlpin told his adoring fans how he "needed to be back in Claston" to help "continue what he started" all those years ago. However, this season has not been without a few bumps in the road, with a number of fans of Scottish football wondering if McAlpin had only returned for an easy ride in what he saw as a sub-standard league.

"The latest problem, or problems, to hamper the man once known as the Highlands Hero, was his very public falling out with manager Fallanks following an uncharacteristically poor performance in the Scottish Cup semi-final against Dundee United last Saturday. Although the Celts did manage to win in the end, with McAlpin scoring the vital penalty in the shoot-out, the game was expected to be a one-sided affair. Yet, despite all his previous successes and obvious class as a footballer, McAlpin was well below par and at fault for the early Dundee United goal. He struggled to impose himself throughout the match, something that did not escape the watchful eyes of his manager.

"After the match, Fallanks lambasted McAlpin live on air, whilst the team celebrated with their fans. Yet that turned out to be the least of his worries that day. Following the match, McAlpin was selected for a random drugs test, of which the results are still unknown. The longer McAlpin is away, the more

likely it seems that he failed said drug test and is facing a lengthy ban. At his age, that could well spell the end of his career. And yet even that would not prove to be the worst thing that happened to McAlpin.

"For reasons unknown, after the match McAlpin went to the notorious Ascension House Estate in east Claston, the scene where he grew up, and seemingly became embroiled in what has been confirmed as a murder investigation, following the death of Claire Duggan: a childhood friend of his. McAlpin was found with Duggan at the scene of the crime, and although Detective Inspector Galloway who is leading the investigation has confirmed that McAlpin is not on any list of suspects, his name must be resurfacing as a potential lead after his disappearance.

"Since that evening, McAlpin has not been seen by anyone, or at least anyone willing to corroborate his whereabouts. Our sources suggest that he may have gone to Bilbao, and an unconfirmed sighting of him was made at the World Arm-Wrestling Championships, although that is expected to be refuted as incorrect.

"Whether McAlpin was actually present in Bilbao or not remains unclear due to his uncanny resemblance of the defeated finalist of that competition, the recently-murdered Sergio Brazofuerte, found in the river just hours after his competition. Whether this has any link to McAlpin remains unclear and only adds to the enigma of the case against him. Whilst McAlpin's presence in Bilbao does remain unclear for now, there will undoubtedly have to be an investigation into the suspicious deaths if it is confirmed he has been in the Basque city.

"Back in Claston, Fallanks has backtracked somewhat over his previous comments, saying that they were in the heat of the moment and that McAlpin still plays an important part in his plans moving forward. Whether that is a decision that has been pushed onto him by chairman Cormac Dundas, although it seems safe to say that he will not feature again if he is suspected of homicide and awaiting trial.

"Within the club the message is seen as "business as usual" with the only official comments being those about their preparation for their upcoming league match against Stenhousemuir and then the Scottish Cup Final a week later. Any questions regarding McAlpin have been largely ignored or dismissed, save from Fallanks's initial statement where he

*indicated McAlpin was still part of his plans and stated that
'Paddy will be back in due course, the club know where he is and
he has our permission to miss training for the time being.' The
secrecy about the matter has, of course, only increased
speculation, with one outlet suggesting he is in a rehabilitation
centre.*

*"There has been one unofficial source linked to the club that
we can try to read into, that of young full-back Mikael Tintoni's
social media account. Tintoni has been responsible for the recent
trending of the hashtag IStandWithPaddy, although to date, no
further release from the Italian has been made.*

*"We will continue to update you with this story throughout
the week."*

Paddy shook his head. There was a lot of truth in there, he
thought. It was then that he noticed yesterday's paper; a blurry
image of him making his way into San Mamés adorned the
front page, and a much clearer image of him competing in his
ring during the final, although that image was captioned:
McAlpin or Brazofuerte? Just as he finished reading, the
receptionist returned and handed Paddy the first aid kit.
Glancing over at the paper she commented how much Paddy
looked like the arm-wrestler she could see on the page, and
then went back to her computer.

Paddy took some disinfectant wipes and some large
plasters out of the kit, reasoning that it was way past time to
thoroughly clean his wound, leaving the rest of the bag on the
side. He did so in the car park, groaning and sweating with
every movement. The wound in his back must have become
worse: it was agonising now. That would not stop him, though.
He opened the notes that Sam Beard had given him and looked
at the two names:

Scholz Vertriebsgesellschaft mbH
Cochran Industries Incorporated

Bizarrely, Paddy recognised the first almost instantly. If
he recalled it correctly, he thought it was a Berlin-based horse
trader from his time playing in Germany. His teammates tried
to persuade him to buy a racehorse in his first season,
something he sensibly declined. He didn't fancy another trip

abroad: he had been gone for far too long and owed his teammates an explanation, and more importantly the other name struck him as familiar. "Cochran". He knew the name, of course, it was a popular one in Scotland, but it meant something to him personally for some reason: it itched in his memory. He was sure it was related to Claston somehow but couldn't remember what or who it referred to.

Grabbing his phone, he had a look for the company. Cochran Industries Incorporated: a local IT firm based in the centre of Claston. Paddy followed the thread that he had begun tugging – "About us... Our team... Owners..." Paddy knew now why he recognised the name...

One short stop close to home to prepare and then unto the breach, as it were, to put an end to this sorry business. He put the Jag into gear and pealed out of the car park, heading north.

Chapter 23: The Road Home

It is a shade over four hundred miles from Eton College to the city of Claston and Paddy knew the route well. Most people would take at least six hours to complete this journey, but Paddy knew each bend and curve like he knew all of his former lovers and took each one with the right speed and timing. Paddy took five hours, his journey completed with a short break for fuel as his only rest en route. Tired and hurting, he was resolute in his desire to finish this. A small diversion as he drove into Claston was a small price to pay to end this nightmare.

He drove through the gates of one of his least-favourite locations: Lightfield Stadium (the Celts fans had an unofficial, rhyming alternative), home of Claston Celts' main rivals, The Claston Wanderers.

Lightfield was everything that San Mamés was not: all Victorian-inspired red brick, with a haunted look about it that reflected the trophyless years since Paddy had come to prominence. The lack of success and subsequent reduced income of the Claston Wanderers meant that the club did not have the finances to maintain their ground in the same way that the Celts did; as a result, the masonry and brickwork in the stadium had begun to degrade, the seats needed to be replaced, and by this late time in the season the pitch was in a desperate state and in need of re-surfacing, but with their hefty wage bill it was unlikely that the funds for this would be found anytime soon. They would have to keep relying on Willie MacDonald, their octogenarian groundskeeper, to keep working his magic.

Paddy strode through the smeared glass doors to the front desk: despite his bruises he was recognised immediately. "Get me yer chairman. Dinnae dick around: if he's nae here in two minutes Ah'll burn this shithole tae the ground." Paddy's tone allowed no response other than a quivering acquiescence and, before two minutes had passed, he was being shown into club chairman Donald MacLeod's office.

"To what do I owe this *pleasure*, Mr McAlpin? Have ye finally decided to come and play for Claston's real club?"

MacLeod, seated at his desk, made no mention of the cuts and bruises that adorned Paddy like the spots on a leopard and held a steely glare, trying to deduce why the greatest star of his most hated club had demanded an audience with him.

Paddy paused at the question, using the time to take measure of this man in front of him. Even from MacLeod's seated position, Paddy could tell he was small, maybe five foot seven. His shiny, bronzed skin had clearly seen better days and his thinning hair was brushed tightly across his pate, in a vain attempt to obscure the baldness that was winning through. His suit was well-tailored though, and it seemed to Paddy that this man's wallet was not suffering as much as his club's.

"Dinnae be so fucking stupid. Ah'm not about tae sell out my boys for a shower o' shite like yer lot. Nah, Ah'm here about yer wife." A flicker of surprise then; or was it fear?

"McAlpin. Paddy. What can ye mean by that?"

"Ye ken what Ah mean: yer wife – Doris, nae? Doris Macleod…or should Ah call her Doris Cochran?"

"Ye ken my wife's maiden name, Mr McAlpin, but Ah fail tae see how that's relevant tae this conversation."

"Ah enjoyed her profile in Highland Life magazine. She's a successful businesswoman, it seems, and owner of Cochran Industries Incorporated." In annoyance, Paddy reached up and furiously scratched his muscular chest and coughed. His injuries were causing his serious problems by now and his chest in particular felt irritated.

"Get on with it, McAlpin: Ah'm a busy man and if ye dinnae wantae turn out fur the Wanderers, Ah dinnae see that Ah have anything tae gain by speaking with ye." His face was flushed now, his annoyance laid bare.

Paddy growled, a low, threatening murmur that stayed MacLeod's complaining. "Ah dinnae think it's a coincidence that one of Ordenadex's largest customers is Cochran Industries Incorporated – based in Claston and owned by yer wife. Ordenadex just happen tae be in possession of vast quantities of thalelamide – the same compound that murdered Claire Duggan, and almost killed me." His rage was building, but at this point, Paddy knew he had to maintain his focus: he couldn't attack MacLeod, not here, not now. He had to find out what was going on.

"So, Macleod. Did yer wife try tae murder me, or is there another story here?" And then, despite his hard exterior, Donald MacLeod's resolve crumpled – he slumped forward onto his desk, his arms resting their full weight down onto the surface in front of him. His left hand reached under the desk, groping for something.

"Alright, McAlpin – ye got me. The club needed money; Ah needed money. Ah've been fixing sports events, loads o' them, all around the world. If ye've seen teams looking outta sorts and losing games ye wouldn't expect, they've been given thalelamide by my associates, whom Ah think ye already ken..."

At that moment there was a crash and the door from which Paddy had entered was flung open and he realised that MacLeod hadn't collapsed onto his desk out of exhaustion or fear; he had signalled that he needed help. A sense of terrifying recognition flooded through his veins as he saw who had arrived at MacLeod's call. Two of the three men were instantly identified; the third was familiar from stories whispered into his young and frightened ears as a small boy finding his way at Ascension. It was clear that all three were well versed in violence and unused to boardroom battles: they were more at home with bricks and bats, with boots and fists and pools of blood. How MacLeod had gotten himself mixed up with these men was a mystery to Paddy. The man who stood in the middle of the three was a ghost, rarely seen by anyone anymore – a huge, terrifying man nearly forty years his senior that Paddy had only set eyes one a handful of times, yet he was one who still haunted his dreams from time to time: IRA Shaun, the founder of The Ghost Mob. The man on his left was instantly recognisable to Paddy, for he was instrumental in Paddy being "known" in Ascension. The scars from The Day The Crowd Gasped were still visible on his face. The last man was an unknown quantity to Paddy, but nonetheless had a terrifying visage: among the many scars that criss-crossed his face, the one that had ruined his left eye was the most chilling.

IRA Shaun spoke first – he was clearly the man with the power in that room. Paddy had never heard him speak before and was surprised at the harsh Northern Irish accent that filled the room with a deep boom. "So Mr McAlpin – do you know me?" Paddy swallowed, hard, and nodded, "It seems that you have once again poked your nose in where it wasn't wanted.

Once again, you have interceded into something that didn't really concern you. Sure, you were drugged; sure, you nearly lost a cup semi-final, but if you had simply missed that penalty like a good little boy, all this would have gone away. Now Bobby and Jamie will have to get their hands dirty, and I hate it when their victims get their blood all over my shoes."

"What's going on? Why is this happening?" Paddy asked, stalling as best as he could. Shaun laughed at the question, but the three men remained unmoved in front of him. Behind him, MacLeod still sat at his desk, finally worrying that these men were not under his control as he had for so long tried to convince himself.

"That's a fair question, Paddy. And as I'm a fair man… Well, I heard Donald clucking like the little chicken that he is…" he raised a finger in MacLeod's direction, silencing any potential complaints. "But I suppose that now you have sealed your own fate it would only be fair to know why this has happened." He paused at this and peered at Paddy, waiting for a sign. Paddy's iron will was nowhere near breaking, though Shaun was right: he was desperate, after all this pain, to find out why. "Well you see, Paddy: on The Day The Crowd Gasped," – Shaun spat this – "as the residents of your little cess pool have come to call it, you dried up my revenue stream. A crowd of people saw my main enforcer being battered in the street by a little boy. Shops stopped paying protection; people started defying The Ghost Mob, trusting the police over us. And when that happened, the police would no longer ensure that my activities flew under the radar. It seems, Paddy, that that final blow you landed was the most lethal one imaginable, at least to me.

"After that I left Scotland. I still had a considerable amount of money – I'm a major investor in Ascension House, you see: I bought up huge amounts of it since it became possible in the 80s: thank you, Maggie, for that. So that provided some income for me, but it wouldn't keep me in the lifestyle to which I had become accustomed, and Paddy: I love the flicker of fear in a person's eyes when they are about to lose everything; I couldn't very well give that up could I? To be what, a fuckin' landlord? Fixing boilers and collecting rents every month? No thank you very much. I even tried to buy your family's flat, Paddy, but Matthew was very…uncooperative. I tried to...convince him many times, but he never relented. It's a shame he had to die so young...

"Well, Bobby was excommunicated after the battering that you gave him. I couldn't be associated with such feebleness." Bobby looked to the ground as if something there were suddenly so very interesting to him. "But he's not completely useless..." Bobby instantly looked up again, like a beaten puppy sensing praise from its cruel master, "and he had heard of an... opportunity for us. He only required a bit of capital to get him started. Well, once he explained about how easy it would be to administer this thalelamide to sportsmen and how we could make a killing from placing large bets against incapacitated opponents I knew that my empire was about to rise again. He even knew of a way to buy huge amounts of the stuff without drawing any attention. All it took was to find someone who was in need of money and had a company that was set up with the paperwork to handle potentially dangerous chemicals. Ha – the government were never going to let me run a company that could do that; not after all the business back home."

He paused here and looked at MacLeod. "The Wanderers have been a spent force for quite some time, Paddy, and Donald here needed some help. Sentiment is a powerful foe, and Donald just couldn't let the club go into the hands of a foreign investor. Well, we came to an arrangement: his wife's company would supply us with the thalelamide, for well-above market value, naturally – but Mrs. MacLeod was smart enough to hide the income in her accounts – and we would make huge amounts from placing bets. We knew the outcome of the games before they even started. Your game, Paddy, is broken and dying. Money rules sport: competition and honour have nothing to do with it. The men at the top understand this, but your kind never will. So, we began to fix matches. We started with football: it was easy, but then we branched out into boxing, rugby, even golf. It's not hard to find someone to insert a little bit of liquid into a water bottle, after all. And most people never even notice the side-effects – they just feel a sluggish and off their game. They blame a bad diet, a late night, a freak incident out of their control. But you: you were a special case. People were falling over themselves to drug your bottle and it seems in their enthusiasm, *someone* made a mistake with the dosage." Again he paused, looking to his side, but this time Bobby wasn't cowed. It was the other man – the one with the scar on his left eye – who flushed with fear and shame.

"**Someone** is lucky to still be alive: I'm not known for my patience! But I was guaranteed that **someone** knew people that could get rid of any witnesses without drawing attention." Next to him, Jamie was itching to defend himself, but clearly knew better than to interrupt the man speaking. "You nearly gave us the slip with your little jaunt to Spain, but I know people, and your old friend Fergus soon let slip as to where you were headed. That was quite the stroke of luck for us, you turning up there. I believe you met my contacts in Spain. Oh yes, Fergus and I go way back. He's told me all about your time at school together. Getting him to work for me was easy; there is little that money can't buy, and certainly not the loyalty of a man like him. It isn't even expensive. After that first pay packet you can keep him loyal through fear alone. And a man like Fergus is easy to scare." Paddy swallowed, unblinking, considering the words Shaun had spoken, realising that Fergus had had more than just their school days as a reason to not want to see him. Perhaps his next visit didn't need to be as confrontational as he had planned. As Paddy developed a genuine feeling of empathy for perhaps the first time, Shaun continued with his tale. He was relishing the reveal, desperate to talk his conquests, about himself.

"Once I knew your location, I made a few calls to contacts of mine in Bilbao. You were supposed to be dead by now, Paddy! And here you are, in all your... glory." Shaun elongated that final word, looking Paddy up and down, focussing on his beaten body, clearly displaying his disdain for the man who stood before him. "Well at least this way I don't get to miss out on the fun." Finally, Jamie could contain himself no longer and launched into a grovelling apology.

"Shaun, Ah'm sorry... Ah..." The voice was cut off.

"Shut it, Jamie. You weren't given permission to speak. You are though, given permission to die." Shaun raised his arm and pointed at Jamie: it was then that Paddy saw the gun in his hand. A single shot was heard and Jamie's body collapsed to the ground, blood coating the wall behind him." Bobby drew in his breath; Shaun's face cracked into a poisonous smile;

MacLeod screamed: partly through fear, partly through the effect the blood had had on his precious office wall.

Paddy though, didn't flinch. He had one final detail to confirm with Shaun before he ended this commotion.

"Ah guess ye'd never have needed Fergus if yer stud trick had worked. Instead, poor Claire had tae die." Shaun said nothing; though Paddy detected a look of confusion on his face, but the look faded as quickly as it had entered, and the sneer returned.

"I have people everywhere, Paddy. You were never going to get away from me." Paddy decided he had had enough. He turned his face to the MacLeod and stated, firmly: "There can be only one."

A moment of confusion, a moment of silence. MacLeod, Shaun and Bobby looked at one another and, led by Shaun, the three began to laugh.

And then the world collapsed: glass shattered and smoke filled the room. MacLeod screamed again. Paddy pulled up his shirt to cover his mouth and nose, revealing the presence of a wire running from his trousers up to his chest, before dissolving backwards into the smoke. Heavily-armed police flooded the room, descending on the three culprits, binding them tightly and marching them into three separate police vans, each with its own escort. The deceased Jamie, leaking scarlet onto the plush carpet, watched on with his one glassy eye as the room emptied.

Walking down to the exit, a team of detectives and plain clothed police officers awaited him. Breaking into applause when they saw him descending the stairs, a familiar face stepped out into a clearing, extending his hand in thanks. "Great work, McAlpin. Ah'm glad ye chose tae work with me after all. We can put these men away for a long time." Detective Inspector Galloway's smile was broad: this would be the feather in the cap of a storied career. He was the only police officer that could ever walk the streets of Ascension House without fear after he had helped Aoife out of that lift all those years ago and this coup would probably propel him to a political career.

Galloway reached out his hand and lay it on Paddy's shoulder, uttering words that would echo with Paddy long after they had been said. "Ye've done a great thing today,

Paddy. What ye do on that pitch makes people happy, ye ken, but today ye gave folks their lives back."

Chapter 24: Confessions of a Troubled Mind

Five days after he had last seen any of the Celts squad, Paddy rolled his Jaguar into the team training ground, trying to act as if nothing out of the ordinary had happened. He made sure to arrive early; he wanted to be the first one there in order to remain low-key but in spite of his early arrival, the press were waiting for him. He should have expected as much – they had probably been camping overnight just in case he arrived under the cloak of darkness. His Jaguar was well-known and instantly recognisable and the press circled it immediately. Paddy refused to wind down his window for the legions of paparazzi and reporters, each of them desperate for a photo or a comment to earn their wages for the day.

The wrought iron gates emblazoned with the club badge, a round shield adorned with sword and crossbow, opened and shut, providing him relative sanctuary from the vipers' nest outside. All he had to do now was face the wrath of his team.

Paddy had thought about how he could explain his whereabouts and his injuries for some time, turning over idea after idea in his mind until he came up with what might just be the craziest idea of all, and the one he decided to stick with: the truth. He would leave out no detail (well, almost no detail, no one needed to know about Marlene or Charlotte) and would have to hope that his team would believe his crazy tale and still have respect for him, and most of all, hope that his manager would believe and continue to select him. He drove past his designated parking space in front of the changing complex and parked around the back in an attempt to make his car less conspicuous, turning off the faithful, purring engine and taking a moment to himself.

In silence he sat, eyes closed, breathing deeply. He stretched as best as he could in the confined space, feeling the tension in each of his muscles and wondering if he would even be able to kick a ball. Tipping his head back and arching his shoulders, he felt the sharp pain in his back from the knife wound he had suffered in Bilbao. He still hadn't seen a doctor about it but was now confident there was no infection as the pain was easing.

With sudden resolve, Paddy opened the door of his now-silent car and stepped out onto the tarmac, making his way reluctantly towards the changing room to await his teammates. The day before a game was always a light training session, with the players meeting for breakfast in the cafeteria first. Paddy had already decided not to join them and made his way into the changing room. He wanted to face the whole team together to give them his story as one. Paddy sat alone for over an hour, running through the events of the previous days again and again. He needed to get this right.

Eventually, he could hear the noise of his teammates as they bounced along the corridor towards where he sat, elbows on knees, hands pressed together, fingers resting gently on his stubbled chin. First through the door was the mild-mannered goalkeeper, Mark Richards. If Richards was surprised, he didn't let it show, with the only the slightest hesitation before calmly walking over to his regular seat, nodding almost imperceptibly at Paddy along the way. Paddy was thankful to his goalkeeper for such a dignified entrance as it set the tone for many of the following players. Unsurprisingly, Joel Johnson was not so subtle upon entry, screeching Paddy's name in a way befitting of a child that has been told that their older sister has broken their favourite toy. What was surprising, at least to Paddy, was when Johnson was instantly hushed by Fallanks.

"Johnson, shut yer wee trap will ye and start acting like a man. We all ken Paddy McAlpin. Although perhaps he wasnae sure if enough people did. Mebbe that's why he's got himself spread across all the tabloids." Paddy looked up at his manager, expecting to see a sneer, but was instead, greeted with a smile.

"Ah'm sure ye've come in here to tell us where exactly it is ye've been, Paddy McAlpin. We're all dying tae' ken, so come on, out with it." Paddy winced involuntarily at the turn of phrase his manager had unwittingly used but could not help but be thankful for his understanding. Paddy took a deep breath and began.

"Ah think it's important tae start with the simple fact that Ah'm painfully sorry for leaving ye all in the lurch these past few days. Mah father, bless him, use tae say tae me when Ah was a bairn, 'Paddy, it takes a big man tae apologise when he kens he's wrong.' Ah always thought Ah understood what he meant, but also never really thought Ah'd been wrong about anything. Ah do understand what he meant more than ever now. Ah hope ye'll forgive me once ye've heard what Ah've been through…"

Paddy related the story from the moment he left them all to go to his drug test until the moment he arrived at the changing room that morning. Throughout the story all sat quietly and listened (even Johnson), with no interruptions. Paddy always had been a story-teller, and with content as wild and unbelievable as this, he couldn't fail to captivate his audience.

"And now, Ah'm back here and ready to play. If ye'll let me, that is."

A silence swept through the room and all eyes turned from Paddy to Fallanks, who took a moment to think before he made his reply.

"Paddy, yer story is totally unbelievable, but it's exactly that fact that makes me believe it. There's no way ye could ha' made that up. Ah'm nae gonnae hold anything against ye for missing these past few days. Everyone in here knows what ye bring to this team and what ye've done for us since signing last summer. Nae one can question yer commitment. But there is absolutely nae way Ah'm going to play ye tomorrow. Look at the state of ye, man. If the rest of yer body is like yer face ye probably look like a leopard with all the black spots ye must have."

"Or a Jaguar, boss!" A round of laughter eased the tension like the relief of loosening a tight belt after a large meal.

"Mah torso is probably a bit worse tae be fair." Paddy said weakly. "But they left mah legs alone, so there's that."

"We aren't gonnae need ye tomorrow, Paddy. But Ah'll want ye tae play in next week's final. Before then, ye need tae get yourself fit! Go tae the physio now. Ah'll see ye on Monday for training!" This seemed both fair and wise to Paddy and hearing it from Fallanks was as unexpected as being offered afternoon tea by a stranger outside Ascension House. As much as it pained him to admit it, his manager was right; with the league already won, the upcoming game wasn't as important to the club, or to him. With a look over his shoulder at the squad who were about to go and do what he enjoyed most, Paddy left the changing room and made his way to the club doctor.

It was nearly four hours before Paddy was released, via the physio, and allowed to go back into the changing room to collect his kit bag and head home. He already felt a lot better and now wished he had been able to seek medical attention much sooner. The physio had eased a lot of the muscle pain from his arms and chest, whilst the cold compressions that the doctor had provided had eased the swelling and soothed the bruising that pockmarked his body. With pre-game-day sessions usually so short, Paddy wasn't expecting to see his team again when he returned to the collect his kit from the changing room. Opening the door, he saw that he was almost right. Sat alone under his peg was the lithe body of Mikael Tintoni. He looked up at Paddy, who could sense that there was something troubling the young man.

"Alright Micky?" Paddy asked, heading to sit down next to the full-back.

"Well, Paddy, I, er... well no, not really." Tintoni offered, a sense of sadness in his usually bouncy Italian lilt.

"Well, what's the problem? Ye ken they often say a problem shared is a problem halved... Although Ah'm not sure exactly who 'they' are."

"I... I need to tell you something, Paddy." Tintoni spoke slowly, timidly, clearly struggling to get the words out.

"Fire away, wee man. Ah'm all ears."

"It's just that, well." Tintoni paused, stumbling over the words that he had planned so carefully while he waited for his idol.

"Ye got women troubles, boy?" Paddy asked with a grin. "Because Ah can tell ye all about that if ye have."

"No," Tintoni said defiantly, and then again, quieter, "no. It's nothing to do with women. It's actually... it's actually to do with you Paddy." At this, Paddy paused. Looking at Tintoni, he saw what others saw: the defined chest and shoulders, the thick, dark hair, his stubble caressing his chin, accentuating his rugged beauty. Paddy was intrigued – he had never considered this idea before, had always been a lady's man...

"You have to understand, Paddy, I never wanted this to happen. I've never told you, but you're the reason I came to Claston. You've been a hero to me for a long time. I had your poster on my wall for many years." Paddy stayed silent, musing.

"But all this time away from home, from my family, my friends… Being in the rain… It's *always* raining in Scotland, Paddy!" Paddy smiled. He knew only too well what the infamous Scottish weather was like. He often said that if you don't like the weather in Scotland, wait five minutes. And learn to like the rain.

"I've got a problem. A big problem. At first it was just to fill the time at home alone, but I couldn't stop myself. I kept doing it more and more." Paddy narrowed his eyes. Perhaps Tintoni wasn't about to profess his undying love for him. Somewhat disappointed (and ashamed of himself for making this about himself) he resolved to help in any way he could, starting with the first step of finding out exactly what the problem was.

"What is it ye're trying tae get at, Micky?" Paddy asked, not unkindly, but firmly. "Ah think it'll be best if ye just say it properly."

"I'm addicted…" Tintoni almost whispered before coughing and finding his voice. "I'm addicted to… to gambling." Paddy exhaled. This was not exactly his area of expertise, but it was something he thought that he could help with, having known others facing a similar plight

"That's nae so bad, Micky. We can find ye some help for that. How bad is it?"

"I'm very ashamed, Paddy. I'm spending more than I earn almost every week. Last week I bet £8,000 on a single horse race." Paddy's eyes bulged and he quickly averted his gaze, trying not to seem as though he was passing judgement. He had known many people, all with their own demons, had faced his own, and knew that passing judgement would be the opposite of helping his friend. "I don't even like horse racing and I obviously don't know anything about it as I lost it all. I make a bit of money every now and then, but never enough. Never enough."

"Ye ken, Micky, it's gonnae be alright. We'll sort this out. I dinnae mind lending ye a few quid, help tae see ye through an all."

"The thing is, Paddy, it's not the gambling that's the issue. That's not even what I wanted to tell you about really. It's just that that information is… Well I'm just trying to justify my actions. What I did to you."

"Ye've done nothing wrong tae me, son." Paddy began to pack up his belongings. Sensing this might be his last chance to tell his tale, Tintoni dove deep into the pool of courage, returning to the surface with exactly the words he needed.

"I poisoned your stud." Paddy stopped still. He was holding his towel in his left hand, frozen midway through placing it in his bag. A shock blasted through him and he felt revulsion, then a pain in his heart. He had always been fond of Tintoni, had once gone so far as to consider him something of a protégé. This revelation couldn't be true. Paddy stood up straight and turned to face the stranger before him.

"What do ye mean, Micky? Ye cannae have? Galloway caught those responsible already. Ah ken cos Ah helped bring them in." Paddy felt the familiar buzzing of his phone. He rummaged through his bag to find it and thrust the screen in Tintoni's direction. "Look, it's Galloway now. He can tell ye all about it himself. Ah'll let ye talk tae him in a moment." Paddy held the phone to his ear, listening to Detective Inspector Galloway, waiting for the opportune moment to interrupt. Behind him, Tintoni reached into his bag and rummaged around for something.

"Hold on, Galloway," Paddy finally managed to get a word in. "Ah've got someone Ah need ye tae speak tae." Paddy turned around to see Tintoni walking towards him, holding the syringe purposefully in his right hand, index and middle finger wrapped around the end, thumb gently pressing the plunger. Paddy froze, dropping his phone. He heard it bounce, once, twice, three times across the changing room floor, coming to a rest just feet away. Through it he could hear the tinny sound of Galloway's voice, clearly unsure what was happening, calling his name, "Paddy? Paddy?" He braced, ready to defend himself one final time.

Tintoni stepped closer to Paddy and held the syringe high before bringing it down hard and fast. Paddy had no time to react, simply letting out a subdued utterance, "Micky, nae…"

He watched on in horror as Tintoni depressed the plunger, sending the lethal concoction straight into the blood stream. Tintoni's hand then dropped away limply and he looked forlornly at the syringe protruding from his own thigh.

He slumped to the ground, the prepared solution taking an instant hold of him. For a moment he sat, legs astride, head slumped, the needle sticking up out of his leg like the mast of a ship, proud against the deck. Then he looked up at Paddy sadly, as the life drained from him.

"I'm so sorry, Paddy," he uttered, every word clearly a torment to him. He screwed his eyes up tightly, contorting his face and biting his lip until he drew blood. For a moment he sat there like that, Paddy watching on in despair at the scenes unfolding in front of him. He had seen too much pain and suffering these past few days already but could not look away. Suddenly, Tintoni's face relaxed and he managed to speak again. "I'm sorry. They told me that if I killed you, they would pay off my debts and that if I didn't, they would kill me." At that, he slumped back onto his elbows, and then slowly lay down, head resting flat on the floor, his eyes looking at the ceiling. Very quietly, he spoke again. Paddy threw himself down beside Tintoni in an attempt to comfort him in what must be his last moments. As he looked into Tintoni's eyes, he saw the eyes of Claire Duggan staring back at him.

"Aw, Micky, ye big fool. We could have helped ye. Ah would have helped yae..." Paddy trailed off, unsure what he could say in this most final of moments. The need to choose his words carefully was removed as, laboriously, Tintoni began to speak.

"I couldn't do it, Paddy. I failed once, thank God, and I was not going to try to kill you a second time." A pause, a deep breath, and then a steely resolve to say his final words, breathing deeply through the pain that coursed through his body, a pain that Paddy knew all too well: "I am glad I am with you for my final moments. At least now I am free from my debt," Tintoni paused, clearly struggling to continue. A cough produced a speckle of blood at the corners of his mouth. After a moment's pause he continued with the look of determination that Paddy had come to recognise from the countless training sessions they had shared, the many matches they had played in together. In the background, Galloway's voice rung though, tinny, far away. "Are ye alright, McAlpin? Paddy? What's happening?" Tintoni took one final deep breath and spoke for the final time.

"I am free… from my… addiction. And… most importantly… free… from them." Tintoni had breathed his last breath, the promising career of the young full-back so needlessly wasted, lost to the most dangerous of foes; oneself. Paddy bowed his head and shed a tear, before trudging over to his phone. Picking it up, he spoke gently, but with a calm authority.

"Galloway. Ye need tae get down here."

Chapter 25: The Fallout

Paddy sat on the changing room floor alongside the lifeless body of Mikael Tintoni, knees held up to his chest, looking blankly at the ground in front of him for what seemed like an eternity, wondering how many more people would die for someone else to make money. Claire, Sergio, even Jamie, all so Shaun could make his ill-gotten gains. And now, another innocent in the backstory of it all, Mikael Tintoni, driven to suicide for the same reason.

Paddy couldn't help but think back to the look on IRA Shaun's face when he asked about the poisoned stud, wondering if there was something else at play. Tintoni had never mentioned Shaun, or anyone for that matter. He pushed the thought away and trudged out to the car park and sat alone on the kerb to await Galloway's arrival.

Eventually, a nondescript black saloon car arrived; after a quick flash of his police I.D. Galloway's unmarked police car was waved through the club gates. Paddy stood up to greet the detective and shook him by the hand. The two men did not exchange any words, both preferring to break their silence in the quiet asylum of the changing room. Once they were inside it was Galloway that spoke first.

"What's happened here, Paddy? Ah heard the conversation ye had with" – he gestured to the body of Mikael Tintoni – "Ah assume this young man," Galloway was unperturbed, clearly well-used to the presence of the deceased.

"Aye, tis a terrible thing, Chief. It seems he was hired tae kill me. He admitted tae mah face that it was him who poisoned the stud that killed poor Claire. Whether he came up with the idea or was given it and the materials by another, I'm nae sure. He said it was tae wipe out his gambling debts. Ah can only assume Shaun O'Neill put him up tae it."

"Seems likely at this stage, Paddy. Ah assume that was the cause of death?" Galloway nodded towards the syringe still projecting from the mid-thigh of the unmoved body.

"Aye. Ye must've heard him say he couldnae go through with trying tae kill me a second time. Ah was tae slow tae react, didn't even move as he pushed that thing intae his leg. Ah jus' stood there like a frightened child." Sadness had begun to overwhelm him as he spoke these words. No tears were forthcoming, but Galloway could see the anguish and dysphoria that languished in his eyes.

"Ah wouldnae blame yerself, Paddy. Ah imagine it seemed like it was happening in slow motion as ye watched, but in reality it would have taken nae more than half a second. Ye couldnae have done anything." Paddy nodded slowly, realising the truth behind Galloway's words, but not wanting to accept it.

"Detective?" He asked slowly, "is there any way ye can make out this wasnae suicide?"

"A cover-up, Paddy?" Galloway snapped his head to face Paddy as the question was asked. "It would look somewhat bad for both of us if any rumours surfaced."

"Aye, but he didnae deserve tae go out like this. Do ye ken a doctor who could be... sympathetic tae our needs during the post-mortem? Say it was heart arrhythmia or something, perhaps? That's not unheard of in elite sportspeople." Galloway looked quizzically at Paddy, trying to determine his motivation for the deception. Ultimately, he relented. He knew of many cover-ups in the history of the Claston Police Force, and the higher he got in the service, the harder it had been not to become involved in any. This, he decided, could be his own cover up. He began nodding gently, almost to himself as he looked once again at the body on the floor.

"Alright, Paddy. That, Ah can do. Call an ambulance now, tell them ye found him like this when ye came in," Galloway removed the syringe as he spoke. "Ah can get rid o' this, and then Ah'll make some calls, make sure we get the right doctor for our needs."

"Dr Piero?" Asked Paddy hopefully.

"What's that?"

"Never mind."

"OK," Galloway continued, oblivious to Paddy's yearning to once again meet up with the Doctor who started off his adventure. "Meet me in the car park in five minutes. Ah rang ye for a reason."

Paddy did as he was asked, and five minutes later, to the second, Alfie Galloway strode around the corner from the far side of the car park. Paddy had no idea how he had got out there, not that it mattered.

"The reason Ah called ye was tae tell ye what we've found out thus far. With regards to the ongoing case.

"Firstly, Shaun has already confessed tae killing Jamie, not that we him needed tae. He's also confessed tae employing Jamie tae poison yer water bottle, again, something we have on record from yer wire. We've checked through the club CCTV. Now, as ye very well ken, there's nae CCTV inside the changing room, but we can place Jamie outside the changing room between yer arrival to drop off yer belongings and the moment ye came back from team lunch. It seems clear enough that this was when he spiked yer water. We had assumed that he did the stud at the same time with the dose strong enough to kill ye, as there's no sign of him after that at all, but now... Mebbe it was Jamie that gave the stud to Tintoni. It's a pretty clever ploy, tae be fair..." Galloway paused for a moment, admiring the audacity of a stunt designed to kill someone before continuing with his report.

"Shaun hasnae said anything abou' the stud, but that's actually good fer us now as it keeps Tintoni outta it. Jamie cannae defend himself now he's dead, so we'll pin the stud on him as well. After ye left to look intae OptimoPharm we continued tae follow up about them. As ye already know, that was the place tae go. Unfortunately, unlike you..." Galloway paused and made a face at Paddy, "we have tae go by the book, and cannae just seize company documents without a warrant. We can't get a warrant unless there is reason tae suggest foul play. Just because a drug that is manufactured by a drugs company was used in a murder, doesnae mean that company has anything tae do with it. We had already asked tae see the documents ye have since provided us, and we will continue tae wait tae get them legally and complete this case formally. If that doesnae happen, we have more than enough tae convict Shaun and probably Bobby. Getting tae Donald and Doris MacLeod may be a little more challenging without the paperwork, but we should be able tae get a warrant tae look through his company accounts due tae the boardroom recording we have from yer wire, and the fact that there is brain plastered across his wall. All in all, it's looking pretty good with regards tae closing this case."

Unlike Galloway, Paddy couldn't bring himself to smile upon hearing this, despite the good news. Yet at least he had nothing further to worry about and could concentrate on getting back to fitness for next week's final. The two men stood in silence for a moment, the sound of a siren twisting its way towards them from the distance. The gates were opened in preparation and the ambulance pulled alongside the two men. As the paramedics jumped out and rushed to get their gurney, Paddy pointed in the direction of the changing room and waited for Tintoni to be wheeled out. The exit of the changing rooms by the pair held none of the vigour of the entrance once they were sure that Tintoni had, indeed, died before their arrival. In the later autopsy he was pronounced dead at scene, caused by a heart attack linked to an undiagnosed hypertrophic cardiomyopathy.

As they watched the ambulance pull away, sirens silenced now, Paddy felt he had to ask Galloway one final question.

"Chief, Micky told me that 'they' told him tae kill me. When Ah asked Shaun about the stud, Ah coulda sworn he had nae clue what Ah was talking about. Do ye reckon there's a third party involved here?"

Galloway shrugged, paused and considered his response.

"We'll have tae see." Galloway replied, simply and cryptically. Paddy nodded again, indicating that he understood what it was that remained to be seen, when in truth he had no idea. Pulling himself together, he lifted his head high and held out his hand to the Detective Inspector.

"Thank ye for all ye've done, Galloway. It's nae surprise ye get tae walk around Ascension unhindered. Now, if ye'll excuse me, Ah've got a match tae prepare for."

Chapter 26: The Final

The day before the final had seen Paddy forced to accept a scenario he had been dreading for many years; when Fallanks ran through his team for the next day, he had been left on the bench. He took it in good grace, assenting to what he knew was a justified decision. He still wore the bruises of his foreign endeavours and some of the pain lingered deep in his muscles, but it was gut-wrenching, nonetheless. He had returned to Claston to win trophies, and there was nothing quite like the winner takes all event of a cup final. That night, Paddy lay in bed, visualising how he would make an impact, perhaps following a teammate's injury, or poor performance. In a disturbed and broken sleep, he dreamt that the whole first eleven dropped down simultaneously after 15 minutes, each one with a syringe of thalelamide sticking out from their thighs. He had to come on alone to try and save the game, but everywhere he ran, he was faced by Shaun O'Neill, prodding the lifeless Mikael Tintoni towards him, whose hands had been replaced with needles. The opposition laughed as he retreated closer and closer to his own goal, with Fallanks berating him constantly from the touchline. He awoke drenched in his own sweat, heart pounding, before eventually falling back into an uneasy slumber.

The day of the final was fine and bright, with the forecast suggesting it would stay that way. Paddy packed up his kit bag with his usual items, ensuring that his personalised bottle was freshly washed and sterilised. Finally, he picked up the parcel that he had had delivered earlier that week and placed it neatly on top of everything else, zipped up his bag, and made his way to the training ground to board the team coach.

Running through the warm up, Paddy tried to act the same way he did for every game, yet it had been so long since he had been involved in an important match from the bench, he found it hard to focus. His touch was off, with the ball running loose more than once. His chest and arms were still suffering from a dull ache from the beating he had received, and if anyone touched the wound on his back a shock of pain passed through him. When the team went back into the changing room for the pre-match team-talk, Paddy, usually so confident, was feeling a shadow of his former self. He knew he needed to pull himself together, that he could be required at any point during the match.

Fallanks began to go run through the team again, emphasising the important roles each member of the team had to play, the key battle grounds and the importance of beating your main rivals in any normal game, but especially in a cup final. Paddy was pleased that Fallanks did not adopt the cliched "it's just a normal match" strategy he had seen used so many times before and was impressed with his diligent preparation. Finally, just before the team were due to go out, Fallanks put forward the question he would always put forward:

"Has anyone got anything tae add?" This question was usually met with a stony silence. The players had learnt soon after Fallanks joined the club that they were not to question the manager's tactics. However, today was different, and something needed to be said. Paddy stood up and pulled the package from his bag.

"Ah know we've all got our black armbands tae wear today, but Ah hoped ye might wear these instead. Ah had them made especially for the match." From the package, Paddy pulled out a collection of black armbands, each embroidered with "Mikael Tintoni – Scottish Cup Winner" in gold thread. "Ah realise that Ah'm jumping the gun a wee bit with these," he said, throwing an armband to each member of the squad, "but Ah ken Ah will give that little bit more today with Micky by mah side."

Solemnly, each player pulled on their armband, replacing the plain black ones that the club had provided for the occasion. And then, the bell rang, calling the players onto the field. An impeccable minute's silence was observed by both sets of fans, and Paddy, along with the rest of the subs, made their way to the bench to await their chance to make an impact on the game.

It was clear from the start that both teams were playing cautiously, waiting for the other to make a mistake. The sun drummed down, beating its incessant rhythm on the players, stifling them. Wanderers began to dominate possession without showing any real intent for goal, making the Celts chase back and forth for the ball. Simple passing, up and down the pitch, always finding a safe option nearby, tidy and neat, never in a rush. Paddy was impressed with the endeavour of the usually lazy Johnson as he chased across the back four, always closing down the ball, but never winning it before it was moved on. This was clearly a tactic the Wanderers were employing in the heat, and it was an effective one. The Celts could only drop deeper and deeper into their own half as they tired in the sun. Paddy couldn't recall the last time a member of his team touched the ball under any sort of control, let alone the last time they had strung a number of passes together.

He was getting nervous now; team captain, William Wark had dropped the defensive line into the penalty area, such was the pressure that Wanderers had been applying. The two full backs, Spelter on the right and Arrol on the left had been forced to tuck in to help secure the centre of the pitch, leaving space on the flanks for an attack. The two wingers were dropping back to mark their counterparts but could not contain the overlapping Wanderers full backs as well, and it was ultimately this that led to the first goal of the game being scored.

The goal would end up going down as one of the greats in Scottish Cup Final history, including sixteen passes and eight of the Wanderers players in the build-up. The move started with a Celts goal kick, with the moment it left keeper Richards' boot the only time a Celts player touched it. A series of intricate passes ended with the ball being rolled down the right for charging Oscar Parah who whipped the ball in towards the far post. A back-peddling Wark could not get there fast enough, and a bullet header from left-winger Mark Burness left Richards with no hope. It had only been 22 seconds from Richards kicking the ball out and then picking it up from of his net.

Paddy slumped into his seat. He had to admit that it was looking bleak, with the Wanderers now dominating in every area of the pitch and looking stronger as the half wore on. Perhaps the shock of losing Tintoni was having a negative effect on the Celts, perhaps it was the armbands tempting fate. A resolute effort from the Celts defensive pair of Wark and Smith kept Cortez, Burness and the rest of the Wanderers attacking line at bay for much of the rest of the half, and Paddy started to think that going in at half-time only one goal behind wouldn't be insurmountable in the second half. He looked up at the scoreboard; the clock ticked over to 42 minutes. The Celts fans were watching nervously, subdued, clearly sharing Paddy's thoughts and praying for the half time break. The Celts players, however, were becoming frustrated, and Fallanks wasn't helping matters by urging his team to shoot whenever they got the ball.

Johnson looked the most frustrated of all, his fiery temper finally getting the better of him after his selfless running early on. When a ball fell to him 30 yards from goal, he snatched at it, sending it high and wide. The Wanderers fans cheered ironically at the first attempt at goal from their bitter rivals. They were enjoying the match immensely and would soon be singing even louder.

With two minutes to go before the half time whistle, Celts midfielder Frank Nolan received the ball on the edge of the centre circle. Hesitating, he was caught by a crunching tackle from Lucio Emanuel. The ball bounced loose and Emanuel was quick to pounce upon it. The referee waved play on and Emanuel coursed forward, devouring the space in front of him. Wark rushed to meet him, the veteran moustachioed defender coming in hard to avenge his teammate and stop Emanuel: Emanuel was too quick though and lifted the ball over Wark's out-stretched leg and continued on his way, unimpeded as he bore down on goal. Hitting a rasping, but ultimately hopeful shot from the edge of the box, he watched as Richards could only palm the ball back into play and straight to the predatory Toby Watts. Watts celebrated before he had even hit his shot, left with the simplest of chances to double the Wanderers' advantage.

A roar was heard from the far end that housed their fans. The Celts fans sat stunned as they watched the ball rippling in the net in front of them. Watts wheeled away, sprinting down to celebrate with his fans, followed by his teammates. Nolan took to his feet gingerly, shaking his head at the referee for his failure to award what, to him, seemed an obvious free-kick.

When the half time whistle went, the contrast between the two teams was immeasurable. Dejected and beaten, the Celts players made their way back down the tunnel, following the substitutes and manager who had already headed in at the sight of the second goal.

In the changing room, Fallanks had reverted back to type, shouting and yelling at his players, bemoaning their efforts, questioning their desire, ignoring the free-kick appeal prior to the second goal and wholly refusing to consider that they were being tactically outplayed by a better team. After what seemed like an age, he finally grew quiet. Paddy waited. And then, the moment he had been waiting for arrived as Nolan spoke up.

"Boss," he said tentatively. "Ah dinnae think Ah'm gonnae get through the second half. That fucker Emanuel came in hard, look at my leg." Nolan pulled down his sock to reveal three deep gashes in his calf. Fallanks looked at him, considered to tell him to get on with it, and then thought better of it.

"McAlpin!" he yelled, "Get yerself warmed up. Ye're coming on."

This was what he needed, what he longed for. After the semi-final he had a point to prove, after the deaths of Claire and Tintoni he had a lifetime's anger and grief to excise. Football was, and always had been, his way of purging his emotions, of expressing himself, and ultimately, of proving his self-worth. He needed no motivation other than a love of the game, a desire to be the best. But today, he had Claire and Mikael, one on each shoulder, to guide him and spur him on. He felt more ready than he ever had before. Today, he would let no one down.

As the second half began, Paddy's influence was immediately felt. His determination to get something out of the game lifted his teammates, his constant battling and running washed away the fatigue that chasing shadows in the hot sun of the first half had brought about. Gradually, the Celts managed to get a foothold in the game. Johnson, in particular, had shown positive intent, linking up play nicely, providing a good chance for fellow forward Daryl Flynn and generally making a nuisance of himself. Had the game been 0-0, there would have been no doubt in the minds of anyone watching that Claston Celts would go on to lift the famous old trophy. Yet, for all their efforts, the score remained at 2-0.

The score may have remained that way, had it not been for the Wanderers' centre back Ismail Folamu. A Portuguese-born Australian who had been signed as a youth prospect,

Folamu was now an imposing player in his mid-twenties, and one keen to wind up the opposition. With the ball off the pitch, he made a fatal mistake in trying to disrupt his opponent.

"Hey, McAlpin," he called over to the great Scot, "Great job on those armbands. Did you get yer ma to sew them for yer? Or maybe it was Tintoni's mum who made you wear them. I guess she expected to see her son on the pitch today, eh?" While Folamu laughed, Paddy gritted his teeth, quelling the rage building inside him. He ran hard towards the side line where Spelter stood, ball in hand, ready to take the throw-in.

"Spelter!" he bellowed as he moved into space. Spelter saw his run and threw the ball into Paddy's feet. Paddy turned towards goal and looked up. To his left, Del-Flaato, to his right, Spelter, and in front of Spelter, Amelié. But Paddy was not interested in any of these options. He looked forward and saw his target. Pushing the ball forward with his right foot, he strode into the space between the centre-circle and the penalty area and, with all his might, unleashed an unstoppable drive towards goal. The ball rocketed away from his foot, seeming to continue accelerating as it flew through the air, swirling towards goal. A deep "ooohh" of anticipation from the crowd built up as the ball flew through the air. Declan Carpenter watched it carefully, judging his leap, springing up towards the path of the ball, his hand outstretched across his body. The pitch of the roar went up a notch –"oooOOAAA!" – as they watched, before breaking into a full-throated, uninhibited, deafening cheer as the ball whistled past the flying Carpenter and into the top right corner.

On the pitch there was disbelief. Amelié wheeled around to reach Paddy, his arms high in the air. Spelter stood, mouth open, staring at the ball in disbelief as if the very last of Scotland's remaining national animal, the unicorn, had galloped into the goal. On the touchline, Fallanks and his staff were laughing in astonishment at what they had just seen. If the Wanderers' goal would go down as one of the greatest team goals, this would surely be considered one of the greatest individual goals. Paddy was surrounded as the Celts players leapt on him, jostling him, embracing him and high-fiving him.

The game was back on.

Johnson ran to the goal to get the ball and take it back to the centre circle for kick-off, and when the mob had dispersed,

Paddy jogged over to Folamu, raised his right arm across his body, turned his head to his right and kissed the armband that clung proudly to his bicep.

It was clear that the Wanderers were shaken, but they still led, and with only 15 minutes to go they had settled into a deep defensive line, holding onto their lead at all costs with every player behind the ball. Try as he might, Paddy could not break down the well-organised pale blue shirts. In the end it was an unexpected source that provided the long-sought equaliser.

Willie Wark, the ageing but legendary Celts centre back, had moved back through the pitch as his pace and fitness slowly left him. Able to read the game better than anyone Paddy had ever played with, his positioning and distribution ensured he remained an integral part of the team. In Paddy's previous spell with the Celts, Wark had been the archetypal box-to-box midfielder that Paddy had based his early game on, and he was now playing his final game before retirement. With the Celts pressing forward at all costs, Wark sat back on the halfway line, ready to soak up any hopeful punts forward and redistribute the ball to start another attack.

No one could explain what made him leave his post in the 83rd minute, but the crowd soon noticed the creaking old warhorse trotting up field. A neat one two between Arrol and Del-Flaato on the left created space for Paddy to receive the ball inside. Turning towards goal, he was faced by Charlie Fraser, and turned back, keeping possession and looking for an outlet. Beginning to struggle under the weight of the injuries that still troubled him, Paddy floated the ball hopefully into the box. From seemingly nowhere, Wark came powering in and, ignoring his advancing years, leapt high above Folamu to thunder the ball into the net. The ageing captain continued his run past the goal where the ball lay and sprinted along the front of the stand where the Celts fans were going wild. As he ran, Wark kissed his hands and raised them above his head repeatedly, whipping up the crowd into a frenzy of delirium and delight.

By now, it seemed obvious to all watching that the Celts would win the game, it was only a question of when they would find the winning goal. Knowing they had to attack or face extra time and penalties, the Wanderers players tried to move the ball forward again, and from kick-off launched their first attack for nearly twenty minutes. Toby Watts, his hair matted with sweat, took up the ball and slipped it through a gap and behind the defence. Paddy watched on in horror as Wanderers' winger Zalik Arik reached the pass and struck the ball first time. Richards dived to his right and got a hand to the ball, but it was not enough; the ball ricocheted into the ground and bounced towards the goal. Spelter came running in and lunged his body in desperation but was unable to stop the ball trickling over the line. Paddy's heart sank as Arik turned to face Watts, beaming from ear to ear, having scored what would surely prove to be the winning goal.

Paddy looked forlornly to the bench, heartbroken, only to see Fallanks looking relaxed, pointing across the field. Paddy followed the outstretched finger of his manager and breathed a sigh of relief as he saw the assistant referee's flag raised for offside. Watching the highlights later on, he was impressed with the vision of the woman running the line: Arik had strayed offside by no more than three inches, a margin that could so easily have been missed.

The jeers rose from the Celts fans, drowning out the cheers that had turned into howls from the Wanderers end. Richards in goal was quick to react to the decision, placing the ball down without delay and playing it out. The Celts were playing with an urgency now, desperate to find a winner in the remaining minutes and thus avoiding any extension to the game. The quick interplay between the Celts midfield, well versed in singing this song, was too much for the tiring Wanderers midfield to keep up with. The sun continued to beat down hard, but now it was the Wanderers players who seemed drained by its piercing rays.

And then, when extra-time seemed inevitable, Daryl Flynn received the ball on the edge of the box, his back to goal, Emanuel tugging at his shirt, hassling him from behind. Flynn shrugged off the defender and played a careful ball into the box for the running Johnson who had raced clear of his marker, accelerating forward. His first touch was heavy, taking him wider than he wanted, narrowing the angle between himself and the goal. Paddy summoned a strength that had been reinforced, not broken, by the events of the previous two weeks and burst into the box, hoping any rebound would fall his way. Johnson twisted back, trying to wrongfoot the goalkeeper, but Carpenter stood tall, not budging. Johnson looked up to see the charging man mountain McAlpin and knew this was not about personal glory.

In an uncharacteristically selfless moment, the young striker zipped the ball back across goal, hoping that Paddy would reach it before anyone else did. The pass was too hard for Paddy to reach comfortably, but he flung himself towards the ball, sliding across the turf, his outstretched legs straining with every sinew to reach the ball, his toes pointed like the finest ballet dancer. Ball met stud and the touch was enough to divert the pass goalward and into the net.

The most unlikely of comebacks was complete. Paddy jumped to his feet and ran to the wild fans behind the goal, standing, arms aloft, nodding his head vigorously. And then, the song he had learnt to hate began, and Paddy, acknowledging the spirit in which it was sung, as if for the first time, conducted his choir in the most rousing rendition of Vienna that he had ever heard, knowing that the lyrics being sung showed just how much this did mean to those fervent, loyal supporters. The song continued without him as he jogged back to the centre circle, his smile plastered to his face with an unbreakable bond. The referee had time to restart the match, only to blow the full-time whistle seconds later.

Wanderers players slumped to the floor, defeated, dejected, disconsolate, while the celebrations of the Celts went on around them.

As Wark led his team up the steps to their prize, Paddy turned to face the fans who had never given up on him. In that moment, he reflected how the present is always more vivid and exciting than the memories we hold, even those most precious to us. And such it was that, in the here and now, this victory tasted sweeter than all his previous success, bringing about a joy that he had forgotten how to experience.

Thinking of Claire, Mikael and his father as he lifted the trophy high above his head, he smiled inwardly, hoping they would be proud of what he had achieved that day.

Epilogue

The three figures sat side by side on the small yet carefully-erected podium, their backs to the now completed project, facing the crowd that had gathered to witness this historic ceremony. The two men were well known in the city, but the woman sitting beside them was a stranger to all in attendance.

Signora Tintoni looked up at the crowd, their hopeful faces reminding her of the son she had lost in this very city three years ago. Time was the greatest healer, but some scars are beyond repair; she was over the worst of the pain now, but every now and again there was the twinge of sorrow, the melancholy knowledge that she would never be reunited with her boy. She had deliberated whether to accept the invitation to this event but now she was here she was pleased with her decision.

Mayor Galloway was well known in Claston now. His sterling police career had ended in honour with the arrest of Shaun O'Neill and the destruction of The Ghost Mob. Not long after, he was promoted to Chief Constable, then had put himself forward for election as City Mayor, and as a man who commanded respect across all quarters of Claston, had been duly elected to represent his home in its highest office.

One of his first jobs was to "fix" the issues faced by the poorest in society, those in need of the most help who had been ignored for the longest. His primary target was the scene of the making of him as a police sergeant: Ascension House.

"Ladies and Gentlemen, please let me begin by saying that Ah ken, like the rest o' ye, what Ascension House stood for. It wasnae how many people perceived it: a nest of lawlessness, a hideout for the destitute, a den for drug runners. It was, in fact, a home. A home to hundreds o' families who had nowhere else tae go. A home that stunted the development that the families who lived there strived for. This was a home that had been neglected for too long, and the cuts ran too deep and were too raw for it tae be saved.

"Thankfully, due tae the arrest of Shaun O'Neill, who had for so long bullied his way intae purchasing these accommodations, and the power invested in me by the Proceeds of Crime Act, we were able tae seize the property, so it is once again in the hands of the public tae whom it really belongs. However, instead of papering over the cracks and painting over the rotten core of those buildings, a new plan was developed, a plan that is more fitting for the people who have, for too long, had to call this dilapidated estate their home.

"Ah've spent much of my time in office devoted tae finding a new home for the noble people of Ascension House, the people who want better. Better for themselves and for their families. Most importantly, a home was needed so the people who lived there could feel empowered and have easy access intae the city, allowing them tae prosper and thrive.

"It has been a long road, and one not without bumps along the way, but today we are able tae end our journey. We have traversed many hurdles, but with the help of Claston's most famous son, we have delivered a home that each and every resident can be proud of.

"The old Ascension House is already scheduled to be levelled and will soon become a place that the population of the whole city will want to flock to as the site of Claston's first nature reserve. In time, this will become a vast green area leading out of the city and intae the beautiful surrounding countryside, guiding those who walk it up intae breath-taking scenes of Scottish wilderness with access to a view o' Claston that has previously been inaccessible tae all but the hardiest of ramblers.

"New Ascension House sits on the land formerly known as Cowie Estates. This land has been donated tae the city by Mr Paddy McAlpin. Paddy has worked with me at every step of the way and Ah am proud to now call this man mah friend. And as we stand here today on Tintoni Pass, the gateway to this new development, Ah think we can all be proud of our city's generous benefactor."

Galloway led the applause directed at Paddy as he stepped down from the lectern and took his seat next to Signora Tintoni. The two of them smiled warmly as the Paddy himself took to the lectern to deliver his well-prepared oration. Although he knew the carefully chosen words by heart, he still found his legs shaking as he prepared to speak. He thought back to all the big matches he had previously played in, to the hundreds of thousands of fans who had expected him to deliver, or hoped he would fail, and realised that this moment eclipsed even the most high-profile of fixtures. For at the end of the day, this moment meant so much more than the result of a football game.

Paddy looked down at the people gathered before him and saw his mother in the front row, smiling up with such pride at her son. In her left hand she held a worn photograph of her husband, Matthew, standing with a ball under his foot, signalling to a very young Paddy. As she caught her son's eyes, she glanced to the photograph and smiled once again. Paddy patted his inside pocket where the very same photograph was safely held. He was ready and stepping forward he spoke clearly and freely.

"Thank you, Mayor Galloway.

"Ah have played in the San Siro, at Wembley, in front of 100,000 people, and today is the day that Ah am most nervous about. This is the first time that Ah've ever used mah words, rather than mah feet, tae send a message. The events that are about tae unfold will hopefully affect people's lives far more than the outcome of any football match, and on this occasion, everyone will be considered a winner.

"For my entire life, this man tae my right has been the man responsible for bringing law and order tae Ascension House. But he was fighting a battle that he could never win. With people like those responsible for the creation of ghettoes like the one in which we were raised, Mayor Galloway was fighting criminals on all sides. Now that he has purged the corruption from the office of government, we can begin tae make real progress.

"People all around the world know mah face. Ah go tae Shanghai, tae London, tae Denver or tae Timbuktu and people scream at me, they call me a hero; but for my entire career all Ah have ever done is do what Ah love, getting paid handsomely for the pleasure. Ah forgot about mah home. Ah never thought about the suffering that went on here. Ah never thought about the exploitation of the people with whom Ah shared a common bond. Ah'm nae hero: this man tae my right is a hero.

"With the New Ascension House Development Project, we aim tae eliminate the need for heroes. We want to remove the barriers in place that prevent each and every one of the people that call Ascension House their home from succeeding in their dreams. Gone are the tiny, squalid flats filled with underfed children; gone are the streets lined with broken bottles; gone are the abandoned cars, rusting out and hollowed from years of neglect, and gone are the broken dreams of residents.

"New Ascension House is a forward-thinking place: Mayor Galloway has had new tram lines installed throughout the city. Now our suburb is connected to the city in a way that Ascension House never was. Each house in the suburb has solar panels fitted to the roof, connected to an electricity supply that feeds the locals before the rich, making everyday life more affordable than ever before. With these innovations, and many more, we aim tae have this area carbon neutral by this time next year. Each house is made out of renewable or recycled materials and each former member of Ascension House has laid a single brick in the foundations of this new utopia! Now we must work together to ensure that New Ascension House becomes a model for the future, nae an empty, unfulfilled dream.

"In the past, each of us found refuge in those things that dinnae matter, those things that obscure the true beauty of life and love and meaning. In television, in sport, in gossip: in a thousand flippant moments. Sometimes, though: something happens – a spark in our reality – that opens our eyes to the inequity of this world that we had a hand in forging. And so together, we take up the baton of those that came before and use our gifts in the right way, undoing the wrongs of the past; we are captains of our own destiny: beacons of hope for those that follow. Even now, after all our work, whilst we congratulate ourselves on our progress, it occurs to me that we but stand at the base of The Mountain, ready tae make our ascension. The road will be long and hard, aye, but it will be the right one tae take.

"Just three years ago, someone told me that my sport was broken, twisted and perverted by money. Perhaps that was true; true for the oligarchs and the oil sheikhs and the shady businessmen that exploit this venerated game for their own foul purposes. It has been said by many that those less salubrious days were when football experienced its death knell, that those were the days when football died. It's nae true, though, for me. It's nae true for the players, nae true for the fans, nor for those people that love the game. For all of us who care so deeply for our sport, football is about competition, togetherness, unity and community. Today, we see the fruition of three years of hard work from Mayor Galloway. Today is the day that football rose."

"Now, Signora Tintoni. When you're ready with the scissors, Ah declare New Ascension House officially open!"

As she was invited forward, Signora Tintoni gently raised a soft fist to her right eye, expecting to wipe away a tear that she had felt forming. Her finger brushed her cheek and came away dry and she smiled, feeling a moment of closure. And as she stepped forward, giant scissors in hand, she was not so much as cutting an entrance to a new home, as cutting the ties to an old life, the final threadbare strands that held so many to an existence without hope being severed forever.

In football, as in life, there are highs and lows and it is the unceasing quest to finish on a high that allows football fans hope that things will get better, that keeps them coming back each and every new season. And such was it in Claston that day, where the desire of one man to allow others to end on a high had brought hope for the season of life that lay ahead.

If you enjoyed this story, be sure to check out Paddy's next adventure:

The Flames That Lick At The Shadows

Years after the events of A Cloud Can Weigh A Million Pounds, Paddy is drawing into the autumn of his career. No longer a first-choice player for Claston Celts, he is working harder than ever to get as much game time as he can. And then, unexpectedly, club chairman, Cormac Dundas arrives at the training ground, calling Paddy away from his teammates and into a conference room. And so begins another foray into solving crime, this time a blackmail being levied against his chairman. With the threat of never playing again acting as his motivation to solve the riddle he finds himself drawn into a web of deceit that has been masterfully spun by a ghost.

Elsewhere in the city, Mayor Galloway has started a fight with a dangerous new drug that has entered the city, a fight that he must win to save his citizens and his reputation. Hoping to stem the tide early on, he calls upon new Chief Constable, William Brackenfell, to stamp out the growing influence of this menace to society, hoping that Claston will embrace the utopia of New Ascension House that he and Paddy worked so hard to create.

The Flames That Lick At The Shadows – Coming soon

For updates on release date, future work and more, go to

www.adstephenson.com

About A.D. Stephenson

Anthony David Stephenson is the creator of Paddy McAlpin and author of A Cloud Can Weigh A Million Pounds. His debut novel was born during the 2020 COVID lockdown and is the first glimpse of footballer turned detective and warrior for social justice, Paddy McAlpin.

A keen football fan himself, Stephenson has a soft spot for Hamilton Academical, but deep down just wants to see real football at all levels (in some ways the lower the better).

He also enjoys good suits and live music.

Before penning novels, Stephenson worked as a teacher in the UK and Germany.

You can find out more about Stephenson by looking at his website:
adstephenson.com, or by checking out his social accounts.

Instagram: A.D. Stephenson

Twitter: @ADStephenson1

Printed in Great Britain
by Amazon